Love
Smiles

Howard McKenzie

Published by Howard McKenzie
Publishing partner: Paragon Publishing, Rothersthorpe
First published 2010

ISBN 978-1-899820-92-4

Book design, layout and production management by Into
Print

www.intoprint.net

Printed and bound in UK and USA by Lightning Source

The Author

Howard McKenzie is married with two grown-up daughters
and a granddaughter and lives near Edinburgh in Scotland.
He was a tenant dairy farmer in Dorset before becoming
a Lecturer in Agriculture and an academic; ending up as
Principal of an Edinburgh further education College.

Dedication

I dedicate this book to Rachel, MY soul mate, and my family
and friends who inspired and encouraged me to write this
book.

Chapter One

It's all gone up in smoke

The starboard engine of the A320 exploded; igniting the fuel in the aircraft and in an instantaneous fireball nearly 29 years of marriage ended and Simon's life was shattered.

He woke sweating and moved his arm over the bed looking for Jane, she wasn't there - she would never be there again. He started to cry, they were tears of abject sorrow and mourning; he had lived the last week in a sort of trance almost like being there but not being there, watching a real life movie but expecting the commercial break to come in at any moment and disrupt the story line.

Simon had left his private school with no qualifications and even fewer prospects; he had worked in an insurance office, the local council and then drifted into working as a farm labourer. After a year, he had got a place at the local agricultural college, won a scholarship to do a second year and had graduated with qualifications in Animal Husbandry and a job as a herdsman. Throughout this period his passion had been rugby, young farmers and women, he had had several girlfriends and quite a few lovers. He had lost his virginity some months before his 16th birthday to a girl he had met at the tennis club; it had been a great way to welcome in the New Year!

His rugby career had been short and rather weak; he had got injured too easily and found it difficult to play with consistency, he had been going to Young Farmers for several years when a neck injury on the pitch ruled him out of rugby for the season. His girlfriend, Felicity, had just dumped him - that is what it felt like - and for the first time, he had struggled with his emotions at the loss. He had liked her a great deal and in later life understood he had fallen in love with her; she wasn't ready for that and left.

A month or so later he decided to audition for the Young Farmers play which was part of a competition between the clubs at area, regional and national level. He wasn't a lovey type; he decided to take part mainly for something to do and landed the part of a policeman; the audition process consisted of a reading of the play at someone's house and then focused on the various parts allocated to individuals.

At the reading, he stretched over the settee to help with a chair and looked below him and saw a new member, he remembered looking at Jane the first time for the rest of his life and she could remember the moment too. Within weeks they were close friends, lovers and inseparable, they were made for each other from the second they met; it was a bond that lasted 32 years. Within nine months of meeting, Simon had proposed in the very unromantic setting of the cow shed where he worked. Their betrothal had not been a surprise to their families; they had all thought it would be sooner and their wedding had been spectacular with a huge marquee erected in Jane's parents' garden and over 200 guests. Jane had looked wonderful in her white toile dress and Simon had worn a traditional English morning suit; they had flown to Tunisia for a two week honeymoon. They had settled into a pleasant and calm life, two years later Jane become pregnant, she was 26 and the result was Fiona.

They struggled financially but gradually Simon had acquired a degree and through a lucky break had landed a job teaching at an agricultural college. He qualified as a teacher and then went on to get a Masters degree in Business Administration and his career moved forward; he ended up in Edinburgh as an academic, running the Business School and then left to start his own business as a management consultant.

For Simon and Jane life had been kind but they had had setbacks, sometimes life just kicked them and then kicked them again. Their daughters had been born and were perfect but the second pregnancy had been difficult, Jane had developed a heart complaint and a third child was ruled out. Simon had been made redundant several times, once when the children were both under four, he had career setbacks and they had to move on seven occasions to support his career.

Three decades later, Simon could think of nothing better than easing off work and spending the rest of their lives together. The world kicked back when his father in law died and he had driven 500 miles overnight to get Jane to her family; he had driven back with Alex their youngest daughter with Jane flying back a week later after the family affairs had been sorted.

Simon sat at home at the computer in the office at their house; it was a fairly traditional detached house just outside Edinburgh. The ground floor had a living room with a very large set of doors that led onto the patio overlooking a garden, the room was decorated with beige wallpaper and a deep burgundy carpet, the lounge suite was covered with a light blue fabric. Over the other side of the corridor was a dining room linked to the kitchen which had traditional white cabinets with a hob, microwave and oven; the floor was covered with a mosaic vinyl in cream, apricot and light yellow, the walls were apricot. Just off the kitchen was a smaller building; it housed the utilities services room, laundry and at the far end the office where Simon worked. Upstairs were four double bedrooms, it was a functional family home.

The phone next to the computer rang, making the computer buzz; it was Jane 'Hiya, we seem to be boarding on time' she said 'my boy I've really missed you and I want to be with you'.

'I've missed you too but it's only an hour and half till I see you again; I will be waiting at Costa Coffee as usual' Simon said; they rang off.

Simon waited 40 minutes and then got in the car, Jane's flight had taken off about 30 minutes ago and would land in about another 30 minutes, he suddenly felt very cold, shaky and a feeling of foreboding washed over him, he shrugged it off. He drove to the airport, he had plenty of time for the 16 mile journey and it was Sunday night and the traffic was non-existent.

When he arrived at the airport he parked in the short stay car park and walked into the terminal; he had to wait as police cars, ambulances and a doctor's car sped past, screeched to a halt and the occupants went inside the terminal; it must be some kind of security alert exercise, he thought.

He walked along the near empty check-in desks towards the domestic arrivals hall, there was a commotion to his left which he ignored and made his way to Costa Coffee.

They were moving people up the stairs, a woman screamed and a stretcher appeared; the police were having a time tonight. He sat down in a seat next to the corridor and luggage belt where the flight usually arrived; Jane would appear from one direction or the other. He looked up at the monitor and saw the flight was delayed but not showing any due time, this was not unusual.

He started to read the complimentary newspaper when two police officers walked past, he asked 'What's going on?'

The woman police officer stepped towards him 'someone fainted, are you here to meet a flight, sir?'

'Yes, my wife is on the Bristol flight' Simon replied 'I see, one moment please sir'.

She trotted over to a group of staff in yellow day-glow jackets; two of them broke off and jogged over to where Simon was sitting.

'Good evening sir, are you here to meet a flight?' one of the women said, Simon gave the flight number and the woman sat down next to Simon unsmiling.

How odd, Simon leant forward and took a sip from his coffee cup, he felt complete dread and turned to the woman and said 'what's happened?'

'I'm sorry sir, the flight er um', she put a supportive hand on his arm, 'there is unlikely to be any survivors'.

The shock hit him like a bullet and his world turned to slow motion, he could not speak or move, his worst nightmare had come true, he had always felt uncomfortable flying.

'Could I have the name of the person you were meeting?' Simon was numb he muttered Jane, my wife, 'could I have your name'; he started to shake, he handed the woman his wallet; tears streamed down his face, his mouth was dry and he could not speak.

His phone rang, Simon looked at it. It was his eldest daughter Fiona; he looked up at the police woman and said 'could you answer this, it is my daughter'.

With his head in his hands, he wept openly, the woman from the airport put her hand on his back. He heard the policewoman saying, 'yes sir you should come here, this is a time when the family should be together.'

'We have a lounge upstairs for you to sit in whilst we wait for news' the woman said.

Simon composed himself, he had to think of the girls and Mary, his granddaughter, the phone rang again; it was Alex his other daughter, she was at home.

'Dad, there's a report on the news that a plane has crashed killing everyone on board' she said crying. 'Mum's on that flight.'

'Alex, it's not good news, go and see Peter and Sheila and ask them to bring you to the airport as soon as possible' he said.

Twenty minutes later she arrived, running into his open arms; it was so good to have the family around; Fiona and her husband arrived about an hour later and met up with them in the lounge put aside for relatives. About ten minutes later, the airline announced that the plane had exploded in mid air and there were no survivors. A member of staff sat down and explained that he had confirmed that Jane had boarded and so had died when the plane exploded. The police woman, who lived just round the corner from Simon, had driven him and Alex home in his car whilst the others followed.

Simon eventually got to bed about midday the next day. Stewart, Fiona's husband and his father had been superb, they manned the phones and started ringing relatives and friends. Manus had visited and a few of the neighbours had come in, his mobile phone had been on permanent charge to keep up with the calls and texts.

The funeral was a week later, there was no body to identify. Alex had given a blood sample for DNA recognition, if needed, and some personal belongings had been returned; there were dozens of friends, relatives and well-wishers at the simple funeral in Edinburgh.

After the funeral came the need to deal with the bureaucracy of death; life insurance, compensation, travel insurance claims, and everything else. By far the worst had been getting Jane's mobile phone account cancelled; they were heartless.

Simon fell to pieces, he was devastated, he felt so alone, no one to cuddle, no one there to console him; but even in adversity there is hope and the son of one of the other victims, Duncan, had asked Alex out and they were dating. Simon put the house up for sale; he hit the bottle, took tonnes of anti-depressants and generally wreathed himself in an orgy of grief and self pity; he didn't deal with his situation well.

He sold the house and rented a flat in Edinburgh in Dundas

Street above the Trout Anglers Club, then bought two semi derelict flats and pushed builders to finish so he could move in; he moved in just before Christmas.

He kept working as best he could, with the Health Trust and some of his regular customers, but it had been very difficult; he scaled back some of the work, the future looked featureless.

Chapter Two

Beaten, humiliated and abused

BK Shore walked into the party at the offices of American Music Inc, it was a warm dry Los Angeles evening, the air outside felt thick and dirty.

Brad Morgan had arranged a party for several hundred clients and others to celebrate 15 years of his company's existence. He was one of the more successful talent managers; he maintained a large group of people who were first rate at negotiations, organisation and keeping stars out of trouble.

He represented and managed hundreds of acts, mainly in America but had small operations in Europe and Asia. At this time his hottest properties were BK Shore who had just released a new album and the Speakers Brackets, a heavy rock band which had just toured America to huge acclaim. He had two major bands on European tours, three in Asia and three on US tours at present and the machinery of his empire was stretched but he was coining in the money.

There were speeches, music and drink served by toga clad waiters and waitresses, with various themes in each of the open plan office areas cleared for the occasion. The office block was ultra modern, with ceiling to floor glass panels, most of the furniture had been moved out and it made a superb venue for a party.

BK Shore circulated and was joined by Hal Riddick who had been her executive manager for some time now; he ran her company Beach; he had worked for Brad but had proved so good she had offered him a job.

In one of the circles she was in, the waiter stumbled and she backed out of the way and into the guy behind.

'I'm sorry' she said. 'Hey don't be, you're BK Shore aren't you?' said the guy.

'Yes, are you Jake Olding?' she said. He was the lead guitarist with Speakers Brackets.

'Yes, like you we are back from tour, I love touring so cool' he said.

They talked about touring, the people around them and gossiped and bitched about everyone in sight, they laughed.

Jake disappeared and came back a little later, he was engaging and charming and he put his arm around her. They parted, giving each other contact details; the next day, he rang up and they started dating.

The next weekend he took her to a beach House in Malibu, they swum in the pool and had sex, lots of sex and three weeks later he moved into her house and they publicly became an item, the paparazzi had a field day. They lived together for nearly a year but gradually BK noticed changes in Jake. He was out and away over night more; he had temper tantrums and was very much more demanding of her in every way; he became very critical of her and everything she did, he became a stranger.

He started to encourage her to do sexual things she wasn't altogether happy with, he started to insist that she was naked in his presence; she wasn't allowed to wear a swimsuit in the pool unless they had guests and then it was very small, he hid her underwear, she resorted to keeping some in her automobile. He used to tickle her if she disobeyed but gradually the demands got more to her dislike and the punishments more extreme, she realised that she was losing trust in him. He liked to see her with other women, some of them had been good fun, she didn't mind it too much but hated sharing him without having a say, if she was going to share her man she would decide when and with whom.

One night, he came back, smelling of perfume and other women and when she refused to have sex with him, he hit her hard; over the next few weeks the violence became more frequent and more brutal. His behaviour became more and more erratic, he seemed to sleep all day and party all night. He started to get very violent towards her and even kinkier in his demands, he handcuffed her, naked to the banisters, left her there for hours. He wanted her to have a clitoral hood piercing and labial rings; she had agreed but hated them and herself for getting them done, she felt cheap and humiliated.

The rumours started about women, the wild parties, the drink and drugs; according to the newspapers, and untrue, she had even found him in bed with two cheerleaders and all he had done was invite her to join in, which apparently she had. He was then busted for trying to score coke. When she confronted him about the women and the drugs, he became so violent he had broken one of her teeth and given her two black eyes.

Brad Morgan and Hal Riddick stepped in and forcibly removed him to a clinic and her to a dentist. When Jake returned, he was the charming, lovely guy she had met and fallen in love with but he started to slip again; she alerted Brad but it was a very slippery slope.

The end came at a baseball match; he had taken her as a trophy, and spent the time talking to two guys from other bands. These two had girlfriends in tow. One, Luke's girl-friend, seemed very nice; the other was a total lunatic who seemed to be enjoying exhibiting herself to all three men. BK and Luke's girlfriend were most put out, they were both annoyed and it created a bond between them; in the lift up from the hospitality Jake had punched her hard in the stom-ach and insisted that she 'did more' for Luke and Ralf; the blow came when she said NO.

She left and went home, the rest of the group followed some hours later; they were high and drunk except Luke's girlfriend; Lizzy, the lunatic, walked in through the door and took her clothes off and lay on the settee with her legs wide open; she had no inhibitions, she was as high as a kite and a complete slut.

Jake picked her up, stroking all of her body, in front of BK, and threw her in the pool; all the guys stripped off and jumped in after her, Luke had pushed his girlfriend into the pool and taken her top off but she refused to get naked. A naked Jake came out of the pool, walked up to BK and smashed his fist into her face, breaking her nose, he started to rip her clothes off 'get naked bitch and then go fuck Luke and Ralf'.

She screamed and ran up stairs, he followed, hit her again and stunned her, she fell on the bed, he handcuffed and tied her and disappeared, returning with a horse whip.

Luke's girlfriend was leaving, she wasn't going to fuck any one and when Luke had jumped on top of that crazy Lizzy and eased himself into her, she realised their relationship was over and it was time to go. She returned to the living room, she heard a scream and a cry for help, she made her way upstairs, and the screams became more urgent. She ran into the main bedroom, there was blood everywhere, Jake was clearly raping BK Shore, she was screaming and he was hitting her with a riding crop with his full strength. Huge red welts had appeared on her breasts, stomach and through his legs, she could see that the area between BK's legs was a mess of blood but he still kept pounding away, raping her and hitting her with the whip and she was screaming in pain and fear 'help, rape, please help' she screamed.

Luke's girlfriend pulled Jake off BK by his legs, he lunged towards her, 'you want some too darling' he said. He landed several writhing hits with the whip but three karate blows and the drunken, cocaine sodden bastard was stunned; she moved forward and undid BK's hand and leg cuffs and relocated them onto Jake; once fully restrained, she kicked him hard in the balls, 'that's one for the sisters' she shouted.

She found her bag and made one of the most important phonecalls of her life; she rang Brad Morgan, who had given her his card at one of the events she had been to, his cellphone rang and was answer almost immediately. She explained what had happened, he had stopped her once and yelled 'Terry, Linda get in here now I need you code red.'

'You have done the right thing my dear' he said calmly 'people will be there momentarily, I am leaving now; by the way what is your name?' he said.

'Emma Button' she replied.

'Are you alright Emma?' he asked.

'No, I'm bleeding too, please come quick I think BK's unconscious' Emma said.

A doctor and paramedics arrived by helicopter on the lawn about three minutes later, a private team on constant standby for the rich and famous, they dealt with drug overdoses and heart attacks mainly; a security team arrived seven minutes later.

BK Shore was an incredible mess, she was unconscious and losing blood from several dozen gashes caused by the whip, she had deep cuts between her legs and Emma could see that her vagina was swollen and bleeding profusely externally and possibly internally; her face was swollen out of all proportion and she had a nose bleed.

Emma felt sick and faint and realised that she was going into shock; she started to shiver and shake.

The paramedics stabilised BK, cleaned her up as best they could but she was still unconscious and losing blood from the gashes inflicted by the whip. They moved her out to the helicopter and told Emma to go with her, Emma had some deep scratches and was bleeding rather heavily from her left breast where Jake had lashed out with the whip, it only now hurt, she looked down and she realised she would need stitches, right across her left breast was an inch wide gash. She watched mesmerised as blood flowed down her breast to her nipple and dripped onto the carpet, she passed out.

They flew to the hospital and BK and Emma were taken into the emergency room; Emma was conscious, holding a bandage to her breast and crying when she heard, 'thank you for helping BK,' the guy was in tears. 'The doctor said he might have killed her if you hadn't stopped him, I'm Hal Riddick.'

Brad and his team and a group from BK's own company, arrived half an hour later and sometime after the helicopter had gone to the hospital. Jake was still there, in the hands of the security guards and Brad was pleased that clearly BK had fought him as he was covered in painful but superficial bruises. Brad rang Hal and talked to him, Brad realised how serious this was and rang his contact in LAPD and this was going to have to be official. Terry and Linda were on their phones talking to the public relations team, the media management team, Brad's and Hal's machines were gearing up for action.

BK was in hospital for nearly two weeks as they reconstructed her nose and allowed the swelling and lacerations to heal. She had needed blood on the first night and she had a dislocated arm, a broken wrist on the other arm and a broken ankle. Emma had over 20 stitches in her breast and was in hospital for overnight, she would need cosmetic surgery as the scar was going to be clearly visible. Hal found out that Emma had no job and offered her a contract to be BK's Executive Assistant; she accepted and started to support BK's needs; she visited BK in hospital every day and, having done some nursing, helped her when she left hospital.

Hal had arranged for BK's mother to be driven from her home in Bakersfield to LA to visit her daughter and stay close to her. BK was born in Bakersfield. Her mother, Erin, was a keyboard player in various country bands, nothing very famous and she had drifted into a series of short-term relationships which were generally destroyed by touring and the need to travel to where the work was. When Erin was 34, she met BK's father and had a tempestuous six month relationship with him, the product of which was Sarah King whose stage name was BK Shore. Sarah's father was eight years younger than her mother and he was a drummer in a successful band. When he found out that Erin was pregnant, he deposited $100,000 in her bank account and deserted her.

Erin had settled in Bakersfield and became a high school music teacher, giving private piano lessons and guesting with local bands; she had brought up Sarah single-handed with only a few 'uncles' to help occasionally. When her mother was playing at the weekends or on tour or away Sarah stayed with the Mexican family who lived next door; they had a girl Martha who was the same age as Sarah and later two boys.

Sarah had attended Buena Vista Elementary and Middle School and then Stockdale High School. BK had grown up with music and musicians and had a natural talent for composition, vocals and arrangement; at school, she had been in the chorus, band and orchestra and was an accomplished pianist and not bad on the guitar. She got a music scholarship to Berkley University, the Centre of New Music and Audio Technology and she was spotted by a scout when 23 and singing herself through College. She signed with Brad Morgan and burst onto the music scene; she had been very successful in her career but her personal life was far more chaotic and unsuccessful.

It was so good to see her mother again; at 71 she was just

beginning to lose it; the doctors said she had the beginnings of dementia. Whilst she was staying in LA and at the hospital BK arranged for her to see a specialist who confirmed the local diagnosis. She was already on a Guardian's Angels scheme with regular visits to monitor her.

BK had asked Emma and Hal to clear the house and rent it out, she couldn't go back; Emma took on the task and started to search for a rented apartment.

BK had the most remarkable invitation as she was thinking what to do next; Brad arrived with his wife Lauren and they offered to take BK into their guest house for a few months to let her recover. Emma moved in too, as in the beginning BK needed to be fed, washed and cared for in every way, BK had found not being able to wipe her own ass and having someone else deal to her monthly sanitary needs particularly degrading but Emma had done everything for her and they grew very close.

She had seen a very different Brad. At work he has the brash, boorish, bully yelling at everyone, hell bent on turning the dollar, at home he was a loving caring husband, devoted to his wife and three kids; he really was a dark horse.

Apart from Emma's love and closeness, there were three things that really helped her recover from the emotional scars.

Lauren had been attacked and had fought off a potential rapist; it had been her idea and persuasion that led to the offer from Brad. Lauren had spent ages talking BK through the recovery, how to forget and how to learn to trust men again; she had been a tower of strength. Brad was a fair bit older than she was, they had met at a charity lunch, purely by chance when he had come to her aid when her car wouldn't start.

Secondly, for a short while, BK was part of a functional family, she had never known her father; in fact she was always given the impression that her mother hadn't known him that well; she had always craved a father and seeing Brad at home made her understand what she had missed; it was strangely curing.

The third event changed her thinking of the world, one night towards the end of her stay; she had woken up with dreadful itching of her wounds, not wanting to wake Emma who was sleeping next to her, she went for a walk in the garden. As she passed the windows of the den, she saw Brad junior with his girlfriend, BK had watched as slowly and lovingly they made love to each other, she couldn't see the gory details but could see their naked bodies writhing together and the tender way he treated her; there has no lustful grunting, no force, no hurry, he was very gentle.

From the sounds coming through the open window, they were holding each other right on the edges of orgasm; when they went over the edge she almost felt relief herself. She had never been with a man that gentle, kind, loving, constantly ensuring that she was alright and comfortable with the process and getting pleasure; she thought only women could do that to women. She realised she had had sex with lots of guys but never made love like that; she was also aware that she had never had the intensity of orgasm that lucky young Karen had just experienced.

For a full eight weeks whilst BK stayed at Brad's, Emma had bathed BK in salt water, sat in the bath with her as she had to soak for a long time to ease the itching and aid healing. She rubbed cream into BK's most intimate areas, masturbated her, defoliated her and dealt with her feeding, hygiene and personal needs, which she could not manage because of the other injuries. Emma's own injuries were healing well, but she still couldn't wear a bra and most clothing itched; she spent most of the time topless. They became very close friends and talked for a long time and in great detail about previous lovers male and female, loves and their relative worth.

Emma even admitted that she had slept with Jake whilst he was going out with BK. At the end of the eight weeks, they moved into a rented flat together and eventually BK had bought a house in Santa Monica and settled in just prior to going on a European Tour.

Whilst BK was recovering she and Emma slept together and shared the same bed but BK was heterosexual by nature and although she liked the closeness with Emma, BK yearned for the bond with a man. It was six months before BK trusted a man enough to have sex with her, she found she was dry and could not orgasm; she was still nervous, it was a one night stand and rather unsatisfactory; she had tried several times since but with similar unsatisfactory outcomes.

She was still heartbroken that the man she had loved and trusted had hurt her so much, maybe her father could have explained or helped her. She felt betrayed, devastated and deeply hurt emotionally and of course was physically scarred. Her music suffered, she had been unable to write any new songs and nothing worked for her. She found that she was both over and under confident, able to sing to audiences but too shy to order a drink at a bar; she had deep psychological scars.

Whilst she was in hospital, she had read a magazine from the Scottish Tourist Board about Edinburgh so she decided to base herself there in the breaks in the European Tour schedule.

Despite Emma being close at hand, BK felt lonely, sad and knew that there was something about life she was missing, she was craving a father figure, a kind gentle man in her life rather than a younger arrogant, up-himself rock star. She wanted someone more her own age where music and the business wasn't what they had in common. Above all, she wanted a normal life doing normal things.

They flew into Berlin for the start of the tour.

Chapter Three

A chance meeting

Simon Macintosh paced the corridor in the Balmoral Hotel in Edinburgh, he was clutching his speech. In a few minutes he would enter the conference room and deliver a key note speech to fellow Chairs and Chief Executives detailing the transformation route he had driven his health trust down in the three years since he became Chairman.

He was used to public speaking; it came easily to him, a natural communicator. That wasn't what was making him nervous, it was months since Jane had died, this was the first time he had agreed to speak and his confidence had been shot to pieces. His mind raced and those black thoughts came back, he cleared his mind quickly, he closed his eyes.

'What the hell are you standing there for like some dork grab hold of this'. His eyes snapped open in time to grab an oval, leather bag from the woman standing in silhouette in the doorway to the street at the end of the corridor. There was a group of people unloading bags from a van, 'hey move arsehole' she yelled. He moved out of the way and started down the corridor towards the conference room, he remembered the bag 'I'm sorry, I can't help at the moment I have to go' Simon said, putting the bag on the floor.

'What kind of concierge does this crappy hotel run to employ staff like you?' she yelled.

'I'm not staff, I'm a guest too' he said calmly; she stopped and turned to him. 'I am soooo sorry, I had no idea er Simon' she said quickly reading his name badge; 'I was just so worried about everything.'

He smiled at her, she was a bonnie lass, mid 40s, well

dressed, very American probably East Coast but he had no real idea; she looked as if she had the cares of the world on her shoulders and somehow she seemed very sad and slightly familiar.

'I'm sorry I really have to go, I've got to make a speech to the conference through those doors, wish me luck' he said with a smile. 'Hey break a leg hun' was the reply she gave as she moved up the stairs and into the hotel.

He turned to the doors to the conference centre, took a deep breath and walked in with a heavy heart and a slight wry smile.

BK Shore walked swiftly round the corner and stopped. 'Oh, Hal, can you believe that I just did that' she said laughing.

'That poor guy was completely confused, but at least it made you laugh' replied Hal.

Hal Riddick had gone through hell and back with her in the last year or so; she had been nearly beaten to death by that arsehole Jake, who had plea-bargained himself out of trouble by admitting assault on Emma Button. They had gone along with the process to avoid damaging news stories for BK and Jake, who claimed it was consensual and got out of hand and they were 'interrupted' by Emma. The facts were he got high on drugs, beat her and raped her. The physical wounds had healed but the emotional ones ran deep; she hardly ever laughed, and hadn't composed anything for over a year. He had to manage the press throughout her time with Jake; it had been a tempestuous relationship at the best of times and keeping the lid on the beatings, Jake's other women and the antics he had got up to had not been easy. All the time Brad Morgan, her manager, had yelled and screamed at him that her music was shit; she hadn't recorded anything new for ages and came across as miserable, sour and reclusive.

He had watched her go downhill, followed by a break-down, she had tried drinking herself to oblivion, suffered depression, hit cocaine, and he couldn't remember when she had last had fun. She spent a great deal of time with Emma, her executive assistant. He was pretty sure they were lovers but wasn't certain, they were close though but Emma was a good influence on her and had managed to keep her reasonably focused.

It was decided that a European tour might get her out of herself. She was so weak, vulnerable and sad it reflected on her music and the European tour was not going that well, dreadfully more accurately. Sales of tickets were OK but not good, there was no new material and the performances lacked passion, sexiness and sparkle. She had insisted they come to Edinburgh whilst the whole road show moved from Berlin to Paris, she refused to stay in Paris – 'the city of lovers and I'm not one of them, it's too romantic, let's go to Edinburgh, I'm told it's pretty' she said.

They entered the Royal Suite of the Balmoral Hotel; it has breathtaking views over the historic Old Town of Edinburgh and is filled with antique and modern furniture, luxurious fabrics and a feature living flame fire in both the lounge and main bedroom. There was a private dining menu; a well-stocked in-room bar and snack basket, interactive television, walk-in dressing rooms, and a mosaic and marble bathroom with a spa bath and double walk-in shower.

Hal had a linked room as did Emma; Hal threw his bags on his bed and sat on the chair in despair; this was going to be a very long and boring weekend with Miss Moody causing havoc. He stripped and walked into the bathroom, switched on the water in the bath, pottered around the room unpacking his things and then stepped into the warm bubbles. He dozed off to sleep, overcome by creeping tiredness and the wonderful warmth of the bath.

Simon sat on the stage with the other speakers, answering questions from the floor, his speech had gone well and now the questions were coming thick and fast. He was enjoying himself; using his skills and knowledge excited him, he felt alive.

The chairman thanked everyone and the conference broke up and people departed to their offices, cars or to catch trains or planes home. He was just leaving when he remembered that he had left his umbrella in the rack in the corridor; he was notorious for leaving umbrellas in bars around town, he joked that he lost them faster than the corporate bodies could give them to him. He hadn't remembered this one until he looked outside to see it pishing it down with rain, a real dreich cold February day in Scotland. He walked across the conference room to the vestibule and through to the corridor. He had been there a lot because the toilets in this corridor had Moulton Brown hand cream, which he adored and something in his Aberdonian genes made him appreciate it so much more when it was free.

As he came out of the toilet rubbing the hand cream in he walked across the corridor to his umbrella. He looked up and there stood a lonely figure, agitated, muttering to herself.

BK Shore decided she needed a drink, not room service but to go to a bar; the guide book in the hotel room said there were lots of bars in Edinburgh. She came to the side entrance in case there were photographers but now she didn't see it was such a good idea; she realised she didn't have the confidence to go outside. 'Get your act together, how difficult can this be?' she said. She was startled by someone talking to her. 'Can I help you? You look lost', she turned realising she had a map in her hand and there was the man from earlier, holding an umbrella, upside down.

'I ... err' she said.

'Did you get settled in and get all your bags to your room, using hotel staff' he said with a smile. BK Shore thought it was a nice smile; especially from a man of this age, she thought bitchily, he had to be late forties and had kind, intelligent but sad eyes.

'Yes I did, I'm so sorry about that, do you know of a good bar in Edinburgh?' she didn't know why she said that last bit, it sounded awful.

He smiled again 'I know lots of bars in Edinburgh, what type were you looking for?' He moved over to help her with the map. 'Do you want a modern bar, an old pub or an ancient pub?' he asked.

Simon looked at the woman in front of him, she was nervous, he could tell, he hoped it wasn't him that made her nervous. She seemed rather sad, he could see it in her eyes and he saw the same thing in his eyes, loneliness; she looked younger than her mid 40s but had not worn well, he guessed, well dressed, quite OK really and she had long blonde hair.

'Are you worried about going out there?' he said.

'It's just a new city and I...' she said.

'Tell you what; I've got a wee while to my next meeting. I'll get you started and then the rest will be up to you' he said.

'Er no it's OK, you don't have to' said BK.

'My name is Simon, Simon Macintosh, what's yours?' he said offering his hand.

'Er my name is er Karen King' she replied.

'OK Karen lets head for the Guildford' he said.

BK wondered if she had gone mad, she was on her own, without backup, in a strange city and with a complete stranger who didn't even recognise her. As they crossed onto the setts outside the pub she stumbled, and Simon put his arm around her to steady her, it felt strange, comforting and kind; they broke contact as soon as she had regained her balance.

They entered the Guildford Arms, she was stunned; it was like entering a different world; it was busy with lots of people at the end of their work early on Friday and quite a few groups of people in white and red shirts. But the architecture was wild, Victorian with great swirls on the ceiling and dark wood walls; this was genuine, not the fake stuff in the bars in LA.

He bought the drinks and they looked for somewhere to sit, they moved into the bar and towards the rear. The seat and tables were all occupied but just as they got to the last table, the couple in the alcove in a pit at the back stood up to leave and they went and took their places.

The two of them sat almost isolated from the pub; few people could see they were there. They chatted about Edinburgh and America; they realised they had very different lives, but got on very well and were relaxed in each other's company.

'Hey' she said 'this place is awesome, thanks for bringing me here'.

'I haven't been in here for ages not since' he stopped talking mid sentence and looked incredibly sad, he looked into the distance.

'Jees, that hurt, what happened?' she said.

'My wife died' he said, she watched as his head went down and his eyes watered.

'I'm sorry I didn't mean to pry, how long had you been married?' she said, prying

'29 years, it's a long time' he said.

'29 years and she just died like that, what happened?' she asked.

Simon explained his story, the plane crash, the grief, the self destruction; he did so in a faltering voice with long pauses; Karen was enthralled, how could anyone deal with that?

'So how on earth did you deal with it, what was her name?'

'Jane, her name was Jane' he said wistfully. 'Karen, I dealt with it incredibly badly, I had dreadful nightmares and depression but luckily the pills from the doctor zonked me so much I hardly noticed. I lost two stone in weight; 28 pounds for you Americans. I drank too much, watched TV and generally hit the bottom. I'm still not really over it, I feel so lonely, empty alone, no one to share with having shared everything; at one time, I had a string of encounters looking for a replacement, I was a bit of a tart, I realised I was deluded' he said sadly, without eye contact and incredibly sadly.

He asked her 'So why are you so sad and lonely just like me?'

'How did you know I was unhappy and lonely?' she said

'Takes one to know one' he replied, shrugging his shoulders.

'He was called Jake, I thought I loved him, he was 26 and I was 34, a toy boy. When he left I fell to pieces, depression, pills, drink; I took noses full of coke; I dated wimps to try to find something but' she broke down.

Tears welled in her eyes and then brimmed over 'I'm lonely, I must be the loneliest woman on the planet, and I have everything and nothing.' She looked up at him with tears streaming down her face.

Instinctively, Simon put his arm around her and pulled her close, he was now crying. They sat there embracing and crying together, they were tears of sadness, and they were tears of suffering in silence. Simon rubbed her back, in the same way that a parent rubs a child's back; he gently kissed on the top of her head but it was like a father's kiss for a heartbroken daughter.

She cuddled into the strong arms, she felt warmth around her and then ever so gently, he kissed her on the top of her head. Bizarrely, she thought it felt so gentle, wonderfully supportive and kind; she became aware that he was holding on to her and realised that he was as scared of being lonely as she was. Simon forced himself to stop crying, he felt comfortable in this embrace and she must too as she had cuddled harder into him; they held their position for several lovely but lonely minutes. Her phone rang and Simon reluctantly broke the embrace; she pulled her phone out of her jeans pocket.

Simon looked at her, she was wearing jeans with a wide sparkly belt and really sexy mid length black boots with an impossible looking height of heels. He noticed she wasn't exactly thin or skinny, probably a size 12 or 14, not that he could talk but she wore those jeans exceedingly well. She had on a vast gray sweater with a big puffy collar that meant he could not see her figure. Her hair was lovely, long and shiny, she had it brushed straight and it flowed like a golden waterfall to about four inches below her shoulder line, it really suited her. She had a pleasant face with some scarring around the nose and as he looked at her, he realised that she was a lot younger than he had first thought.

BK was annoyed that her phone had stopped their embrace; she had felt safe, supported and warm for the first time in ages; the call was from Hal, he was raving at her.

'Where the fuck are you missy, do you know how dangerous it is for you to go out on your own in a city?' he yelled.

'Calm down Hal sweetie, I'm with a friend' she was aware of Simon looking at her and mouthed sorry to him. He smiled, that was a nice smile she thought, his eyes were not smiling though, they we set back, sunken and sad, she recognised the look. He went to pull away and remove his arm which was around her shoulders; she stopped him.

'Hal, don't worry' she said. It occurred to her, he probably should, she was in a bar with a total stranger, they had just emptied their hearts to each other and now she had stopped the stranger, who was much older than she was, from breaking physical contact with her; she knew very little about her new friend but then he didn't seem to know her either.

'BK you're vulnerable, you could get drunk, lost, kidnapped, raped; your mind isn't all straight, get the hell back here, before you end up on the front pages of the papers or worse'.

'Hal, I really don't want to leave what I'm doing now, ring me in an hour and I will tell you where we have been, if I need help I will ring you, please Hal, I need this' she said.

It wasn't the defiance; they had seen her defiant and pushing the self destruct button with the urgency of someone stuck in an elevator. What shocked him was that she hadn't sworn and that she was not shouting at him and was calm, she had never simply asked.

'Who are you with?' said Hal.

'Simon, the guy in the hotel I thought was a porter' she replied.

'He'll just want to take advantage of you BK; they are all the same just another gold-digger, hanging around the rich and famous' Hall said.

BK laughed and said 'No Hal ring me in an hour and ask nicely for Karen and I will see if she will speak to you'.

She laughed thought Hal 'He doesn't know who you are?' he said.

'On the button sweetie' she rang off.

'What's going on?' Emma said, shaking Hal.

'She is in a bar somewhere in this city with a bloke she met in the hotel' he answered.

'What!! The stupid bitch what is she playing at?' said Emma.

'It's worse, he doesn't know who she is, when he finds out he will either walk or screw her up again, like that guy in Chicago and after all the time we've spent putting her together again'.

BK turned to Simon and said 'I'm sorry about that but people are worried about me'.

'Was that your boyfriend?' he asked.

'Oh boy no, Hal is a colleague of mine and he's a confirmed fag' she said smiling.

'I told you Simon that I'm lonely and alone just like you; we have a lot in common in our grief, so let's just enjoy each other's company' she said touching him lightly on the arm.

'That sounds like a plan' he said and they embraced again.

Their eyes met and they sat holding eye contact for a long time, comfortable in the silence and stare; when they broke eye contact they both realised that their hands on the table were holding each other, neither broke the contact.

The rugby supporters started to sing, the bar was now very crowded and noisy, they decided to leave and find somewhere a little quieter. BK handed Simon the VIP card that the concierge had given her; Simon suggested they made their way to the Opal Lounge, one of the bars listed.

They walked out of the side door of the Guilford Arms and turned left along outside the Cafe Royal, along the street towards Tiles and St Andrews Square. As they turned into the wide alley to St Andrews Square she stumbled again and Simon put his arm around her and she put her arm around him.

'I would carry you over the cobbles but I'm far too old' he said.

'Oh come on buster, you can't be a day under 40' she said, they both laughed.

'You're right; I'm 54, how old are you?' Simon replied.

'36' Karen said adding 'God that's nearly 20 years younger than you'.

'Thanks for pointing that out, I feel so much better,

perhaps you should carry me' they laughed again.

'Are you wearing five inch heeled boots?' she said.

'No, I can never get them in my size' he said, they laughed again.

As they walked they started to tell each other more about themselves and their lives, they were forming a bond of friendship and understanding.

Chapter Four

Kissing and hugging in the Opal Lounge

They walked along George Street, Simon pointed out the Dome, Hard Rock Cafe and Tempus Bar. BK realised that they had walked the entire way with their arms around each other; Simon had stopped to talk to various people as they walked along; it was the end of the working day and the offices were emptying out and mixing with large numbers of England Rugby fans, the street was alive and buzzing with excitement.

Simon was enjoying feeling relaxed and the first glass of wine had cheered him up from the sadness of their last conversation. He was slightly embarrassed when they met David and then Manus in George Street. David, who was a young auditor, had looked at Karen in a very strange way, Manus had asked how she knew such an old man, and he had been very funny and winked as he left.

They went down the stairs into the Opal Lounge, the two rugby supporters in front of them were turned away by the doorman. BK flashed her VIP pass and the doorman with a second take opened the door and gestured to the host who greeted them. The bar was packed but the greeter, in an immaculate black outfit complete with a plunging shirt down to his navel, guided them through the throng and into the member's area at the back; he ushered them to a table but BK saw a nice secluded alcove and said 'we will sit there', he looked at BK, smiled and nodded, 'yes, of course, madam'.

The private members area consisted of a long bar to the left and to the right a series of semicircular alcoves seating between six and two people, each alcove had white muslin-like material stretched and pleated from ceiling to the top of the semi-circular seating; affording privacy but making the area bright. BK had seen that at the end of the row of alcoves there was a small table for two that half faced the fire exit and half faced a table of six. It was very private and could not really be seen from the doorway and or from the bar; you would know that someone was occupying it but could not see by whom.

They sat there and the waiter arrived to take the order. BK said 'some sparkling water and your wine list' the waiter turned. It was hot in this bar and they both removed their coats and jackets; BK took off her sweater and sat down next to Simon, the waiter returned with the wine list. She turned to Simon and said 'What is a good European wine?' He answered 'Red'; she laughed and turned to study the wine list and ordered.

Simon looked at her again, she was rather good looking and she did have a nice cleavage, he could see the nice rounded edges of her breasts held in a white laced bra and covered with a white blouse which clearly was well tailored. He guessed she was probably C cup but with modern technology it had become difficult to say; as he scanned her body he thought she was about average size, she certainly wasn't skinny but had a slim waist but larger hips and thighs.

'What is rugby and how come there are all these people from England here?' she said.

'Well, Scotland plays England at Murrayfield tomorrow for the Calcutta Cup' he replied.

'That hasn't actually helped a great deal' she said, laughing; she hadn't laughed for some time and now, with him, she was doing it regularly, he had charm and he was so relaxed. She watched as he suddenly became very animated and a broad smile crossed his face; he explained rugby.

As he talked, BK looked him over, he was about 5ft 10ins tall, he was well built but didn't have a paunch like a lot of guys his age, he had wide shoulders which, she knew from his grip were powerful, he must work out; he was not very over-weight, she could see he had lovely legs quite athletic and she was sure he did not look his age; but it was his wit and smile she was enchanted with, his relaxed manner, she realised that came with maturity.

'I've lost you haven't I?' Simon said.

'Yes honey' BK said, concentrating again.

The wine arrived, the waiter filled their glasses and Simon said 'Failte a Alba, Slainte mhath, Welcome to Scotland, good health, cheers'.

'So tomorrow is a big day England v Scotland?' she said.

'Yes, I've got a spare ticket if you want to come along and see the game for yourself, I'd hate to go alone or waste the ticket' Simon said.

'Do you know, I would love to' she heard herself say, why did she say that, she knew nothing about rugby or him, Hal would crap himself, they would argue but she didn't seem to care, she was also relaxed with him and had her arm around him.

'When did you last go to a major sports event?' he asked.

She stared into the distance; I went to a baseball game; I was very miserable and about half time went home in a taxi. She started to cry, Simon put his arm around her, it was an instinctive move and he regretted it almost straightaway and pulled his arm back.

'No don't, please leave it there' she said.

She cuddled him harder, she liked that 'what *is* that after shave you are wearing?' she said.

'It's called L'Occataine, it's French' he said.

'It smells very different but I love it, it's such a gorgeous smell, it's very you' she said.

He leant forward to get his wine and was surprised to feel her rising up, she pushed him back and they kissed full on the lips, he was shocked, it wasn't where he thought things were going. Maybe it was the wine and the warmth, maybe he had missed the signs, anyway he kissed back.

'You're quite a good kisser, for an old guy' she said.

'Practice makes perfect, I once won a kissing competition in a pub in Glasgow' Simon smiled and told her the story.

She laughed and her phone rang again, she answered it still giggling like a little girl, there was a pause.

'BK what's going on, where are you are you all right?' demanded Hal Riddick.

'I'm OK, actually I'm better than OK' BK answered 'I'm enjoying every minute, we are in a great bar with a real nice quiet lounge and we are sat on a settee in a nice private place' she said.

'BK at least tell the poor sucker who you are, has he only got one head? He must be from a different planet if he doesn't recognise you; look, tell us where you are and we will come and get you' Hal pleaded.

'Hal, I know you are right, but I'm enjoying myself and Mr Riddick, I'm going to the rugby tomorrow' she threw the phone on the table in front of them.

Back at the hotel, Hal and Emma had listened together, when the phone went quiet they looked at each other in exasperation and they both said 'what the hell is rugby?'

BK took Simon's hand and kissed him again on the cheek.

'Simon, I have to tell you something and I expect it will mean I can't go to the rugby,' she said; his face fell but she moved closer to him.

'I'm BK Shore' she looked deep into his face for a reaction

but saw no recognition.

'Is that like HIV positive?' he asked; she roared with laughter, in the back of his mind he did know who BK Shore was.

'No, I'm an international singer, I've sold millions of records and I'm on a European tour and have a few days off her in Edinburgh; I've lied to you my name's not Karen' she said sadly.

'I also lied to you' Simon said 'I don't have another meeting to go to, it's Friday night and I was going to sit in my flat on my own; I was lonely, wanted some company and I met a woman called Karen, who is still here with me and who has just tenderly, very tenderly kissed me, I don't care what you are, I feel more alive than I have for months. I will call you Karen, so when you are with me you are Karen and when you are in your other world you are BK Shore; so Karen, will you come to the rugby with me tomorrow?'

Hal whispered to Emma, 'the sucker doesn't know who she is'. Emma waved for him to be silent; the two of them huddled closer to the phone. BK was clearly unaware that when she threw the phone down it went onto speak phone and they could hear everything that was being said; Emma pushed a note pad and pen between them so they could 'talk'.

Karen giggled, Hal couldn't remember the last time she had giggled like that but it had been a very long time, probably before she met that arsehole Jake.

Karen leant forward, they kissed, long and hard; Simon felt her body next to his and the slight touch of her tongue, she moaned just a little; he could feel himself becoming slightly aroused, naughty boy.

Hal scribbled 'what are they doing?' Emma replied 'kissing'.

Hal mimed fuck fuck fuck; Emma wrote 'no just kissing if they were doing that, there would be more noise!!' They were giggling now but silently.

They heard the unmistakable sound of two people finishing a long kiss and shifting in an embrace.

'That was very nice, Karen' Simon said.

'I think you deserved your kissing award' she said.

'In the competition, that was just a level two kiss,' he said.

'So when do I get level three?' she asked.

'When you ask nicely, drink your wine' he said and winked. 'By the way it's not a three point scale' and smiled at Karen, she thought it was one of the naughtiest and enchanting smiles she had seen.

They sniggered like school kids, she realised she was very relaxed in his presence, probably too relaxed, the wine was beginning to kick in, it was a very nice wine and it was lovely and warm in their little alcove. She felt strange, light headed and er young? She recognised it; she knew what it was she was enjoying herself.

'OK, so tell me what happens at a rugby game?' she said.

'A band plays, we sing and Scotland gets beaten, we go and party' he said.

'So those guys in the shirts and the guy in the town crier's uniform are England supporters? But you got on with them really well' she said questioningly.

'Ah this is rugby, no crowd segregation, no problems and five minutes after the game no one can remember the score; he's dressed as John Bull, a mythical English character' Simon replied.

'So do the Scots wear kilts?' she asked.

'Of course, even I will be in my kilt tomorrow' he replied.

'Is it true about what a Scotsman wears under his kilt?' she asked with an impish smile.

He leant forward, very close to her, she liked that, she arched back ready for a kiss but he said 'There is nothing worn under the kilt it's all in perfect working order.'

He kissed her briefly on the lips, looking down her cleavage and he saw a small mound on her breast, so she was enjoying and slightly aroused by his company.

'What do I wear?' she said.

'Clothes might be an idea, I'm sure you look good in a bikini but it is a little impractical for Edinburgh in February, it might even snow tomorrow' he said. Simon leant forward to get his wine but detoured and he kissed her this time, she responded and they cuddled each other in the throws of another kiss.

Back in the Balmoral, Hal and Emma were entranced; neither had seen this side of their employer, friend and charge. It was an incredibly personal almost intimate conversation they were listening too, Emma felt quite emotional and a little jealous; she and BK were or had been intimate friends. She wrote to Hal 'should we be listening to this?' He wrote back 'I can't think of anything I want to do more.'

At the Opal Lounge, Simon and Karen sipped their wine; it was a mighty fine Barolo and had gone down rather easily despite the distractions.

Simon said 'I'm not the best person to ask but most of the young women wear Tartan miniskirts with legging type things or is it tights, I don't know, with a Scotland home strip. I have no idea what they wear underneath, but it would have to be thermal this week, obviously a big warm coat and they take a big Arran sweater for the match; it's Baltic at Murrayfield this weather.'

'Where do I get them?' Karen asked.

'Jenner's opposite your hotel or the shops in Royal Mile, the hotel will know' he replied.

'What pattern, sorry tartan?' she asked.

'Macintosh, if you can get it, not Campbell, my family have a history there and not Buchannan which is a dreadful colour' he replied.

Back at the hotel, Emma had made a note of everything and as it was still early, she might still get them; she wrote on the pad, Simon Macintosh, Edinburgh – Facebook now!! Hal went into his bedroom and brought back his laptop.

Karen leant forward and kissed Simon again, this time their tongues met tentatively and then urgently as they did she wondered if this was a level 3 kiss. She felt an arousal in her and a tension in him, this was stupid, they were both lonely; he was 20 years older than she was and they had only just met, but it felt so right, so nice, so good, so mmm.

Back at the hotel, Emma hung up; Hal objected 'Why did you do that for?'

'Hal, unless I'm mistaken she is about to ring us to tell me to get these clothes, I'm off to Jenner's to see what I can get' she said, looking for her coat and bag.

Emma added 'lighten up Hal, think what you have just heard, she called you Mr Riddick, she wasn't yelling at you and she was laughing; hey mister get that plug out of your ass and start thanking our lucky stars.'

'He's an old guy, look'; they looked at his photo on Facebook and said 'Elton John!!' the guy's Facebook photo was one of Elton John. Hal clicked the icon on his explorer bar that said 'LinkedIn', the business network was great for finding out about people, up came Simon's profile, and a real photo, you know he does look like Elton John, he clicked the link to Simon's website.

As Emma was leaving the room, her phone rang; it was BK.

In the Opal Lounge, several of the group of people who were sat opposite Karen and Simon, stood up, the group was a mixture of young men and women, the men in business suits and the women in twin sets or trouser suits. The girls had undone several buttons of their blouses, exposing far more of their breasts than they would in the workplace, the men had responded, removing ties, undoing buttons and rolling up their sleeves. It was clear to Karen that some of them, especially the girl in the red blouse and the guy next to her with black hair, were more than work colleagues.

Part of the group started to leave, casually putting on their coats but leaving their jackets; the taller of the three guys turned to the group and said 'we're just off for a fag anyone else want to come?'

Karen turned to Simon 'what did he just say, Simon?'

'Ah, a people divided by a common language, in Scotland you are not allowed to smoke in a public place, so he is going outside to shag a homosexual instead' he said.

She laughed and jabbed him playfully in the ribs, they kissed again; their kisses were getting more relaxed and deeper.

When they parted, they could see the couple opposite had been left on their own and were attempting to climb down each other's throats. The guy was gradually moving his hand over the girls right breast, she was clearly enjoying the moment.

'That's a level three' Simon whispered.

The couple broke for a moment and the guy looked around then turned and kissed his girlfriend again. This time, his hand ran over her breasts and under her blouse and into her bra. He gently massaged her naked breast, they parted and he removed his hand as their friends returned to the table; Simon and Karen could see their mutual arousal.

Simon and Karen said 'level four' at the same time and they laughed.

They stared at each other; Simon stroked her face, they kissed; Simon moved his right hand up Karen's body and gently cupped her left breast in his hand. He felt the wee bump of her erect nipple and gently rubbed the little nub. 'mmmmm' she said, still in their kiss.

She laid her head on his shoulder and said 'that was so nice', she pushed him back onto the settee and kissed him again, she moved her hand over his left hand and moved it up onto her right breast, then put her hand on his chest and played with his nipple, tit for tat she thought; they parted and looked at each other.

They ordered some soft drinks, they were now quite merry and relaxed and enjoying each other's company. Simon was aware that they had started a mutual touching process as people do. Karen said 'I'm getting very tiddly and you are looking wonderful'.

'Must be the wine, you are gorgeous but above all, I am enjoying being with you too' Simon said.

They continued to chat, Simon was interested in her world and her job, and he asked her 'so how does the agent, a manager, a production company and record label thing work'.

'Everything is protected by someone's union and the performer is the last in a very long line of people to get any money out of their own talent. I can't even use my own name and my stage name is registered and trademarked' she replied.

'So Belinda Shore isn't your real name?' Simon said.

'No, I can't use Belinda either; I'm registered as B.K. Shore' Karen replied.

'OK, I'm confused what is the name on your birth certificate?' said Simon searching for clarity.

Sarah King/Karen/BK/Belinda/Sarah said 'I couldn't register my stage name under my own name, my mother's name is Erin Belinda King, I hate Erin as a name, so BK, it is also an abbreviation for Bakersfield, I can't remember where Shore came from I think we tried Shaw,' she said.

He leant forward, kissed her briefly on the lips and said 'I'll stick with Karen, Karen'.

'The business is very complicated, I will simplify the system; I have my own company called Beach and I have a share in a record label called Blue which is jointly owned with some other acts. Brad Morgan is my manager and Hal Riddick is the CEO of Beach; he negotiates with my manager, agents etc for my services and fees. Larry Packman is the promoter and his company organises the gigs and then there is the recording company, I still have three years to run on a contract.

Beach employs Hal, who organises my work and my business and Emma who looks after my personal interests and our secretary Carolyn, a publicist and her department, lawyers and accountants who look after my business interests; there is also a production team, the band and touring manager who look after my music. At present, whilst on tour, I employ about 170 people. I own another company called BKSM, BK Shore Music, which owns the copyright to everything I write and record, I have written some songs that are performed by other people, BKSM has its own legal team and executive of five and lastly, there is SLK, Sarah Linda King, which is my real name, SLK looks after my personal investments, property and assets' she said.

'And I thought traded derivatives were complex, I wish I hadn't asked' Simon said.

'Now you know how I felt about rugby and like you I've left out almost as much as I put in' they laughed and he tickled her around the waist, they hugged each other.

Karen said 'if we are to meet up for the rugby tomorrow, we should exchange contact details'.

Karen typed on her phone and said 'OK, let's Bluetooth,' she laughed out loud. Simon's face was a picture, he had his phone in his hand and the look on his face was so comical; he had to admit to her that he knew all about Bluetooth but had no idea how to get it to work on his phone. He also apologised profusely for being too old to understand technology, she smiled sweetly at him, took his hand and placed in on her breast and said 'You are only as old as the woman you feel', they kissed again and were interrupted by a smirking waiter.

They ordered their meal; neither of them had really looked at the menu so Karen went with Simon's recommendation.

They returned to the phones and they managed to exchange their contact details straight onto each other's phones, Simon was very impressed, Karen saw nothing unusual in the transfer of data. Karen had used her personal contact details, not her business contacts, her personal phone was hers and it was paid from her personal account not her businesses.

As Karen was working her phone and Simon's, Simon turned and looked at her, long blonde hair hung over her shoulders, her blouse slightly open revealing an interesting amount of lightly tanned flesh, her body looked sweet and well filled, her jeans and thighs were tight; she looked great; but it was how they got on, her personality and charm that he really liked; he was aware he was beginning to fancy her.

'Do you know a guy called Gary?' she said 'several, why?' he said.

'Hey! Look at this, someone called Gary has sent a series of photos by Bluetooth and I've picked them up on your phone,' there had been no security code, like she had used.

'Oh my god, it's that girl sat opposite,' she pulled Simon in beside her and they conspiratorially cuddled and looked at a series of five photos called 'and here is one I had earlier'. They were highly sexually explicit photographs of the girl about to or having sex, presumably with the guy she was with, only one part of his body was clearly visible. 'That bastard is sending those photos to his mates' said Simon.

'Have you ever done anything like that? Karen asked 'No,

I always used to have naked photos of Jane on my phone but it never crossed my mind to share it with anyone, it was my special album.'

'Did you delete it?' she asked.

Simon smiled and said 'No, a bit like the fourth photo in that series, I backed it up'; they both gave a loud laugh and bashed against each other as they shared the joke.

Karen looked at him, his hair brushed neatly, his pinstripe suit, his shirt now undone showing some of his ginger chest hair, his smile, she felt his hand next to hers and she breathed in and could smell his aftershave. He was such good fun, so caring, she felt safe and protected with him in a way she had not done with other men, for some inconceivable reason, his maturity and humour really got to her, she realised that she was beginning to fancy him.

They ate their meal chatting and joking all the time, when the bill arrived and Simon went to pay, 'no, honey' said Karen 'this meal is on expenses and deductible, so let me pay for it, there are some advantages of running a business, but you know that don't you?'

'Being of Aberdonian stock, I will accept a free meal from anyone, thanks that is most kind of you, BK' he replied, she looked at him, 'you haven't called me BK all night, please don't, please call me Karen, I don't want to be called BK by you.'

'By the way' said Simon 'where the hell did Karen come from in your encyclopaedia of names?'

'I'll tell you one day' Karen said, he looked her in the eyes and said 'Thank you for a lovely evening and meal, Karen' and they kissed.

It took some time to climb into sweaters, scarves, coats gloves etc, Karen pushed Simon back onto the seats and kissed him firmly on the lips, their tongues played together and Karen guided his hand under her coat; they were there for a long time and afterwards sat looking at each other, Simon's hand cupping her left breast.

Karen stepped forward and said 'I really enjoyed that'. She replaced his hand and said 'I have enjoyed your company, I like your hand there, and I know you like putting it there.'

He removed his hand 'I'm sorry, I am going to have to drop you off at your hotel, I can't' he looked at the floor.

Karen said 'Don't be sorry, I'm not, I do understand what you mean. Look, Honey, we have another day tomorrow, so why don't you walk me back to my hotel and kiss me good-night and we will meet up for the rugby tomorrow and see how things go. I am so glad I met you' they kissed again, the hand moved in circular motions. Simon could not believe his luck, she was 20 years younger than him and gorgeous; Karen thought she had been so lucky to meet such a nice kind and gentle guy.

Chapter Five

Scrum down, play begins

Simon was woken by the buzz of his alarm clock; he reached out and tapped the top of the clock to put it on snooze. He had slept incredibly deeply despite being excited by the turn of events the previous evening; indeed he had had to take himself in hand to get to sleep at all, but once asleep he had drifted into a deep and unusually dreamless sleep.

He snuggled under the covers and wondered if all that happened was true; he ran the movie of the evening in his head. He had always had the ability to run a kind of movie to see what was happening, he thought it was one of the gifts of his dyslexia; it enabled him to portray abstract things in a very concrete manner. It had been a curse with the six months of constant nightmares and horror movies imagining the last moment of Jane's life; he shuddered under the covers. The gift meant that although his occasional foray into writing fiction had been relatively unsuccessful, he was good at writing articles, academic papers and speech writing and delivery.

He was suddenly aware that he had not dreamt of Jane, he often did, things during the day would trigger thoughts; God! What would she be thinking if she was watching, dirty old man? He remembered discussing with her what her reaction would be if she found out that he had been unfaithful, several times she had pushed him to find out if he had been; she was a mild-tempered woman but had left him in no doubt that she would have fought for her man. A wave of sadness washed over his thoughts, he would give everything to be waking up next to her; his hand instinctively stroked the bed next to him.

Their's had been a loving relationship, lasting over three

decades, despite opportunities he had never fallen in love with anyone else, they had done so much together and achieved such good things, in particular the two fantastic young women, their daughters. God! Fiona, his oldest daughter would kill him, if she realised he had kissed someone more her age than his, she could never adjust to her father with a different woman and Simon had had to keep his other female friends well away from her and Alex. Alexandria, Alex, their other daughter was very much more laid back, after she finished her PhD, she had got a job at a research institute just outside Edinburgh and she lived with her boyfriend, Duncan, in a flat near Haymarket Station a couple of miles away.

Fiona and her husband, Stewart, lived in a house in Livingston, 16 miles away with Simon's granddaughter Mary; they were very happy and quite successful and content with life, what else did a parent want?

The alarm erupted from snooze mode, he threw back the covers and leapt to his feet, he had always slept naked since the kids had been older and he and Jane started each day with a nice close cuddle or made love, how he missed that; he walked across to the dressing table and switched on his laptop.

Dorcas O'Hare, the interior designer he had employed, regarded his bedroom as 'very male' not at all girlie and dominated by the king size bed. He had laughed when she had said 'if you get a woman into that bed she will start to redecorate in her mind; it's like staying in a Travelodge'; Simon loved it.

The room had two almost full length windows that looked over the roof of Waverley station four floors or so below, there were net curtains at the windows and Simon pulled the cord and the first of the full length bright red curtains opened to reveal the day beyond. It was a dry day, with just an occasional flake of snow fluttering across the view; there had been a light dusting of snow but not even enough to affect the

Edinburgh traffic. He turned into the room; the wall opposite the windows was floor to ceiling mirrors along it entire length; behind was wardrobes, chests of drawers and storage space, the pelmet at the top housed the tracking and the lighting that shone onto the ceiling. Simon opened the other curtain and moved over towards the dressing table, this wall had the door to the living room and a large dressing table and an enormous framed mirror. The fourth wall had a doorway to the bathroom between the windows and the king size bed; the bedside tables and a double shelf across the bed were all in dark cherry veneer, they also house lights shining down as reading lights for the bed and up to bounce off the ceiling to give ambient diffused light. The bed had a white sheet and pillow cases, a black duvet cover and a red runner over the end of the bed, matching the curtains.

The dressing table was made of the same wood as the bedside tables and shelving; Simon leant over his laptop and clicked the icon for the Vodaphone Music Store and typed in BK Shore, a list of songs appeared and he downloaded three at random, plugged in the speakers for the room and pressed play.

He walked into the bathroom and used the toilet; an old man's thing, at least the morning glory had been impressive, he thought. The music started to play and he listened in, oh dear, not his kind of music; he was a Rolling Stones, Eric Clapton and Mark Knopfler kind of a guy and this was very much pop mush, Spice Girls meets Bananarama and Status Quo. He opened the door and walked out of the bedroom into the living room, this was a triangular shaped room with one wall straight and the other tapering the room in width from 35ft to 16ft, with the fireplace in the middle of the 16ft 'apex' wall; he walked into the kitchen and through the door on the left into the utility room.

This room housed the boiler, the hot water system, the washer dryer and had a sink and drainer. He picked up the black leather boots and buffed them to a shine; best to do this naked then everything gets washed off in the shower. He remembered doing this when dressed for a ball in full highland dress and got polish all over his only white dress shirt, ironically he had to wear a black dress shirt instead, since then Jane had insisted that he cleaned his shoes whilst naked, actually she rather liked it, he smiled, frisky, he thought, he felt the stirrings of arousal between his legs.

He walked back through the kitchen, it was black and white; all the cupboards were black lacquer with frosted glass fronts, the work surfaces were white marble, it wasn't actually marble, it was a sort of plastic marble substitute, the floor was a tiled vinyl which reflected the colour of the dining and living room. The dining and living room walls were very light purple, one side of the triangle had four windows including the one in the kitchen by the sink, the other three, one in the dining area and the two in the living room were nearly full-length and had long deep purple curtains. The other wall by the entrance to his bedroom had two full-length windows and the wall with the doorway to his bedroom was painted the same deep purple as the curtains.

The room had a large screen TV on one wall and the fireplace, with a pile of logs neatly stacked next to it; a large 'L' shaped white leather settee dominated the room which was carpeted in the same speckled carpet as in the bedroom only light purple and gray. Against the wall to the bedroom stood a dark wood Welsh dresser which looked just a little out of place, its shelves were full of photographs and ornaments. On the lefthand wall stood a china cabinet, which had been recently restored and again was full of family 'treasures', the sorts of things only families keep, a lock of hair, a damaged pottery cat won in a shooting gallery and commemorative plates.

A corridor ran between Simon's bedroom and the front door, the walls were covered with artwork, his artwork, abstracts, photographs, watercolours of buildings and views from all over the world. Simon was very creative, but totally crap at it; he displayed his work mainly to remember the sympathetic and supportive smiles Jane would give him when he presented her with his latest masterpiece, regardless of its quality.

A door opened to the right that led to the second bedroom, it was quite small but comfortably took a double bed and had a small shower room en suite; this bedroom had one window and was decorated in blue. A closet and another very small shower room led off the corridor just to the right of the front door. Opposite these was a spiral staircase leading upstairs and behind this a small, box room just big enough for a double bed and precious little else. This room had one window, looking over Waverley station and was immediate behind Simon's en suite bathroom.

When Jane had been killed, Simon could not bear to be in the house they had shared, and he had put it on the market with what Fiona thought was unseemly haste. From being his pride and joy it turned into a bête noire, it had sold quite quickly so he rented a flat in Edinburgh, in Dundas Street, above the Trout Anglers Club. He then set about looking for a flat to buy; he wanted to take his time. But about six weeks later; one of his friends rang him to tell him about flats for sale in Cockburn Street, part of a conversion of a corner building that had been council offices; the builder had gone bust having failed to complete the roof replacement. They were going cheap if you had cash to complete the roof quickly and then continue with the conversion; he had walked over, looked around and bought them subject to survey; the legals and transfer took four weeks.

Simon had contacted Alistair, an architect friend and they redrew the plans for the flats and redesigned the roof to make a roof garden, installed a spiral staircase, the office glasshouse and the unique feature, at the end of the roof garden, was a hot tub; the plumbing is a bit complicated but it did work.

'What the hell is that noise?' Simon muttered to himself as he turned into the bedroom; BK Shore was belting out some god awful song, she's a lot nicer than her music he thought.

The music changed and he walked into the bathroom, he could still hear the music from the speakers in the bathroom; a song called 'Love smiles' came on, he thought, that's better but would be much better sung slow and with passion rather than screamed down a microphone, he felt old.

His bathroom had gold, brown and cream mosaic tiles on the floor, which were heated, beige tiles up the wall with a ceramic Rennie Mackintosh dado rail in art deco turquoise, terracotta and cream. The window had a very heavy net to provide privacy but was not frosted; long curtains in dark brown hung either side draped back with a tie to cover part of the window.

On the far wall was the toilet, a cream coloured square pan and seat with the cistern tucked away behind a false wall, to the right and along the wall facing the bedroom were two sinks with storage underneath, the sinks were set in the same 'marble' as the kitchen and the storage units were made of the same wood veneer as used in the bedroom. On the far wall, that faced the box room, was a vertical towel rail with big flurry, dark bronze and black bath sheets; the rest of this wall and the corner leading across to the toilet was a large walk-in shower with a monsoon shower head; Simon hit the start button and lashings of hot water washed over his still sleepy body.

He washed his body with Dove shower gel and his hair in a combination of shampoo and conditioner from the Moulton Brown collection; the soft suds and the warm water were so gorgeous and relaxing, he didn't want to leave but the phone rang; he switched the shower off, grabbed a towel and walked into the bedroom, snapped the phone by the bed onto speak phone and said 'Simon Macintosh'.

'Hiya Simon, its Manus, you dirty old codger, that was some young totty you were with last night'.

'You're only jealous, old boy' Simon replied.

'In your dreams, anyway we have a game to watch, where do you want to meet, we don't want you on your own' Manus said.

'I'm taking Karen with me, the woman you met me with last night' Simon said.

'Rock on you old dark horse you, well done' Manus chuckled.

'So do you want to meet up after the game, Sarah and I and the others are off to the Hampton after but we will meet in the beer tent in the north car park first, up for that?'

'Aye, I expect so I'll text you if anything different, we're off to the Jamhouse for dinner' said Simon.

'Ok and Simon it's great to see you with someone' Manus rang off.

Simon walked out into the kitchen, switched the kettle on and took out the porridge packet, mixed in the milk and microwaved some breakfast which he took through to the bedroom and settled down in front of his laptop.

He had to tend to his farm. Alex, his daughter, had introduced him to Farmville on Facebook and he had been hooked ever since, great, his cranberries were ready and he had a stack of trees to harvest; he started at his tasks. He also Googled BK Shore and read about her, she had certainly had a different and difficult time; the reviews of her Berlin concert were simply dreadful, there were quite a few insulting comments.

He looked up and it was nearly eleven o'clock, hell where did the time go, he'd been up about an hour and a half, had breakfast, done a bit of browsing but still hadn't put any clothes on; he would have to leave in an hour and still had to tidy the flat.

He bustled out of the bedroom; he had a weekly cleaner who came in on a Friday and she cleaned the toilets, flung the Hoover around and generally dusted. He remembered his mother having a cleaner Mrs Willet; in the end his mother used to clean the house before Mrs Willet got there so the old girl didn't have too much work to do, they were all dead now, he thought sadly.

He emptied the dishwasher and put away its content then reloaded it with the stuff on the drainer and his breakfast things, made a pint of blackcurrant squash and walked back to the bedroom. He opened one of the mirrored walls and started to lay out his clothes for the day. First, his rugby kilt, then the sporran, the belt, a thick long sleeved black t-shirt, the Scotland home strip and big cream, woolly Arran sweater, his hose and the boots he had cleaned earlier.

He crossed to the dressing table and clicked on his music library and listened to some music whilst he shaved, the Philishave razor made light work of this stubble; he dare not let it grow because it came out gray, in his youth he had had a big bushy red beard, those were the days and he smiled. It was vanity, the same vanity that made him dye his hair, it used to be red but now he had to be blonde red as his natural colour had all but gone; at least he had hair which was more than could be said for many of his male friends.

He took the bottle of Vaseline Intensive body cream and started to rub into his body, walked into the bathroom to floss and clean his teeth; he gargled some mouthwash and then went back to the bedroom to dress. His father had always told him that the kilt is the last thing you put on, so he pulled on the hose, strapped on his boots, put on his t-shirt and Scotland top and then put on the kilt; he was running out of time. He was putting on the big wide leather belt when his mobile rang; he looked at the caller and it said Karen, his heart sank, she was ringing to cancel.

'Good Morning Simon' Karen said 'this is BK er Karen'.

'Good Morning Karen, hope you had a good night's sleep, it's going to be a busy day, unless of course you are ringing to cancel?' Simon said dreading the answer.

'Hell, no' Karen said; he choked back tears.

'Hal fixed the Jamhouse, we have a table at 9pm' she said 'Listen hun, how much money do I need, Hal says I should try not to use my credit cards because it shows who I am, so I need cash, will £500 do, Hal has already paid for the meal and drinks for tonight?'

'How the hell did Hal fix the Jamhouse, that's very impressive; we'll struggle to spend £500, take a couple of hundred and we will be in clover' he replied.

'I am really looking forward to this Simon, Hal and Emma are crapping themselves, I have promised to ring occasionally, I'm all dressed and ready, Emma got everything you suggested even a Scottish flag, the one with a white cross on it' she said with the excitement of a small girl.

'A saltire, it's called a saltire, now if you let me finish getting dressed I will be over' he said.

'Listen, honey when you get here, ring me and I will meet you in reception.' Karen said.

'OK, no probs see you and Karen, thanks' Simon said, he really meant it, he thought she had rung to cancel, she hadn't, he was overjoyed.

He tucked the sporran chain behind the belt loops and realised he was shaking as he did up the buckles. He took his black leather jacket out of the wardrobe and started to look around the bedroom for the things he needed. First, he loaded his small wallet with his personal credit cards, money and the ever so valuable tickets for the match; he put them in the zipped pocket of his coat. Phone, keys, mints – might need those - a couple of business cards, a pen in the sporran, handkerchiefs, lip salve and a comb; loaded and ready to go.

He went to his laptop and went to the flat website; the flat was wired so heating, some lights, the burglar alarm and front door access codes could be set remotely. The main front door to his flat still needed a good old-fashioned key but the door at the bottom of the stair could be coded and the code given for deliveries which could be dropped off at the bottom of the stairs. He reset the timings for the hot water and heating and the times for the security system to come on, he then switched the laptop off, took his jacket off and slipped on the Arran sweater and put the jacket and scarf back on; he was lovely and warm.

He looked in the mirror, tidied his hair then walked down the corridor to his front door, he picked up gloves; he paused, he looked at the photograph on the wall, it was of him and Jane on their wedding day; his finger traced the outline of her face; he looked into her eyes.

'God, I wish we were doing this together, sharing this day, like we had planned, love you sweetheart' he said. He was in deep thought, shook himself and walked out of his flat, slammed the door shut and walked down the stairs.

Probably the quickest and easiest way was to walk down the hill and across Waverley Bridge, but he needed to go to the cash machine so he walked down Cockburn Street turned right into Market Street and entered the station, used the cash machines near Cafe Nero then up the escalator and walked up the Waverley Steps which were right next to the Balmoral Hotel. Before he left the cash machine he rang Karen and they agreed to meet in the residents lounge behind the concierge desk in the hotel.

The door to BK's bedroom in the Balmoral Hotel opened silently and Emma walked in, she was wearing the heavy high quality bath robe from her room and carried two mugs of coffee. Last night, Emma and Hal had looked on in astonishment as BK related her story of a chance meeting; she had no idea that Emma and Hal had been eavesdropping, she didn't mention kissing and they had thought they might have misinterpreted what they had heard. BK had gone for a shower and Emma had gone with her, they often had showers together, these days it wasn't actually together but it was their special girlie time.

BK stirred and rolled over in the bed, Emma put BK's mug on the table next to her and jumped onto the bed and sat crossed legged with her back to the headboard. BK sat up and started to drink the coffee, she was wearing silk pyjamas with little pink and blue bears all over them; the set had short sleeves and very short shorts, she kicked the covers down and sat with her back to the bedhead, next to Emma, well not exactly next to Emma; it was a Queen sized bed and there was enough room to get at least another couple between them. BK had woken from the most wonderful deep sleep, the room was beautifully warm and she had dreamt of being safe, being loved and being with people - belonging. She yearned for a domestic life, of going to a supermarket, cooking a meal and having a home rather than a house and a kind man to look after and be looked after.

Emma and BK drifted through to the sitting room of the suite for breakfast, as they finished a package was delivered to the room.

'What's the parcel?' said BK, 'it's the last of the clothes you wanted' Emma said.

'Oh, let's look at them now' said BK; there was excitement in her voice, something very rare.

'BK I have a confession to make' said Emma, 'I bought a set for me, I thought it would be fun and I hope to go out later today.'

'Emma, what a wonderful idea let's try them together' smiled BK, they gambolled into the bedroom.

They laid the clothes on the bed, there were two of everything, a thermal vest, a Scotland Rugby top, one Macintosh tartan ladies kilt for BK, one Royal Stuart kilt for Emma and packets of thick black tights and in the new parcel were two thick woollen jumpers with cable stitching down the outside.

They stripped and started to dress; Emma looked at BK and could see the scars from the beating Jake had given her on her thighs and buttocks. They quickly dressed; they stood looking at each other in the mirror. It was BK who spoke first, 'not exactly my choice but it doesn't look too bad, it must be very warm with the tights or leggings on.'

'Tell you what' said Emma 'it feels very sexy like this with your tush hanging out but I think we should wear underwear' they both laughed and went back into the lounge and finished breakfast.

BK ran the water in the large Jacuzzi bath, added some of the bubble bath and skin cream provided and stepped into the warm water. She sat and reached over for her fresh coffee and started to read the Scotsman newspaper. She didn't really ever do this but she thought she would read the rugby pages and the local news, she nearly fell to sleep twice but she enjoyed her soak.

Emma walked in and said that Hal had found a recording of a rugby game on the BBC iplayer that she might want to watch, BK got out of the bath and stepped into the shower to wash her hair.

She walked out of the bathroom still drying her hair, went over to the dressing table and took out the hairdryer. Once dry, she walked over to the wardrobe, pulled out the drawer and looked at her underwear; she could wear really sexy stuff but then with all these clothes, he wouldn't get to see, what on earth was she thinking!!!.

She selected a comfortable, wonder bra and matching panties in cream silk lace, once she was semi-decent she yelled to Hal to come in with his laptop. The advantage of having an outrageously gay executive manager was that he never tried to jump your bones and you never need to worry too much about your privacy. Hal walked in and said 'how much cash do you think you need today, I've only got about £500, I don't think you should use your personal credit cards stick to the corporate card it's got BK Music Corporation on it'.

'I have no idea' said Emma and BK together.

'I haven't a clue how much things cost here' said Hal.

'I'll ring Simon' BK said, she got her mobile, selected and rang a number; she turned her back on them.

Hal looked at Emma and made a sign and mouthed 'get that number' Emma nodded.

BK came off the phone and said 'he suggests £200 and Hal, he's impressed by you getting us into the Jamhouse.'

Hal hooked the laptop to the screen in the bedroom as BK and Emma continued to dress, a recording of Edinburgh v Cardiff in the Magners League appeared.

'It's very butch' said Hal, camply and they all laughed. They watched the highlights of the match and were completely bemused about what was going on, great heaps of men, running, crunching tackles that people walked away from, bizarre.

'Simon described it as 'American Football without all that faggish body armour'' BK said.

'Pretty accurate' said Hal.

BK put on the thermal vest and a t-shirt; it was a BK Shore t-shirt one of the promotional set created for the European Tour. She put on the Scotland Rugby top, she thought it odd that she was going to support a country she had never visited before and had only been in for 24 hours, how life surprises. She tried on some very thick panty hose and put the skirt on over the top, it was certainly going to be warm; she went over to the wardrobe and took out her knee-length leather Gucci boots which were in a mock alligator style and zippered them up.

Emma had taken BK's thick suede and faux fur coat out of the wardrobe, BK stepped across and put the coat on and looked in the mirror, the style didn't look too bad, a $7000 dollar coat and $2000 dollar boots worked really well with the $200 tartan skirt. If those stuck up assistants at Gucci and Louis Vuitton in LA could see her now they would pass out.

She filled the pockets with her ID, her purse with money and a corporate credit card and some makeup and other things she needed. Emma moved close to her and said 'you might need this and handed her a breath freshener spray' she kissed BK on the cheek, BK wondered why Emma had given this to her, she hadn't told her that she and Simon had kissed; maybe she just thought they might.

BK slipped the coat off and touched up her makeup, treated her hair, brushed her teeth and doused herself in perfume, she had wondered which perfume to use but had settled on Bulgari, Omnia Green Jade; she liked and used Britney Spears, Fantasy perfume, but she decide against it, Simon had told her that Jane had used one of the Britney Spears perfumes, the nearest thing he had got to a rock star he had said; she took a small atomiser and placed it in her coat pocket; travel light, Simon had said so she didn't even have a handbag.

Her mobile rang, it was Simon, she rang off and was aware of a different feeling, it ran through her body, she was slightly shaky, she had butterflies in her stomach and she was really looking forward to this, how could she be excited about meeting a guy she hardly knew and going to a match of a sport she had never seen?

She put her coat back on, checked herself; she walked through the lounge with Emma and Hal in tow. 'You could have met him up here' said Hal.

'No' said BK 'you might meet him, but not now, not yet, please guys cut me some slack'.

As the door of the elevator closed BK Shore said 'By the way, he's 20 years older than me' the doors shut, funny she thought that revelation didn't have the effect she imagined; the doors opened at the ground floor, she stepped out and she smiled to herself, she was now Karen.

Simon turned the corner of the hotel and a chill breeze flew up his kilt; kilts are actually very warm, far warmer than trousers but not when a February breeze comes up the Waverley Steps and tries to blow away your sporran.

He entered the Balmoral Hotel; the doorman opened the door; dressed in his rugby finest, he raised the suspicions of the concierge.

'Yes sir and how can I help you?' he said.

'I'm here to meet one of your residents in the lounge around the corner' Simon said.

With that Simon walked around the corner, he hoped he wasn't going to be asked her name, the entrance was full of folk and he didn't want to tell everyone, there was a guy there with a video camera too.

He walked into the lounge and Karen was sat on the settee just inside the door. She was sitting on the edge of the seat, excited and in expectation; Simon walked in and said 'Good morning Karen, welcome to rugby day'. She stood up and they faced each other, it was a very awkward moment, neither of them knew what to do, how to pick up where the heat of the previous night had ended.

Simon leant forward and kissed her on the cheek, his right hand moved around her waist, she moved closer. They looked into each other's eyes, they were both embarrassed, awkwardly but slowly, very slowly and with hesitation, their lips came together and they kissed, long and slow.

'That was nice' Simon said; 'I do like that aftershave; can we do that again, please' Karen said.

They kissed again, Simon felt her tongue on his, he felt her teeth as he pushed his tongue into her mouth and felt her tongue pushing back; it felt very good, nice comfortable.

'Excuse me!!!' someone said in the distance, they parted.

Jeremy Guscot of the BBC, Dewi Morris of SKY TV, Bill Lothian of Edinburgh Evening News and a host of other rugby reporters and the captains of England and Scotland had come into the room together with a radio team and a TV camera crew and the concierge; Nathan, the Scottish captain smiled and gave Simon the thumbs up.

Karen started to shake, Simon turned to them and said 'thanks guys, we don't need your help, I was just getting going.'

Bill Lothian looked at him, God he knew Bill and Nathan. They all looked at Karen, and they definitely recognised her, he thought.

Dewi Morris said 'well someone has scored even before the match starts' everyone in the room laughed.

Simon quickly ushered Karen out of the lounge, passed the grinning bell captain, around in front of the reception desk and down through the side entrance to Hadrian's. They turned right and walked up the bridge; Karen was amazed by the view; directly in front of them on the right was the Scotsman Hotel and a large old building; the Carlton Highland Hotel on the left, she could see the sign on the outside, the wide bridge was choked with traffic and large numbers of busses. In the distance on the right were a church and a bank which she knew was a bar because Simon had pointed it out to her the previous evening. The pavements were thronged with people in a variety of outfits, in the distance she could see a group dressed as chickens, several knights in plastic armour and a group of Loch Ness Monsters walked by with a huge red and white flag, shoppers mixed with the rugby crowd, to her eyes it was all a little strange or odd.

Simon stepped into the road and hailed a taxi; Simon said 'Bar Italia on the Lothian Road please' he sat down next to Karen and took her hand.

'I thought you would cancel, I thought you might not want to spend any time with me, I was scared of being alone today' he said.

'Honey, I was worried you'd do the same, I'm so glad we kissed like that in the hotel, that we were still more than just friends, even if we did get caught, did you see the look on their faces when they clocked the age difference and then possibly who I was? They laughed.

'One of those people was Bill Lothian, the Scotsman newspaper rugby correspondent, I vaguely know Bill, I think he was in shock, and he will be when he remembers who I am, Nathan is the Edinburgh Rugby captain, I know him well' they chuckled.

Chapter Six
Kick off together

The taxi turned around to drive back over the North Bridge, turning left by the Bank Bar and then down by the Radisson Hotel to drive along the Grassmarket to Lothian Road. They sat in the back of the black taxi, it was a bit tense, neither of them knowing how to move forward.

'So where are we going, what are we going to be doing?' said Karen.

'Well, first we are going to see the Loggies, a group of family, friends and others Jane and I met about 10 years ago in a pub after one of the games and we have been friends ever since and been going to these pre-match 'readies' for years' Simon said.

'Don't worry, these are nice genuine people, realistic, you will find them easy to get on with; just be yourself and be scrupulously honest but remember, you are Karen when you are with me' Simon reassured her; Karen put her arm though his and smiled.

'I don't think I said, but you look fantastic in a kilt, I've never seen one close up; I always thought the idea of men in skirts as rather feminine but it's incredibly macho' she said.

Simon took her hand and placed in on his bare knee just inside his leg. 'There is only one way for you to find out what is worn under a kilt' he moved her hand slightly up his leg. 'But beware of the ancient law of Culloden'. He placed his hand on the inside of her leg just under her skirt.

'What you do to me, I will do to you' he said; she kissed him on the cheek and whispered 'Oh Good'.

The taxi swung into the side of the road and stopped

parallel to the curb and right outside Bar Italia. Karen got out whilst Simon paid the taxi driver.

As Simon handed the cabby his fare, the cabby asked 'Isn't that BK Shore?'

'She does look remarkably like her, I should be so lucky' Simon said with a smile.

'Enjoy the match, pal' the cabby said winking and hooting as he left.

Simon put his arm around Karen and said 'you'll be fine, just relax, they will welcome and accept you, just be yourself. I know that you might not be feeling too confident about this, but listen they don't know you and you will enjoy socialising and having a personal life; I'm here to support you, if it is too much we will leave' she smiled and hugged his arm.

Karen was terrified but she remembered what her counsellor had said 'face up to what happened, never forget, but get on with life, try to make it as normal as possible. She really hadn't recovered from the mental scars of what Jake had done to her and felt a crushing lack of confidence. She also did not trust men, she had tried but maybe it was too early; she felt so safe around Simon, maybe it was because he was older, and maybe it was because he was hurting too; she had known Simon less than 24 hours and yet she was trusting him to take her around a strange city and introduce her to people she had no idea about, maybe Hal was right, this was madness. She pushed back just slightly and was aware of Simon's arm around her back; guiding her towards the door, supporting her; it felt nice. He leant forward and kissed her on the top of the head and ran his fingers down her cheek, he stopped, froze and then relaxed; she thought she saw guilt in his face.

'You will be fine, we will be fine, by the way have a starter and a main course you'll need it' he said reassuringly.

The outside of the bar was quite old, a plaque said 1901, it had recently been painted brown and cream with the letters picked out in burgundy; it had large windows with rounded corners. Karen had looked down the street, she was puzzled by the mix of shops and businesses she could see. There was a Japanese restaurant, an American diner, three strip joints one called Bottoms UP, a large banner offering saunas, a bar, a pizza hut and a child's toy store, she squinted into the distance, her sight was not that good at that distance, oops it was a toy store but maybe it wasn't a kid's toy store!!!

They entered the restaurant through the vestibule; Karen took in the sight, she instinctively pushed back, to find Simon's reassuring hand at her back.

The restaurant was full; most people were in Scotland tops and she assumed kilts or tartan skirts. A few were wearing white and red tops with a rose on them; England colours she knew this from yesterday; in front of her was a riot of about 150 people all laughing, joking and enjoying themselves. Karen had never seen quite such a broad mix of different types of people in one place; she also noticed that there seemed to be talk between the tables and exchanges of more laughter; attentive staff, squeezed between the tables supplying drink, a lot of drink and food, a lot of food.

To the left of the door was a long table with about 25 people around it; above this on the wall from shoulder height to the ceiling was a 50ft wine rack half full, she noticed several waiters taking bottles from the rack; when this rack was full it must contain at least a couple of hundred bottles. The wall to the right of this doorway was mirrored from ceiling to waist height and had been hand painted with scenes of Rome, Venice and Naples. The passing buses and other vehicles reflected from the road outside gave a strange moving image to the whole wall. There was another long table that stretched from the doorway to the servery in the far right corner of the restaurant; it must have another 20 or 30 dinners. The wall directly in front of her had another wine rack along part of it and then painted scenes of vines, grapes, olive trees and Italian looking people, almost cartoons. The middle of the restaurant was packed with about 20 tables seating four or six people, along the window was the biggest table; this was where they seemed to be heading.

'This is Karen everyone' Simon said, Karen gave an embarrassed half wave and took off her coat, jumper and scarf and handed them to a waiter. People stood, there was much shaking of hands, Simon was hugged by men and women and there was much air and cheek kissing; Karen got pulled into the activity.

Karen was delighted at what happened next, an older lady, Mary said 'now you must be petrified come and sit next to me and Ken here and we will look after you dear'. Mary took Karen's hand and led her along the window side of the table. They sat down and to Karen's relief Simon was sat right opposite her, he looked at her and smiled, she watched as he instantly engaged with an older man, yes; even older than he was, she thought.

Simon poured two glasses of red wine from the bottle on the table and two large glasses of water; the wine bottle was now empty and she watched as it was replaced with a full one by one of the staff.

Karen chatted with Mary and Ken and several other people around her, she was relaxing and enjoying herself; Karen took another gulp of wine and looked across the table at Simon he was in a furtive conversation with young Kirsty, it was quite a serious conversation and she saw a slightly different side of Simon in use, he seemed to be coaching or advising her; was that his professional side or his father side?

Terry Loggie was a 6ft 2ins tall, bearded man, with a sense

of fun that struck you when you first met him; he seemed to be the one 'in charge' as much as anyone could be in charge of such a diverse rabble; he was sitting at the end of the table with his back to the door of the restaurant. He called the table to some degree of order, and was greeted with a hail of light-hearted friendly abuse for his efforts; Karen thought that is what Simon called 'banter'. 'Friends and relatives, there is a difference, friends are here because you have been invited' there was general uproar 'OK OK settle down, the sweepstake will be going around, a quid a punt, and here is a toast to the newbies Kirsty - who is Steve's girlfriend - and Karen, who for some obscure reason has agreed to go to the rugby with Simon; the newbies' they raised their glasses and sunk into conversation; the volume level of the conversations on their table and the restaurant was gradually increasing.

'So how long have you been walking out with Steve?' Karen asked Kirsty.

Kirsty blushed and stammered 'Six weeks, this is the first time I've been to one of these'. Karen looked at her, Kirsty was clearly terrified, Karen reached forward and held her hand 'hey, welcome to the club, we're the newbies' she said.

Karen noticed that her glass had been filled again by Mary; the waiter arrived to take their orders, Simon ordered, the waiter said something she didn't understand and he said 'Auch, aye'. The waiter turned to her, she ordered a minestrone soup and a seafood pizza and again the waiter asked a question that sounded like 'jezwantashipsatha' she nodded.

Simon had seen her puzzled look and winked from across the table; he had noticed Karen talking to Mary and Ken and several others, she was coping very well. He had had a difficult conversation with Kirsty, not only did she instantly recognise Karen as BK Shore; she was a member of her fan club and owned every record. God, he had felt old, he felt like her grandfather giving her advice; he had said that Karen/BK was on her day off and didn't want to be disturbed but he would swap places with her so Kirsty could sit next to her, but she wasn't to text friends until afterwards or make a scene. Kirsty was only just on board with the whole idea when Karen leant forward and held Kirsty's hand, the young girl was shaking.

He felt positively ancient, he looked across to Karen, she was looking very attractive, her long hair neatly brushed over her shoulders and looked dead sexy in her Scotland top and wee tartan skirt, he was so glad he had asked her to be company today, he was so scared of being alone, she seemed to be enjoying herself; he simply could not believe his luck.

The piper started a rendition of Flower of Scotland and the restaurant erupted into song, this was followed by Loch Lomond and Scotland the Brave. Karen knew these songs because of a party she had attended thrown by Rod Stewart's manager in November where there had been pipers.

By the time the singing stopped in a round of applause, the wine was beginning to kick in; Karen was feeling warm, relaxed and increasingly part of the proceedings. She had been to several long tables in restaurants with road crew, staff, colleagues and even the band but never anything like this; at those events she had longed for them to finish, this event she thought, no, she knew, she was enjoying herself and she felt - safe? She smiled to herself, looked up and Simon was looking at her, he reached out and held her hand.

'I'm really enjoying myself, thank you for bringing me' she said.

'You're doing really well' he said and winked.

He was so reassuring; thought Karen, he was such a kind man, he had no idea, how generous it was of him to share his friends, she had never had a circle of friends, yet alone the many different circles that Simon seemed to have, he was so very funny and looked mighty fine in that kilt.

Karen looked along the table. At one end was Terry and at the other end was a woman breast-feeding, she was aware of the incredible age range which seemed to be from 3 months to 75 years, but everyone was talking to everyone. The thing she noticed most was that conversations were struck and closed and then people moved on to talk to someone else.

Ken leant into the conversation 'Karen, have you been to Edinburgh before?'

'No' answered Karen '*no*, I was working in Europe and came here entirely at random for a weekend off'. 'So how did you meet him' Ken asked, Karen was aware that Mary was listening and so was Sue the other side of Mary; Karen explained their chance encounter.

'When was this?' Ken asked 'yesterday' Karen replied.

'The old sod' said Mary and they all laughed.

Simon was talking to Gary, Kirsty and Steve and occasionally Terry, as he did so he kept an eye on Karen to make sure she was coping; several times their eyes met and they smiled at each other. It reminded her of how Brad junior had helped and supported the other Karen at family mealtimes when she was staying at the Morgan's.

Ken butted in 'Let me get this right, you met him yesterday, some random bloke in a hotel corridor, you went out for a drink together and he asked you to the Scotland v England rugby match and you didn't even have to sleep with him.'

'Yup, that's about it, I did kiss him though' Karen said.

'Yuk' said Ken, 'mind you, for a ticket to today's match I would kiss him too' they laughed.

'He's actually a very good kisser' Karen smiled.

She looked across the table towards Simon but he wasn't there, her stomach turned; he soon returned, her reaction to him not being there startled her, he had the right to go to the bathroom but it focused her on how much she had come to rely on him, no that wasn't right – it was how much she trusted him!!!

The main course arrived; she looked at her pizza, mussels, scallops, anchovies, tomatoes and a bed of French fries and cheese on top; she looked puzzled across at Simon and he leant across and said 'jezwantashipsatat' is 'do you want chips with that?' they laughed. There was more wine, beer and water but although Karen ate heartily, she didn't really notice the food too much because she was laughing, talking and listening so much; she was aware that pizza with French fries was not as bad as she thought, it was an unusual combination but definitely not a diet option; she was so enjoying herself.

Simon pulled the table out and Karen went to the end of the table and talked to Pam, the nursing mother; Terry had waved to Karen from the other end of the table so she went to talk to him.

Terry sat Karen on his knee and talked to her; she was in full view of the restaurant and aware of several people taking photos with their cellphones. Terry said to her 'we're really pleased to see you here, keeping Simon company and it's an honour'. She didn't have friends like this, who cared for her as a person, not because of what she did or because they were paid to do so. As she stood to leave, Terry said 'I've seen your videos and always admired your buttocks' he smiled at her and she grinned back and said 'be my guest' and he gently fondled a buttock and said 'thank you'.

'Careful' she said 'Sue might just kill you' pointing at his wife, they all laughed.

She sat down next to Kirsty and looked across to Simon who was in deep discussion with Ken about rugby. Karen thought Simon looked very attractive, why did she suddenly think that, maybe it was the drink, she realised, she was attracted to him, she fancied him; she wanted to kiss him and feel his touch.

'I've got all your records and I belong to the fan club, I'm going to one of the concerts in London' Kirsty interrupted Karen's thought process; she looked at Kirsty, she was 19 or 20, petite features and very cute, she was also blushing from every fibre of her body.

'I never thought I'd meet BK Shore, you're my hero, I wish I could have your autograph but Simon said I mustn't ask because it's your day off, are you dating him? Why aren't you in Berlin? I've got tickets for London, I've said that already, haven't I?' she blurted out with the enthusiasm and speed of youth.

'Kirsty, Simon is right, it's my day off, I'm not dating him but I think I might like to, and I'm in Edinburgh because it's my day off. Kirsty, give me your email address and I'll write to you and then send you an autograph, give me your cellphone'. The two girls sat cheek to cheek as Karen handed Simon the phone to take a photo of her with the youngster.

'Thank you, thank you, BK, thank you' said Kirsty, throwing her arms around her and kissing her on the cheek.

'Taxis are here!! £40 per head for the meal'.

Karen asked Simon to pass her purse from his sporran where she had put it when her coat was taken away, she handed him the money clip 'I'll pay for you honey.' Simon took out four £20 notes and handed the clip back to Karen and the notes to Terry.

Terry said 'You must really trust him Karen, you didn't even count the money he handed back' she smiled back, looked at Simon who was looking out the window, she knew he was trustworthy or was she just being her normal rotten judge of character.

Simon took her hand and said 'this is your ticket; guard it

with your life, if we get separated I will meet you at the seat.'

She pushed against him and smelt his aftershave; she found it rather exciting, he put his arm around her, he could smell her perfume and her hair, that gorgeous fresh smell of women's hair washed cleaned and then warmed, only newly mowed grass had the same effect on him; thank god for the smoking ban.

Karen realised that she was quite drunk, however it felt warm, comfortable, happy and a somehow appropriate thing to be. She remembered drinking to forget, she knew Simon had done the same at some time, this was different this was drinking to be sociable, this was drinking to remember.

She looked up at Simon and said 'That was so nice, these are good people, they are good friends to you' he kissed her gently on the head and said 'You were superb'; she didn't want this to end.

Chapter Seven
Rugby rules OK

A taxi arrived and they piled into it with Ken and two people from one of the other tables and they drove off, down the road towards Murrayfield Stadium.

The taxi stopped and they jumped out into the middle of a huge crowd; Karen looked around she could see a railway bridge, a factory belching out steam, there was a strange musty smell and buses and taxis everywhere but she could not see a stadium. They followed the mass of people, she held on tightly to Simon's hand; it was lightly snowing, a few flakes then a flurry, on the grass railway embankment the snow had settled to a light dusting. Simon was aware that Karen was gripping his hand tight as they walked towards Murrayfield, she was getting very cuddling, must be the drink he thought.

They moved into the dark under the railway, Karen felt the crowd push around her, she nearly lost hold of Simon but recovered and gripped harder; they emerged into the daylight and on their left was an enormous stadium surrounded by a sea of people. This was Murrayfield Stadium, the guide book in the hotel room had described it as the home of Scotland Rugby seating 67,500 people and today it would be full, it looked like any other stadium in the world.

'Look, Anne is here, sorry; can you see that flag up there, the first on the left?' Simon said, pointing to the four flags. 'That is the royal standard of the Princess Royal or Princess Anne who is the patron of Scotland Rugby' he said.

The crowd had dispersed a little from the bottleneck under the railway and Karen but her arm around his waist and he reciprocated, they had to separate to go through the turnstiles. Simon went through first and waited for Karen. As she emerged she flung her arms around his neck and kissed him on the cheek and said 'God I missed you' they laughed and walked off down the hill with their arms around each other's waists.

'Hey! Simon, over here'; they looked around and saw a group of people who were waving, they made their way over and Simon said to her 'this is my Edinburgh Rugby crowd'.

They started to introduce themselves to her 'honoured to meet you welcome to Scotland' they said and they gave both Simon and Karen a pint of beer each.

Barry said 'are you BK Shore?' Karen stared at him, she had an idea; pointing at Simon she said 'how long have you known him?'

'Seven years or so' Barry said. She knew she was a bit drunk but it just felt the right thing to do. 'Hold this' she said passing her beer to Barry.

She stepped forward and launched herself at Simon and kissed him, she darted her tongue in and out of his mouth, it was a sloppy kiss, someone grabbed Simon's beer and he enveloped her in his arms and she felt him kissing back. They parted, Simon looked shaken and she turned to Barry and said 'Still think I'm BK Shore?' Barry shook his head, she smiled, took Simon's hand and said 'Well, I am' and Karen and Simon walked up the steps and into the stadium which loomed above them.

They went up the stairs to section 14 of the East stand, got to their seats and Simon carefully stowed their drinks, he seemed to know a lot of people around where they were sitting, especially the red round face guy sitting next to him. Simon shook hands with several people behind and in front and one or two pecked Karen on the cheek. She was wearing a big bobble hat, a scarf and a big coat and wouldn't have been recognised now by Hal let alone anyone else.

Through the light snow, Karen could see the teams lined up with their backs to them, she rummaged in her purse and brought out her glasses and suddenly the distance came into focus, she could also see the big screens and see a woman talking to the teams.

'Who's that?' Karen asked Simon 'that is Princess Anne, she inspects the teams and wishes them good luck and then we have the national anthems then the game starts' he replied.

He looked at her and was startled 'I didn't know you wore glasses' he said.

'I need them for distance, I usually wear contact lenses but with the drink and snow etc I couldn't be bothered today; I feel like Ugly Betty in these' Karen replied.

'Well I can tell you, you look bloody sexy in them and thanks by the way, I am sure I went up a peg or two in the eyes of my Edinburgh Rugby pals' he said.

She whispered in his ear 'I have wanted to kiss you from when you held my hand in the restaurant'.

The Tannoy crackled to life 'Your royal highness, lords, ladies and gentlemen please, be upstanding for the national anthems, best of order, best of respect.'

The band with drums, pipers and trumpets struck up a chord and a man with an immaculate white beard appeared on the large screen and the Scottish national anthem started.

'Oh flower of Scotland!'

The crowd took up the song, and Karen was struck by the passion by which those around her sang and the volume of the singing. The atmosphere was electrifying and Karen thought she could nearly reach out and touch the tension.

The crowd erupted into shouting and cheering and then fell silent as the first bars of the English national anthem came out.

'God save our gracious queen'.

The atmosphere was still very tense but a little cooler; she looked around and saw that as many of the kilted fans were singing this one too; she would have to ask Simon about this later.

She also made a note that Simon could definitely not sing; not even Clive Thompson, her production wizard and his magic box of electronic mixing desks could help here, still she thought, I'm useless at business.

The stadium fell deathly quiet then erupted as the teams kicked off.

Simon unpacked and placed the saltire over their knees and took her right hand and put it underneath the flag and on his knee; she took her hand away, took off her glove and replaced it slightly further up; she kissed him momentarily on the lips but she saw that his eyes were turned not at her but at the match.

Karen had no idea what was going on, Simon was clearly highly animated, deeply knowledgeable and utterly engrossed, shouting, yelling, criticising the referee and moaning at mistakes. At one stage Scotland got a penalty kick and the stadium went very quiet, she looked around and thought, naughtily that if she stood up and stripped she would get told off for obscuring the view. She smiled to herself, men and sport but this was so very different from her experiences in the States.

She enjoyed the atmosphere, the spectacle was one of the world's greatest, better than any concert she had held or been at. Simon had tried to explain what was going on but the game was scoreless at half time and she noticed that despite the swirls of snow and the sub zero temperatures Simon was sweating with nervous energy; he was jumping, his knee bounced up and down and he leant forward and back like the films of children in orphanages.

He said 'The game is on a knife edge, the snow makes running and passing at speed almost impossible, so we do get a lot of ping pong. I expect in the second half this game will be won or lost on kicks and penalties; not the best match to bring you too.'

She tugged at his arm 'I wouldn't miss it for anything, listen honey, you just concentrate on the game in the second half, I'll ask any questions if I need any more information.'

'Karen, I appreciate that, you are wonderful, I'm so glad you're here with me, you look and feel fantastic' he said and with that his mind went, the second half had kicked off.

Scotland won 9-8 on the very last kick of the match, the last ten minutes of the match had been so exciting, even for her and she didn't know the rules. Even Karen could see that Scotland had played bravely; she felt the tension in the spectators and the sheer guts of sportsmen, on both sides, obviously playing beyond their personal bests. Indeed, for the last five minutes everyone had been standing, shouting, cheering, yelling and screaming, Scotland holding the English team yards from the score line.

Scotland had won the Calcutta Cup and it was presented to the Scotland captain by a real live princess; Karen was watching the big screens. There was a huge roar as Nathan MacLean, the captain of Scotland, who BK recognised from the lounge in the hotel that morning raised the cup above his head. Karen looked to her left and saw two men weeping openly with joy and hugging each other; she could see the women screaming and crying at the same time. Simon hugged her and kissed her on the head, he hugged the guy next to him and turned around and hugged and kissed the people behind them who were complete strangers, Karen was hugged by everyone around too. They were making their way to the exits, when Simon hugged Karen and kissed her on the lips, there were some raucous comments. 'Hey, Simon that's a terrific performance, superb, that's the way to beat the defence, the rugby was good too' or 'is that a maul, could be a ruck later.'

They slowly left the stadium, Simon was on his phone; Karen heard the texts and emails coming into Simon's phone and remembered her own phone and dialled Hal.

'Hallo sweetie' she said.

'Did you enjoy the rugby?' Hal asked.

'Yes, very much so, the atmosphere was fantastic but I have no idea about the game, those players have balls though; we are now off for a drink; did you get to your folks?' she asked.

'Yes. I'm in a place called Perth about an hour by train from the hotel, so easy, I'll ring you regularly if you want' he knew by her voice she was happy, a sound he had not heard for a long time; she'd talked to Brad Morgan the night before and he had rung Hal and they had discussed how to manage the situation.

'Hal, I'm OK, there is no need and I'm having a ball,' BK replied.

'Where's Emma?' Hal asked.

'Simon suggested a pub she could go to watch the match and get some local colour but that's all I know, if I get a chance I'll ring her' BK said.

'OK, talk to you soon' said Hal 'BK, it is so wonderful to hear you happy' and he rang off.

She felt Simon's arm around her waist, she looked up at him and he looked back, their eye contact lasted slightly longer than normal; they said nothing and everything. She looked in his eyes and knew she wanted to get closer to him; she wanted to lie in his arms, he knew he desired her and wanted her but was frightened, he also felt a bit guilty.

Simon said 'Manus and a couple of others are over there; we will quickly say hallo and then walk back to town or get a bus.'

They walked down the steps towards a large marquis; it reminded Karen of the so-called smoking tent outside the Hyatt 'hell house' in LA.

'Karen, this is Manus, my best pal, we met him briefly yesterday in George Street' Simon said, introducing her, she noticed, with pride.

'Karen, careful with this old bugger, he's a bit of a smoothie you know' Manus said. 'Oh Good' said Karen.

Simon put his arm around her 'Listen, Karen, you won't remember all these characters, indeed I've known them for years and can't remember who they are, but the next time you meet them may well be in a police ID parade' they laughed.

There were discussions about the game, which Karen simply didn't try to understand, the women drifted into a group and the men in another. The women asked Karen about family, America and how she met Simon and told her funny stories about him, they knew who she was but no one said anything, Karen realised that as far as they were concerned she wasn't BK Shore, she was Simon's friend.

'So what are you going to do with her now' Manus asked winking.

'Get to the Black Bull on Grassmarket for the atmosphere and a drink and then change quickly before heading for the Jamhouse for dinner and dancing' Simon explained.

Karen realised from the discussion she was having with the women, this was a very special group of friends, his inner sanctum, and his very closest friends in the world; she was also aware that she had been temporarily admitted and very much on approval.

Sheila said 'Neil and I have known him for years; we all met through rugby and every time we meet up with him and Jane,' she paused, 'he did tell you about Jane?' Karen saw them all suddenly look sad. 'Yes' Karen said, 'anyway every time we have been anywhere something magical or weird or both happened.' They all nodded.

They stayed about another ten minutes drinking and exchanging stories; Simon was asked to tell the Agen story.

'We', he pointed to most of the group, 'went to Agen for the Edinburgh Rugby versus Agen Rugby European Cup match. It's in France, that's in Europe by the way, in the middle towards the bottom, south of Paris; it's a typical French regional town with 100,000 people; history as long as your arm and a rugby club that dominates the life of the town. It is also the capital of the world prune industry; the town motto is 'we keep you regular"; one of the women explained that prunes have a laxative effect and were used for children by their mothers, who in their day were obsessed with whether their children pooed regular, it went back to the war days.

'We went to the match, Edinburgh lost, and afterwards we walked back to town, four guys in kilts and various wives and female friends, we decided to get a drink in the first bar we came across. So in they went, I was longer because my knee was playing up and it was like the scene out of Police Academy when the cadets go into the gay bar. Everyone had moustaches, which they preened, tight t-shirts, jeans and denim jackets and drooled at the new flesh coming in through the door, dressed as women; even the women in the bar eyed up the females in our party and came over and talked to them.

When Neil, here, wanted to go to the toilet the whole bar stood up and when Neil asked me if I would go with him they all sat down again with a sigh of disappointment. They absolutely loved Neil, the shaved head, rugged looks, the chance to bugger a lawyer; even Sheila disowned him and told him he was on his own and not to catch anything. That said, they were very hospitable and produced some fantastic bread, sausages, cheese etc; we left to applause with Neil reversing out of the bar: another night out together when you have difficulty sleeping because your sides hurt from laughing'.

They laughed, Karen could see them remembering the event or story; she realised it had been embellished over the years of telling but it was clear it had enriched their lives and she understood how Sheila said things happened around Simon.

They left together, the majority of the crowd had dispersed and the others turned left outside the stadium and walked up Roseburn Street and Simon and Karen turned right under the railway bridge to walk to the bus stop. As they got to the bus stop a number 22 bus appeared and Simon said 'on you hop and tapped her buttocks'. They climbed the stairs to the top deck and found two seats together near the front; Karen nestled into Simon and whispered 'that was lovely, they are good friends, do you know this is the first time I have ever been on the top floor of a bus, I can't remember the last time I was on a bus'.

Simon suddenly stood up 'Excuse me bus, I am here with an American friend who has never been on a bus before and I have just told her about the tradition of applauding newbies on busses' he made a gesture with his nose. 'Can I ask you all to give her a round of applause for her first bus journey?' The bus erupted into applause and laughter was followed by a series of jokes.

Karen buried her head in her hands and giggled. Simon but his arm around her and squeezed her and kissed her; as people passed her to get off they shook her hand or slapped her on the back 'well done hen, enjoy Scotland' they said.

Chapter Eight

Wanting each other

They got off the bus when it turned into Lothian Road; it was still snowing but only lightly, they crossed the road and walked down the hill, the castle loomed 400ft above them on top of a sheer cliff, to their right was a multi-storey car park. They walked with their arms around each other until they entered the Grassmarket and continued to the Black Bull; Simon pushed through the throng, ordered some wines and then made his way to the back where it opened out to a large room. There was a group just moving and he quickly nipped in after them; this was a partition, just above waist height that jutted out into the room, when not so busy it probably housed a table and chairs but all the furniture had been removed to make more space.

Simon stood with his back against the wall, leaning against it, Karen stood in front of him with the partition on her left as she faced Simon. Their coats, sweater and scarves were piled up on the floor behind Simon, their drinks sat on a small shelf on the partition and they were very snug and warm.

Karen was pushed from behind as someone went passed, Simon but his hand on her waist to steady her, she was very close to him and got a wonderful nose full of his smell, as she pulled back his hand slipped to her buttock and he looked at her and gave it a tweak but left his hand in position. She pushed forward and kissed him on the lips and said 'so far this has been one of the best days of my life'.

He looked at her and gently stroked her cheek and said 'this has already been the best day of my new life.'

Karen smiled 'That's really sweet'. Simon replied 'We

won the Calcutta Cup and I have been able to share it with a gorgeous, caring person, I have liked being with you'.

They kissed again and Simon took a swig of his wine, he smiled, he was out at the rugby with a beautiful girl, twenty years younger than him and she was very attentive and he knew she wanted more.

The group of England rugby supporters on the other side of the partition started to hand Simon condoms.

'Here mate, carry on like that and you will need these' they said.

Karen blushed and one of the supporters said 'look, gorgeous, he's a bit old for you, when you've exhausted him give us a ring and I'll take over' they laughed.

'I'm not actually that old, I'm only 35 but she's very demanding' Simon replied.

'Way to go mate, way to go' the supporter said.

'I am so warm' BK said, she went to pull off her rugby shirt and inadvertently flashed her bra at the entire pub, Simon stepped forward and pulled her vest and t-shirt down, she squealed, the pub roared approval.

A woman standing next to them said 'I thought I recognised you, you're BK Shore'. BK realised her mistake, she was wearing a tour t-shirt with BK Shaw Rocks written on it and a picture of her on stage. She turned to Simon and said 'Help'. He looked down and saw the t-shirt. 'Hey guys, this is Karen, my BK Shore look-alike, she's the spitting image'. He put his drink down and pulled off his rugby shirt, he had an Elton John t-shirt one with Rocket Man on it, everyone laughed. He cuddled her to him and said 'Go to the bathroom take the t-shirt off put your Scotland top on instead,' he handed her the Scotland shirt and she held it in front of the motif on the t-shirt.

When she returned she stood in front of Simon, put her

arm around him and moved to one side with her hand, slipping her hand under his kilt to just fondle his right buttock. They were having an animated and excited discussion, every now and again there was a joke with some of the people around and Simon always explained it to her; all the time he had his hand up her back, under her Scotland top and was running his fingers, gently, very gently up and down her back, it was rather exciting.

Simon and Karen stood comfortable in their little niche, every couple of minutes someone pushing past would push Karen towards Simon, he would hold her there, close and she liked that. She thought about how the last 24 hours had passed in a way she never imagined, Simon was just an ordinary guy, who helped her out and now she was sitting, well standing, in a crowded bar with her hand on the top of his thigh, under his kilt and his arm around her under her shirt feeling her skin, she was loving every minute and wanted more. They stood like that for some time just watching other people then Simon said 'It's nearly 7pm so I suggest we grab a cab, it can drop me off and then take you to your hotel and I'll pick you up about 8:45'.

'Fine, but what do I wear?' Simon put his hand up the back of her shirt and pinged her bra, 'as little as possible?' Simon kissed her and brought his hand around to the front and briefly fondled her left breast under her shirt through her bra, he could feel her nipple hardening. She was pushed hard against him and she kissed him hard on the lips and he pushed his other hand down the back of her tights and fondled her bare buttock; she looked him in the eyes and said 'that's nice'.

'We will be eating, dancing, drinking and maybe walking so whatever you feel comfortable in and whatever I can comfortably feel you in, it's not very posh or upmarket' Simon said.

They spent a few minutes just holding each other, she

looked at him and said 'you are a lovely man, I do like being with you, I'm looking forward to spending more time with you'. He hugged her, 'Thank you, this is so much fun and it's just wonderful being with you'.

They collected up their clothing and made their way towards the door and outside where they gradually put all the clothes back on in various orders because there was more space; Karen noticed that there was now a queue to get into the bar they had just left.

It took a couple of minutes to get a taxi and they got inside; Simon said 'Balmoral Hotel but can you drop me off at the junction of Cockburn Street and Market Street please then take the lady to the Balmoral'.

They kissed in the back of the cab and the cabby coughed 'excuse me; this is where I drop you off, sir'.

'OK my sweetheart, see you in the residents' lounge 8.45' Simon said to Karen.

Simon stood in the gentle snow and watched the cab disappear up Waverley Bridge, and he walked around the corner, tapped in his pin number and walked up to his flat. He walked straight into the bedroom with his post and put it on his dressing table and switched on his laptop, then stripped and walked into the bathroom, switched on the shower and lapped up the freshness and especially the warmth of the water.

He stepped out the shower, shaved, cleaned his teeth and tidied up the bathroom after him by which time he was dry. He went to the wardrobe and selected his clothes for the evening, sat at his dressing table and rubbed cream into his face whilst looking at his emails, nothing vital. He took out his phone and plugged it into the laptop, it would charge; he had just over an hour, he set an alarm and lay on the bed under the covers and drifted off to sleep.

BK Shore walked into her bedroom, walked over to the walk-in wardrobe and took off her clothes; she looked along the racks, looking for something to wear; her phone rang, it was Emma.

'Hi, Emma, are you OK, what are you up to?' Emma Button looked at her phone; BK never started a conversation asking her how she was!

'I'm swell, I went to that pub, the Shakespeare, that Simon recommended and I met a group of girls and I've met this girl, Carrie who is quite fit, are you still with Simon?' she said.

'Emma, he is such a nice guy, we have had a ball and now I'm back at the hotel getting changed. Have you got any idea what I could wear for this Jamhouse thing?'

'Hold the line BK, I'll ask the girls' BK heard Emma say, 'it's my boss she's going to the Jamhouse what should she wear?' There was a buzz of girls talking, BK heard a lavatory flush so knew where they were, BK smiled and heard one of the girls say 'You'll have to ask her what she wants to be polite, tease him or shag him'.

'Did you hear that?' Emma asked; BK thought for a moment and answered 'Oh boy, do I definitely want to shag him'. There was a roar of approval from the other end of the phone.

'Don't hold back any BK, the consensus here is that you should wear what they call here stockings and suspenders with a tutu skirt and a revealing top with bare shoulders so he can see down your front and a big coat over the top, is that any help?' Emma said.

'I think so' said BK.

'BK, I've got this white Lousa Stennson gathered top in my closet which would go with that dark blue Alexander Wang skirt of yours' Emma suggested.

'Hey, thanks Emma worth a try,' BK rang off.

She tried on the combination suggested by Emma, but it didn't work that brilliantly, she swapped the skirt for a bright red one slightly shorter, the combination looked stunning; with red make-up and brushed hair it was just right.

She took everything out and put it on the bed; she took her Agent Provocateur, girdle, stockings and strapless bra and panties, he was going to see these she thought. She tried the top on without a bra and decided that it was a little too revealing even for her and she wasn't sure what would happen if she was dancing, although she was pretty certain that Simon was a breast man, she was sure he didn't want them flopping out on the dance floor. She then went back to the bathroom, brushed her hair, three times and blending in a little shine oil during the last brushing; she wandered into the bedroom, drank some coffee, ate a Danish and panicked because of the time and put on her make-up including some bright red lip gloss.

She had another task to do before she got dressed, she went over to the dressing table and looked at a group of studs, bars and rings, she giggled and selected a favourite one, she lay on the bed and inserted her clitoral hood ring; it felt tickly and stimulating, it always made her feel naughty. She found and inserted her diamond belly button stud; she selected a pair of matching diamond earrings, no necklace, if dancing.

She wafted perfume over her body and stood by the bed to dress; she looked at herself in the mirror in her underwear and thought she looked pretty good for her age. She finally, dressed, first the skirt and then the strapless, gathered top, it opened at the front to reveal her studded belly button, it would also mean that Simon could touch her naked stomach and back with his hands; she shuddered slightly in joyful anticipation. She remembered how he had touched her, how soft and gentle he was and how she had wanted more, she wanted to take him to bed, she knew this now but also knew he would be nervous.

She slipped on her Christian Louboutin red stringback shoes that matched perfectly with the skirt, she remembered now it was an Yves Saint Lauren skirt, she hardly ever wore it but now she looked stunning. She walked into the closet and took the full length faux fur coat and slipped it on over the outfit, she went up to the mirror and slipped the coat off her shoulders; she knew she looked good, she felt good. She hadn't felt this good about herself for a long time, this was Simon, he had done this and she hoped he felt the same.

Simon woke and made himself a cup of coffee and a peanut butter and jam sandwich, he carried it through to the bedroom. Once finished eating and drinking, he brushed his teeth again, gargled and then dressed. He put on his black Church's brogues, black socks, black shirt and bright red tie, his dress kilt, not the rugby one but the formal one, he always said that the difference between the rugby kilt and the dress kilt was that the dress kilt had a very much better quality of red wine spilt down it.

He dowsed himself in aftershave; it was time to go, he quickly tidied the bedroom, went over to the dresser and reloaded his sporran and pockets and grabbed his full length tweed coat. He looked at himself in the mirror, he was sure he looked younger than his age and he did look good in the kilt, he felt better than he had for a long time, he felt wanted.

He bustled over Waverley Bridge and right along to the Balmoral, he stepped into reception and the clock struck 8.45, she would never be ready, he turned the corner and she was stood there in a fur coat

'Bloody hell, dead on time, I'm impressed' he said.

She turned and locked eyes with him and let the fur coat drop from her shoulders, he took his coat off and threw it onto a seat. They dissolved into laughter and held each other in their arms; they were both wearing red which matched perfectly, they kissed holding each other tight, in the middle of the deserted lounge. Simon put his arms around her waist and she could feel his touch on her stomach and back, the gathered blouse allowing him free access, she loved that touch.

'You look stunning, red seems to be our colour, I'm so proud to be going out with you tonight' Simon said.

'Simon, you look so sexy in that kilt, I'd like you to know I only have eyes for you tonight; Pweeor!' Karen said.

Simon broke the touch and bent down and held out her coat for her then put his own on and they walked out arm in arm and asked the doorman to get them a taxi to the Jamhouse.

Chapter Nine

Foreplay at the Jamhouse, love in the Balmoral

The taxi pulled up outside the Jamhouse on Queen Street, this was a live music and dining venue for about 800 aimed at the 'older' middle of the road customer, no ska, no acid, no house more pop, rock and glam. The building was the former BBC studios in Edinburgh, the broadcaster having moved to a small hi-tech studio near the Scottish Parliament.

The building had been sensitively converted so the studio was now a performance and dancing area with a sophisticated sound and lighting system, with bars and sitting areas. Upstairs, in the large gallery and former camera storage area was another bar, a large sitting area with settees and a restaurant with 120 covers neatly fitted in the balcony overlooking the dance floor and stage. It was very popular especially during rugby weekends and with stag and hen nights; Simon wondered how Hal had winged a table for tonight.

They left the taxi and made their way passed the smokers and the queue of people waiting to enter. Karen went up to the desk and said 'we have a table for 9pm under the name of Shore'. The girl at the desk looked up and said 'Yes, Miss Shore, you are more than welcome' she spoke on a walkie-talkie and the manager arrived to great them personally. 'Welcome to the Jamhouse, Miss Shore' he said 'let me escort you to the restaurant'.

'Certainly, this is Simon Macintosh,' Karen said introducing Simon 'Welcome sir' said the manager without making eye contact with Simon; as they walked through the first bar,

Simon said 'I don't usually get this kind of welcome'. Karen smiled and held his hand.

They went up the stairs and were introduced to the restaurant manager who said 'Welcome Miss Shore, welcome back Mr Macintosh and thanks for the recommendation and bringing Miss Shore here, may I take your coats?' Simon turned and helped Karen off with her coat, she looked a million dollars and the manager looked appreciative. 'Miss Shore you looking positively radiant tonight' he said, leading them into the bar and sitting area. They went over to the bar and ordered drinks, Simon had a gin and tonic and Karen asked for a bloody Mary.

The bar steward said 'Welcome to the Jamhouse, we were all sworn to secrecy about you coming here tonight BK, I love your music.'

'Well thank you, Sandra' Karen said reading her name badge. 'If you would like to sit down I will bring the drinks over' Sandra said.

They sat on a settee in the corner, just behind the curtain; they were very close to each other and Karen said 'the only way Hal could get the booking was to use the BK Shore card; they have been asked to be discrete which means they might not bug us too much but will tell the press everything'. Simon put his arm around Karen and they kissed, 'my publicist says that as a single female, if I talk to a man twice the press think we are lovers and if they are sure you have slept with him you are pregnant and if you deny it, it's twins!!!!!' she laughed. She continued 'the Press made a big thing about Emma and I being lesbian lovers, she nursed me when I was injured and we are more than friends, that's true, but they made a big thing about us having showers together, at the time I could only just stand so Emma used to come and supervise, god this sounds awful.'

The manager returned with a waitress to take them to their

table, 'Special occasion?' he said 'No, we just want a quiet evening to ourselves' Karen said 'we won the Calcutta Cup, that's pretty special'. Simon said 'Yes, it was a good match, some of the team are supposed to drop in later'. They walked around the gallery to the far side, Simon sat at right angles to Karen who had her back to the gallery but got a good view of the stage in front and the dance floor to her left, their knees touched, Karen slid her hand under the table and placed it on Simon's knee, kilts are good for this she thought.

Karen looked around; the building was an art deco Odeon style design with terracotta and turquoise and cream walls; hanging from the walls were opaque angels which looked like frosted glass but clearly couldn't be and were probably moulded plastic. Hanging from the ceiling about 8ft above where they were sitting was a modern remote controlled lighting system and a large 'disco' mirrored ball.

The manager said 'please feel free to use this staircase to get to the dance floor, it's usually only used by the performers but I've made an exception tonight so you don't have to walk through the crowds' he said.

'That is very thoughtful of you' Karen said.

'May I introduce you to Gemma who is your waitress tonight' he said.

Gemma was a 20 something and about 5ft 8ins tall with small features and a tiny waist, clearly serving at table kept her fit, she was very sweet and courteous and extremely nervous. 'Hallomynamessarahiwillbe servingyoutonightwouldyoulikesomedrinks' she said, so quickly neither Karen nor Simon heard what she said.

Karen noticed that Gemma was shaking, she held her hand and said 'now, deep breath, calm down'; Gemma breathed in and out and said 'Hallo my name is Gemma, I will be serving you tonight, would you like some drinks.'

'Hallo, Gemma I'm BK Shore, but you know that, this is Simon my friend, you may call us BK and Simon,' Karen said.

'Thank you, Miss Shore; BK' Gemma said.

Simon said 'a bottle of the Etchart, Malbec reserve 2005 and a large pitcher of water please' he turned to Karen and said 'we will need the water later.'

Simon turned to Karen and said 'you do look stunning tonight, it is doing my ego a power of good, so thank you' and he kissed her.

The wine and water arrived and they ordered their food, just as the band was starting its first set, it was cover versions of the popular hits, wedding music as Karen remembered singing at weddings whilst a poor student. The band was not great musically and to the trained ear some of the backing singing was dreadful but overall the performance was passable and she expected most of the people were drinking and enjoying themselves and wouldn't notice or care.

After a few glasses of wine, Simon asked Karen if she would like to dance, she had noticed him working up to it, he was clearly nervous and maybe intimidated because she was a trained dancer and danced on stage, they had discussed that. 'Simon, I thought you would never ask, I would love to dance with you, don't worry I will be gentle'. They made their way to the dance floor and really enjoyed themselves, there was a slow number and they enjoyed the closeness and she found herself relaxing again.

As they made their way up back to the table, Simon stopped her on the small landing and pushed her gently into the corner, they kissed, it was long and passionate and he fondled her breasts, she ran her hand up his right thigh under the kilt. He looked her in the eyes and said 'I love your bare shoulders and soft skin' and kissed her shoulders, she guided his hand to her stomach, they were about to kiss again when they heard someone below and gambolled off to their table giggling.

They chatted about their respective lives and their hopes for the future, occasionally leaving the table to dance, they had drunk the bottle of wine and most of the water, both of which were refreshed. The place was now very busy, pretty warm and had a wonderful relaxed atmosphere, there were groups of people, couples, and singletons, in the darker areas couples were kissing; the average age had to be forty or so.

In a break in the music Karen asked 'what is it like to be married to the same person for thirty years? I have no idea what it must be like, the longest relationship I have had was about two years'.

'It's wonderful; it's really like ten, three year sequences. First, there is just the two of you, then the kids come along, they get more independent, start to contribute to and become a part of your life, they leave and then there is the two of you' he said.

'How did you stay in love with the same person for so long?' Karen asked.

'Jane and I used to have dates where we went out separately and met up as if we were single, and fondle and kiss each other, we had dirty weekends, we booked in under different names and she pretended to be my secretary. Throughout there is being in bed together, not necessarily sex but cuddling each other, there are times when sex is abundant or scarce, when neither or both of you are too tired or stressed to perform; you tend to get into a rut and use the same positions but then there are times you come back and just do it over the kitchen table. I suppose you merge socially, psychologically and sexually; it's very nice, I feel sorry for people who don't feel that. I simply cannot start to describe the sense of loss; it's like part of you is missing, a leg or an eye' he stared into the distance.

Karen put her hand on his and said 'I will never meet Jane, but I think I would have liked her, anyone who could inspire you like that must have been special' Simon smiled 'If she was alive today and we were here together, she would probably scratch your eyes out!!!'

'I wouldn't blame her' Karen said kissing him on the cheek 'I think you are probably worth fighting for'.

They ate, drank, danced, chatted and kissed and generally enjoyed the evening; towards the end as they walked up the stairs and got to their landing, Karen pushed Simon into the corner, kissed him and put a hand up his kilt and fondled him, he put a hand around her and fondled her buttocks. As they stood there enjoying each other, Simon's eyes darted above her shoulder and saw a small CCTV camera blinking in the corner, so much for discretion; as they got to the top of the stairs Simon stopped and pointed it out to Karen.

When they asked Gemma for the bill, she told them it was being charged to an account, as Karen gave her a tip she asked, 'we have noticed there is a CCTV camera on those stairs, where does it go?' Gemma went scarlet blushing to her hair roots.

'I'm sorry I have been watching from the monitor by the kitchen to see when you came back to the table, you two should go home to bed' Simon and Karen both laughed and looked at each other.

It was about 1am, when Simon suggested that they should go, it had been a tiring day for him, Karen was quite please as she wasn't used to quite so hectic and changing days. She and Simon had danced for hours and really enjoyed themselves; they had returned to their table in the restaurant; she had enjoyed it when they cuddled on one of the settees and kissed; she could feel his body heat and his sweat on his clothes. His aftershave and natural musk mixed in a strange but rather nice odour and she found it a bit of a turn on; he had been attentive and loving and their dancing had been sexy; she had expected 'dad dancing' from Simon but he seemed rather good, not at the level she trained to, but acceptable.

They had laughed and joked the whole day, it had been a fantastic experience, normal people treating her normally.

She leant forward and gave him a long kiss and pulled him closer towards her. 'I'm having the time of my life; I like being with you I feel alive, I don't want it to end' Karen whispered, yelled actually over the music, into his ear.

'I feel the same' he said 'I've enjoyed your company, friendship and being close to you' he said, they kissed.

'Well you old bastard, how did you get a lovely like this then?' a voice boomed; it was Nathan MacLean, the Scotland and Edinburgh Rugby captain.

Nathan said 'I recognised you two at the Balmoral this morning when we caught you doing that earlier, you old fox you, you two left looking really sheepish' they could see other members of the team arriving.

'Excuse me' he said putting his hand on Karen's bare shoulder, his hand looked enormous, mind you at 6ft 6ins, everything about Nathan was large – allegedly; 'you are BK Shore aren't you? Everyone this morning was convinced you were, they even tried to get it out of the bell boys? I love your music, crap choice in blokes,' he said pointing at Simon, Karen thought he has unwittingly accurate except about Simon - she hoped.

Karen leant forward and put her arm around Nathan and pulled him towards her, he stooped and she talked in his ear. Simon was nudged from behind and turned to see several of the other Edinburgh and Scotland players behind him; they started talking about the match and Rory Little said 'Nathan said he saw you with a decent bit of stuff in the Balmoral,' there was a general cheer and some gesturing imitating a sexual act, they all laughed and without any ceremony or warning handed Simon the Calcutta Cup.

Simon glowed, he took out his phone; put it on photo mode and handed it to Rory and he stood holding the cup with Nathan. Nathan rounded on Karen, lifted her off the floor, Simon handed her the cup and cameras flashed, everyone was laughing. Andy stepped forward and pushed Karen's skirt up, revealing her outer thigh and the head of her stockings, her upper thigh and some suspender, cameras flashed. Simon stepped forward and pulled the skirt down to a more respectable place, turned, wagged his finger and said 'mine'. They all cheered, Simon got Rory to take a photo of him with the cup and another with him and Karen and the cup.

The band struck up Brown Sugar and Simon and Karen skipped off to the dance floor; in the pause between songs, Karen nestled up to Simon's ear and said 'Thank you for putting my skirt right, I would like to be yours.' They left about ten minutes later; both bathed in sweat from dancing, tired and happy.

Simon was thinking that he had planned to drop her off at her hotel, say good night and might try his hand for a day together on the Sunday; as the day had gone on he thought he might get more than a kiss and a cuddle in the hotel lounge. He had enjoyed her company so very much and didn't want to leave their relationship at the door of the Balmoral Hotel but knew that tomorrow she would be BK Shore the star and he would go back to being Simon the management consultant. He was also aware that he was quite aroused, sexually interested in this woman, he knew that in his mind he wanted to have sex with her, he'd like that, it felt right this time but he didn't want to push her, and spoil it. What should he do?

Karen was in turmoil, their chance meeting was clearly

meant to be, they had found a lot of common ground in their shared pain and they had become closer as the time had gone past. She had had a simply wonderful day, such rich and memorable experiences, such wonderful people and to see someone so at ease in so many different groups had been an eye-opener for her. She loved the way he looked after her, protected her, no-one had ever done that before; she longed for his touch, his smell and especially his kisses; she didn't want the night to finish, she wanted to stay closer and maybe get closer, she decided that she did want to go to bed with him but didn't want to push him too fast or he might leave her. What should she do?

They walked down the steps, turned right and made their way up the hill, Karen pulled Simon into the shadows and kissed him, she moved his hand down to cover her right breast, Simon's hand gently kneading her and they both felt her nipple harden with excitement.

'I have had a wonderful day and evening, I really don't want it to end; please, please do come back to my suite,' Karen said.

He looked at her 'I would like that very much' they laughed from relief; they put their arms around each other.

They continued their walk down the hill towards the Walter Scott memorial and then left along Princes Street to the Balmoral, they never looked at the view, the valley, the castle floodlit dominating the city; they were both deep in their thoughts. They got to the front door of the Balmoral Hotel and walked in arm in arm, over to the lift; they kissed in the elevator, parting quickly as the doors opened.

They entered the suite; Karen took his hand and led him into the sitting area of her bedroom; the fire had been lit and on a table was some hot chocolate and Danish pastries. Simon sat on the floor in front of the fire with his back to the settee, Karen poured some hot chocolate and handed a mug to

Simon who sipped it; Karen sat down on his right and sipped her chocolate. Karen had her back to Simon and he had his other arm around her shoulders, gentling stroking her skin.

Simon kissed her on the head and then slowly pushed his hand under her blouse and under her bra to feel her naked breast for the first time; it was tight, pert and the nipple was very aroused. 'That's nice' Karen said 'I have wanted you to do that for some time'.

He very gently circled her nipple with his finger, which drove Karen wild, she was beginning to feel very horny and turned on, indeed she had that pleasant warmth of sexual excitement and her ring began to twitch. Simon felt her naked breast and enjoyed the feeling of soft flesh; her nipples were extremely sensitive, he thought, he knew that he was pushing it but her reaction had been complimentary; she hoped he would go further.

'I've wanted to get my hands on these all night' he said; he was very aware that his own body was reacting to the stimulus too and that difficulty getting an erection wasn't going to be a problem this time.

He removed his hand and pushed her forward a little and undid her blouse at the back, he also undid her bra and let the clothes fall off. She still had her back to him, he had his arm over her right shoulder and was stroking both her breasts, Karen found this unbearably exciting, she felt the first movements in her towards climax; she had always had sensitive breasts but this was just heaven; clearly reaching an orgasm wasn't going to be a problem with Simon.

She leant forward and turned towards Simon giving him the first view of her naked breasts in the fire light, they kissed and he gently fondled both of her breasts. She started to undo his shirt, 'I love chest hair it's so sexy' she said. Simon pulled his shirt off and Karen leant forward and suckled on his left and then his right nipple, she could feel him sticking lightly into her side. He fondled and kissed one then the other breast, a level five kiss he joked, Karen thought her nipples were going to explode, she was now very excited. He placed his right hand on her knee and his left hand was around her top holding her up as she looked at him, he leant down and kissed Karen, his right hand moved up to the top of her thigh. She stopped him, 'I want to find something out first' she moved his hand and then stood up. She undid her skirt and stepped out of it and her panties, leaving her in just her suspenders and stockings and straddled his knees with her buttocks on his calves; she glimpsed her own breasts and was pleased how pert and erect they were, they ached for attention; she needed and wanted him.

She slowly moved her hands up his thighs and under his kilt, she was going to find out! As she did so she rose up slightly and Simon put his right hand straight onto her and played with her. She couldn't help herself, her hands pulled back and she arched backwards, 'You are very naughty and that is... is... is,' Karen said. She had not achieved an orgasm with a man since Jake, in fact she hadn't had an orgasm of that intensity since before Jake, long before Jake, she gasped and moaned appreciatively.

She sat on Simon's knees with her legs open and she took his hand and placed it on her; he was soon rubbing and play-ing. 'I'm still going to find out' she said 'that is lovely, keep doing that' she said. 'Glad to be or service, madam, would you like me to take your suitcase to your room next?' he smiled.

He had undone the buckles of his kilt and she now slid her hands up his thighs to the very top and parted the kilt, she moved the material to one side and she now knew for sure, what a Scotsman wears under his kilt.

She caressed him, 'I've never had an old world one before'

she said. 'I've never had one with a stud before,' he said tweaking her clitoral hood ring. 'Actually, I probably have to admit to never having been awfully good at finding my way around down there'. She laughed, this was way too nice.

He moved down slightly and she moved up his legs, she took hold of him, shifted and impaled herself; he had given her total control. She had another orgasm after which she dismounted, took of the last of her clothes and took Simon's hand. He stood up, naked and erect and she led him to the waiting bed.

Simon gently laid her on her back, she opened her legs to welcome her new lover and he lay on top of her. He stopped 'I am about to enter you, are you happy and can I have your permission?' She moved and pushed down so she 'entered' him, as it were; she looked up at him and said 'Yes, but please take your glasses off,' he took them off and threw them to the other side of the bed. He replied 'then let's have a level 12 kiss, they kissed long and hard in rhythm with his thrusts, idyllic thought Karen, he is so gentle, so n-i-c-e.'

This time they climaxed together, a lovely warm feeling seeped through Karen's body and they fell asleep in each other's arms. The last thing Karen thought before she went to sleep was 'Thank you, daddy'.

Chapter Ten

Deeper, harder and colder

Simon woke at 5.30; he walked over to the fire and stacked it with a few logs and a little more coal, the room was warm and he was comfortable wandering around naked. He sat on the seat overlooking the view across towards the castle; he swung his legs up and put his feet against the opposite wall of the alcove. Below he could see the snow and tracks where a few people had driven. Being sat so close to so much cold was deeply satisfying, he could remember doing this when it had been snowing when he was a boy and his mother would strip his wet clothes off him and sit him by the open fire to warm up. For a moment, he thought of his mother her tender touch, that special love; he sighed, she had been dead 20 years or more.

Karen stirred in the bed, a sleepy head appeared and she sat up more asleep than awake and walked off toward the bathroom. She returned and walked over to him, wearing her glasses, there was no light in the room except the firelight and that coming through the open curtains where Simon sat. Karen moved over to Simon and stood next to him admiring the view of Edinburgh, he put his arm around her and fondled her right buttock, and he could feel some scars. She moved his leg and sat between his legs and leant back into him, he moved his arm over her right shoulder and fondled her breasts.

Neither of them said anything they just sat there adoring the view and the closeness, Karen slowly drifted off to sleep and then woke up with a start. They returned to the bed and laid down in the spoon position, they were both sleepy and with the duvet over them they fell back to sleep. Karen just loved that Simon's arm and hand was draped over her hip and just rested on her pubic area, it felt so protecting. She had no pubic hair because it grew different lengths and styles where Jake had whipped her and too much of it had grown back grey, it had to go; she and Emma had become experts at defoliation, waxing and shaving.

Emma Button covered her body with her blouse and pulled on her panties and sweater. She hated the morning after a one-night stand, it was so difficult, she felt cheap and dirty, Carrie avoided eye contact. Emma had gone out to the Shakespeare Arms to watch the match and had met a group of girls at the bar and they had watched the game together, they had got on really well, and gone round the corner to a night club called Subway and she and Carrie had ended up in bed together. Emma had enjoyed the sex, Carrie was good and Emma had a satisfying night, they had not woken until 9.00 and Emma always woke BK at 8.30 maybe 9am on Sunday; she was in for a row. Carrie had made Emma coffee as she dressed, they exchanged telephone numbers and kissed goodbye and she got in the taxi Carrie had called for her.

Emma ran from the elevator, unlocked the door to the suite and walked in, it was quiet. She put her things down and put her ear to the door of BK's bedroom, all she could hear was snoring, she recognised BK's snore; Emma decided to have a quick shower.

Just before she got in the shower, her phone rang.

It was Carrie 'Emma, look, I wondered well, North Berwick would be nice today, would you like to go look or something?'

'Carrie, I would love to, where do we meet?' Emma interrupted Carrie's faltering delivery; they made the arrangements and Emma stepped into her shower feeling better with herself.

Karen and Simon woke; they turned towards each other and cuddled; they made slow, delightful love, no great thrusting, just gentle in each other's bodies, this wasn't the sex of the movies or the lust of the lovers, this was everything that Karen had ever wanted.

They had made love and climaxed together, Simon had flipped her up so she was on top with her legs either side of him. She had remembered this was exactly what Brad junior had done with the other Karen, Simon's hand had moved down in her buttocks and caressed her from behind; he had held her at the edges of orgasm and then let her go. Karen had lain on top of him for some time afterwards scared to break the contact; it was lovely, just sublime. Simon lay with Karen on top of him, they had made satisfying, enjoyable love, he was nearly in tears, it had been wonderful but it brought back memories.

Karen rolled off, stood up and picked up the phone and rang room service 'Hello, this is the Royal suite bedroom - full American breakfast for two, yes, pancakes and muffins, one moment' she put her hand over the phone 'anything extra you want Simon?' she asked 'Yes, toast and can you ask them for Marmite please, plenty of Marmite' he answered; she shrugged her shoulders 'and toast with lots of Marmite.'

Simon was lying sideways on the bed with a pile of pillows propping him up, he gestured for her to join him, 'just look at this' he said. She nestled down with her mouth resting in his chest hairs; she looked in front of her and saw his penis, just lying there, sleepy. He shook her, not there, she lifted her eyes and there was the most stunning view across the valley to an Edinburgh Castle encrusted in frost and snow, 'eat your heart out Walt Disney' Simon said.

There was a knock on the door and Simon darted into the bedroom and Karen slipped on a dressing gown. Jenny, the female suite assistant brought the trolley into the room and BK asked her to leave it at the end of the bed. Jenny took in the sight, the fire was roaring in the grate, they would need more logs; there was a man's kilt, belt and sporran and a woman's skirt and bra on the floor by the fire and a pile of other clothes. A pair of woman's panties was draped over the clock on the mantelpiece, the bed had two dents in it and the room smelt of sex; lastly, someone had just started to run a bath.

Jenny smiled and turned to BK and said 'I trust you slept as well as you could last night' BK looked at the 'evidence'; 'I slept as well as could be expected under the circumstances' she said smiling back, they both laughed.

The spa bath was huge; Simon wondered why posh hotels had beds that could fit eight and baths that could fit four, what did the other four do? This was a fancy model with a double sitting area, ledges and various hydrotherapy settings; it also had an auto fill mechanism, which he couldn't see because his glasses were in the other room. He could see 'auto fill' and there were some words next to that which he couldn't make out; as soon as the maid left he went back to the bedroom and got his glasses. Next to auto fill were the words 'please fit the bath plug before operation'. He thought the bath was taking a time to show any signs of filling, he inserted the bathplug and returned to the bedroom to see Karen throw the bathrobe onto the bed and start to pour some coffee for them.

The bath finally filled as they poured a second cup of coffee and finished the muffins.

Karen said 'you can't eat muffins in the bath' Simon replied 'that definitely gains something in the translation from English to English' with a very impish grin.

'What?' said Karen.

'I'll explain later when my mouth is full' Simon said, Karen looked at him quizzically.

They settled in the bath, the water was soft, warm and gently caressed their naked bodies; the bubbles were fragrant and caring.

'Honey, would you like some toast?' Karen said 'yes please is there any Marmite?'

'What the hell is this Marmite, what is it like' she found several small sachets or tubs of stuff called Marmite. 'Do you spread this on toast?' she said.

'Usually,' said Simon 'but today I think I will eat it off something else – you'.

He pushed her back to the wall and took one of the small tubs of marmite and opened it, he smeared it onto her left nipple and breast, and then slowly smeared it onto her right nipple and breast.

Karen felt a building, strange stinging sensation in both her nipples, this was so good, no, this was fantastic, and the feeling of well being was increasing; she squirmed on the edge of the bath, this was so too nice.

Simon brought his hand up and gently played with her ring, he thought these rings were great, a bit like a light house, he would never think of Trinity House again in the same way.

Karen did not know whether it was the warmth of the bathroom, the stinging from the Marmite, his touch or the tickling sensation but she was feeling really good. Simon started to lick the Marmite off her left nipple, the consistency of the spread, its stickiness, its stiffness meant that the licks were long, clinging and hard and he lingered, she just savoured every tiny contact, shivering with delight.

She could not help herself; she screamed in delight and then shouted at the top of her voice 'No, no not again please.'

All Emma heard was a scream and then the word no; she had just got out of the shower and was drying herself, she had had a long shower as she felt slightly soiled when she arrived back in her room but Carrie's phone call had stopped the feelings of guilt.

She dropped her towel and sprinted towards BK's room, she flung the door open and turned right to the bathroom, she heaved the door open, to hear BK scream again and say 'Jesussssssssssssss that is so tickly.'

Simon felt Karen tense and freeze under his grip; she started to say 'um, um'.

Simon turned around to see a totally naked young woman with wet black hair and stunning jet black pubic hairs, she had a very tight pair of large breasts and her left breast had a discernable red line from armpit to cleavage. She instinctively tried to protect her modesty and then just stood there as she disintegrated into laughter; Emma had thought BK was being attacked and had burst in to rescue her – again.

What she saw was her close friend and employer perched, totally exposed, on the side of the bath, with her lover's hand caressing her and him paying attention to her right breast, her left one was brown and had lick marks on it. It was a very private, intimate, sensual and sexual thing for her to see, what made her laugh was that when the guy turned towards her, licking his lips and he had a brown substance spread all over his face and had his glasses on - it just looked so comical.

Karen said 'Emma, this is Simon, Simon this is Emma'.

Simon stood up and shook Emma's hand and said 'Pleased to meet you'.

'Yes' said Emma looking down 'I know you are,' Simon sat down quickly.

'I'm really sorry; BK I thought you were being attacked' Emma said.

'Emma, thank you, but this time I have just found out about a hidden secret of Marmite' BK said.

'Marmite?' Asked Emma 'Guess, you won't need me today,

could I have the day off, I have a friend to meet' Emma continued.

'Emma, darling, I won't need you at all, but if you could order some extra Marmite it would make my day' said BK.

Emma left the room and Karen got out of the bath and walked out after her.

'Emma, I er sorry but I er,' BK said.

'BK, he wasn't hurting you was he?' Emma asked.

'Oh no honey, I was enjoying that more than I can explain; have you made a friend in Edinburgh too?' she replied.

'Yes, Carrie I met her last night in a bar, I thought it was a one night stand but she just rang me and wants to go out for the day; I'm so excited' Emma jumped up and down.

BK cuddled her, Emma moved to the door, looked at her breasts and ran a finger over a rivulet of brown liquid which had transferred from BK in their embrace and she turned to BK and said 'Marmite,' you say.

Karen turned back to the bathroom but the moment with Simon had passed.

Karen and Simon sat in the alcove of the window looking over the blizzard raging across the valley in front of them. They had got out of the bath after Emma's arrival and played in the shower as she washed her hair and they washed off the remnants of the Marmite.

Simon had helped Karen dry her hair, he used the dryer on her long blond hair running his fingers through her hair and she just loved the caress; she said 'I've never had a man that dried my hair before, other than in a salon, it's nice'.

'Do you dye it?' he asked.

'It is forever being dyed, blonde is my stage colour, my hair is always fluffed up and given volume, I only ever wear it like this in private, people don't always recognise me because they look for the big hair,' she laughed. 'I was going to say you know my natural colour but of course you don't,' she said caressing her shaved mound; he smiled looking at her in the mirror.

'I'm slightly darker and redder that this blonde, there is bit of Celtic blood in my mother's family' she said.

He brushed her hair with long sweeping movements; she found it very relaxing and strangely romantic; Simon had returned to the bedroom as Karen brushed her teeth and went about her morning 'toilet'. When Karen emerged from the bathroom Simon was sat in the alcove with the duvet from the bed wrapped around him, looking out at the weather.

'It's snowing quite hard, come and watch' he said.

She walked over towards the window, putting her glasses on, he flung the duvet open and she nestled into him, sitting as she had before in between his legs and facing the far window. They snuggled under the duvet and watched the blizzard below.

'This is wonderful, all snugly bugly watching the cold and next to a gorgeous naked woman' he said gently, touching her breasts and stomach.

'Not bad for me either' she said, playing with his feet; as she did so she found out he was quite ticklish and as she gently rubbed his ankle and shin, she could feel him getting aroused.

They sat there in silent watching the snow and the people far below scurrying around, Simon and Karen were just pleased to be close and in each other's presence, his arms were around her and she held the duvet tight shut around them; it was heavenly.

They started pointing out things they were seeing to each other, like a taxi driving sidewards, skidding down the hill on Waverley Bridge; the flags on the Bank of Scotland Building blowing in different directions and the shadowy presence of the castle, a bus turning around covered with snow on one side and untouched on the other.

Simon asked 'does it snow in Bakersfield?'

'Not usually,' she said 'I was staying with Mom in 1999 when there was a fall as heavy as this, it's very rare, for Bakersfield, at least the white powder from the sky is, there is plenty of the other stuff.'

'Have you ever done cocaine?' she asked.

She was surprised by the answer 'Yes, once, never went near it again, it was just too nice and very addictive. Recently I took some sherbet, it's a sugary lemon white powder sweet for kids to a party and snored it like cocaine, when it hit the mucus membranes if frothed , it was incredibly painful and white froth billowed from my nose, won't do that again either. Have you done Charlie, I expect you have.'

'Well, yes but I didn't really like the change in me, yes I was relaxed, horny and wanton but I felt so empty and dirty afterwards I stopped doing it, a large number of people around me use it, that is Jake Olding's problem; complete coke head' she said, adding, 'I like smoking pot, occasionally use it to relax before gigs, it makes me very giggly though'. She replied.

'I love it. I could smoke it all the time, but it's so illegal here, and in my position I can't afford a bust, I used to visit Amsterdam on business and enjoyed sloping off for a puff in the cafes' Simon said.

'You can just walk in and buy it, over the counter?' Karen said.

'Yes, it's totally legal, I once took Jane to Amsterdam for a dirty weekend, we went into this cafe and I ordered some coffee and a Colombian medium, Jane said I like the look of that cake, can I have a slice of cake. The guy behind the counter looked at me and I asked for a large slice; she had eaten about half before the penny dropped and that was only because I started smoking, I never smoked cigarettes so it was unusual' he said smiling.

'Did she get high?' Karen asked.

'High!' Simon laughed 'I had to tie on a piece of string to her to stop her drifting off into the clouds, it also made her incredibly horny, it was a very dirty weekend' they laughed, he squeezed her close to him.

'What do you want to do today or do you have plans?' Karen asked.

'I was rather hoping you would spend the day with me' Simon said.

Karen half turned and kissed Simon on the cheek 'I would like nothing better, but I guess the grand tour of the city is out for today, what do you usually do on a Sunday?' she asked.

'Nothing spectacular, long lie-in, occasionally church, tidy the flat, read the papers in the hot tub and family around for lunch, ah, that reminds me I have to make a phone call' he said.

Simon pushed Karen forward and stood up, replacing her in his place, he moved over to the fireplace, stuck a few more logs on the fire and searched for his sporran and took out his phone. Karen watched him; it was an unusual sight, a fully grown 50 year old man wandering around butt naked making a phone call, her part of the conversation was stranger.

He laughed a loud, infectious, kind laugh and walked back towards Karen 'That was my daughter Alex, she's a cheeky madam' he said.

'I wonder where she gets that from; did you just bounce her for me?' she said; she stood up and they sat down as before except Karen took his hand and replaced it for him.

'It's an informal arrangement, don't worry, she is very laid back but very practical, would you like to come to my flat and I will cook you traditional roast beef and Yorkshire puddings, we may have to go to the shops first,' Simon said.

Karen squealed with delight 'your inviting me to your

home, it's an honour' she said.

'What was your line then? You said to Alex *that's my line*' Karen said.

'When the girls went out I used to say 'be good and if you can't be good be careful and if you can't be careful use contraception" he replied.

'You said that to your girls!' she exclaimed. 'Yes I'm a caring father, unwanted pregnancies ruin lives'.

'Maybe this is the right time to say that I'm taking the pill for period pains so I have that base covered – sorry daddy' she said gently squeezing him.

Simon started to tell his story. 'I'm not sure it's all in working order; when I was a tenant dairy farmer I went out to check on my cows late one night. Being a bloke, I decided to have a piss, pee to you, and aimed at a thin piece of wire and hit it; I had forgotten the basic laws of physics about water conducting electricity. A charge the equivalent of a car spark plug shot up the water stream and into my body, I passed out.'

'Ouch, no way' said Karen.

He continued 'I came round with the Hereford Bull standing over me, licking my face, George had a lovely temperament, he could have killed me but instead he was helping me, all the cows were stood behind him in a big semi-circle. I went home and cleaned up but within the hour I was pissing lumps as the charge had damaged my urethra and kidneys, I went to hospital. Anyway I ended up being nursed by Jane, only able to get up to stagger off to the toilet, I was on a massive dose of antibiotics, this lasted for a full four weeks; I thought I had broken him, I couldn't get an erection at all.'

Karen felt him feel himself with his left hand, she smiled.

'After four weeks, they took me off antibiotics and one day, he sprang into life, I called Jane and we made the most of the moment or she did, there wasn't much I could do, other than lie there and enjoy myself. The radio was on and tuned to the BBC, the news bulletins are preceded by the pips, a time check, we timed ourselves to the pips. Beep, beep, beeeep. The result is Alex, she was conceived at 5pm exactly; we never had any more children so I could be firing blanks here.'

'It seems to be working satisfactorily from my point of view' she said and tickled his right foot.

They sat there for a few minutes longer, neither of them wanting to break their hold or leave the warmth under the duvet, but eventually they stood up and Karen went across to the walk-in closet; she selected, and put on a white Sofia bra, camisole and panties set from Agent Provocateur, a white cross over blouse from Jaeger and some Thallum faded blue flares by Calvin Klein with a large buckled Jason Conran belt some boot socks and her black Warren, quarter boots from Kurt Geigar, she would wear the thick white cable stitch Arran jumper Emma had bought her and her faux fur coat. She was confident that in the short while she had known Simon he would only notice what she wore, when she took it off.

She came out of the wardrobe to see that Simon was completely dressed except for his kilt which he now wrapped around himself and attached the belt.

He wolf whistled and said 'You look fabulous; those jeans really show off your best bits'.

There was a knock on the door, Karen moved to the door and opened it and invited Emma in.

'It's lovely and warm in here' Emma said 'Hallo Simon, can I say you look good in that kilt'.

'Glad you recognised me, I nearly didn't recognise you with my clothes on' Karen laughed loudly, Emma blushed and Karen thought she had never seen Emma blush before.

'BK, I'm going out now, Carrie's picking me up and we are going to drive to North Berwick, I will ring you every now and again. Hal is in Perth visiting his relatives and is due back later, so you're on your own, what are you guys going to do' Emma said.

There was a pause as they all looked at each other then exploded into laughter, no dialogue was needed. Emma and Karen embraced, laughing and kissed, Simon came forward and put his arm around Emma and whispered in her ear, 'you may need these' and handed her something.

Emma turned to leave, smiling and Karen said to Simon 'What did you just give her?'

That impish grin appeared, 'two pots of marmite' he smiled; Karen laughed and went next door after Emma; she was standing looking at the pots in her hand smiling.

Karen said to her 'leave it on for a couple of minutes, it's really good, have a great time and enjoy yourself, I'll be fine with Simon'.

Emma bustled off out the door putting on her coat as she went.

Karen returned to the bedroom to see Simon using a stylus on his phone, 'what are you doing?' she asked 'I'm booking a car, I belong to the City car club, it's great, I pay an annual fee and a monthly subscription and I can use any of the cars for up to 50 miles. There a couple of parking bays right outside my flat; I suppose to an American the fact I don't own a car must be really strange?'

'Spooky more like' she said.

'That's it I've booked us a car so we can go to the supermarket, the roads look OK but if this keeps up things will get really difficult, whilst I'm on the phone I will reset the heating and water in the flat'. Karen stood next to him and he showed her the flat's website and he switched the heating to continuous and then increased the temperature by 4 degrees, too warm for sweaters he thought. He then switched the water heating on for the tank that supplied the hot tub, they may need that later.

They put on their sweaters and carried their coats, gloves and scarves and took the elevator to reception where they put on their coats and wrapped up against the snow and cold. The weather station on the concierge desk said it was -1c outside; they stepped out into the snow. They turned left and walked along past the deserted bus stops and down the hill towards the Waverley Bridge, they had to walk on the road because the pavement was too slippery. On the other side of the bridge, they crossed the road and Simon walked up to a car, took a card out of his wallet and held it to the windscreen and the doors unlocked. They got in and Simon punched a pin code into the keyboard on the dashboard and the glove compartment opened, he took out the keys and started the car.

They sat there for a while whilst the windscreen defrosted. Karen said 'that's three things that are different between our language; windscreen is windshield, pavement and sidewalk and flat is apartment and what's this with muffins?'

'A muffin is this' and he placed his hand between her legs, she jumped with surprise 'so you see you could eat muffins in the bath, but that would be a level 10 kiss' he said, Karen laughed, turned towards him and kissed him.

'Naughty boy' she said, he went to remove his hand and for a moment she held him there.

He turned and said 'OK let's go to Sainsbury's'; he put the car in gear and it stalled; they both laughed. 'It doesn't happen like that in the movies' he said restarting the car. 'Unlike you Americans, we drive on the correct side of the road' Simon said turning left up the hill towards the Mould.

Simon explained the view 'that tall tower you can just see through the snow is the Sir Walter Scott memorial. When I was a young boy, we used to visit Edinburgh occasionally, we had relatives here and it was always covered with scaffolding, in fact, I thought that Sir Walter Scott invented scaffolding. After about what seemed twenty years, they took the scaffolding down and it looked just like it had before they put the scaffolding up. He was a writer and historian in the 1820s; you probably know him for writing Ivanhoe, Brigadoon and Rob Roy. Waverley Station is named after one of his novels; he was linked to railways I think.'

He continued 'I remain convinced that the memorial is Thunderbird Three from the 1970s puppet show and I expect it to blast off and save some one in true International Rescue style, not sure you will understand that?'

'No, honey, you lost me with the Thunderbirds, it's cheap liquor for us' said Karen. 'Google it' he smiled.

They got to the top of the hill and without stopping Simon turned left up the Mound which luckily had been gritted so there was some grip.

'That big tall black building there is the assembly of the Church of Scotland and the School of Divinity of the University, the new Scottish Parliament first met there in 1999.' He turned right and up the Lawnmarket and then down the Castle Esplanade, it was quite slippery and he made a mental note to avoid the hills on his return. They entered the Lothian Road and Simon drove towards and along the Western Approaches, he said nothing he was concentrating on driving, the weather was getting worse.

'We drove along here to Murrayfield, at the bottom of this hill is where we were dropped off' he said.

Karen saw the factory on the left which was still belching out steam, she now knew this was a brewery; they went through the dip and under a railway bridge and on the left was a large supermarket called Sainsbury's. The car park was covered in snow and largely deserted; Simon parked the car in a space near the door but reversed in so he could drive out. They got out, grabbed a trolley and walked in, arm in arm like a married couple out to do the weekly shopping, Karen was quite excited and there were very few people in the store.

Simon whizzed around the shop with Karen in tow, she hadn't actually been shopping like this for ten years, in LA, she would be so pestered and it wasn't worth it and probably quite dangerous. He had no idea, this was the exact domestic life she craved, shopping with her man and she enjoyed just being a person not BK Shore in her strange isolated world.

She adored watching him, as he selected items he needed for the next few days like bread and milk; she thought it very homely when he bought toilet tissue, cleaner and bin bags, strangely something she found rather sexy. He led them down an aisle and took some ketchup and then turned to her and said 'you seem to like this' and gave her an enormous jar of Marmite; they laughed and she hugged him, she was so enjoying being with him.

'Thank you' she said placing it in the basket; she kissed him on the cheek, she thought the gift was such a caring and romantic thing to do, she hugged his arm.

They paid for and packed their shopping and went out to their car, it was covered in snow and Simon opened it and started it, as Karen loaded the shopping into the boot as he called it or trunk as she called it.

Simon let the clutch off and the car gradually moved forward, he turned right and then crawled along the road at about 10 mph, visibility was very poor and the roads very slippery. He turned left under the railway bridge, Murrayfield Stadium loomed on the left as they drove along Roseburn Street; the going was a little easier when they got to Corstorphine Road. Karen looked across at Simon his face was a picture of concentration, it really was atrocious weather.

They drove slowly along to Shandwick Place and then Simon drove, illegally, along Princess Street, as they got to the far end the traffic lights turned red, Simon braked and the car continued on sideways. A taxi coming up from the Waverley Bridge saw what was going on and stopped, Simon pumped at the accelerator and the back of the car shot around as he pulled the hand brake then the car straightened and shot down Waverley Bridge; Karen held on for dear life. The car went up the hill on the other side over the junction and entered Cockburn Street going the wrong way up a one-way street, Simon drove to the right and straight into the first parking bay they had vacated earlier.

He stopped the engine and opened the boot, took out a couple of the bags and walked across the street to a doorway; he typed in a code and opened the door, wedging it open with the two bags. He then walked back to the car and opened the door for Karen. She was very touched, how romantic she thought, until he handed her a couple of bags and pointed at the doorway. He took the final bag, locked the car and returned to the doorway, the snow was very heavy and with a cruel wind, the chill factor was very high.

Once inside, he closed the door and they struggled up the four flights of stairs to the top; Simon searched in his jacket and removed a key and opened the door, he closed the door behind them.

Chapter Eleven

Making love at home

'Welcome to my home' he said.

He opened the door to the closet and took off his jacket and jumper; he took Karen's coat and jumper too. As he was hanging things up Karen saw a wedding photo next to the front door, that had to be Jane, she looked at her and thought 'lucky bitch'. They picked up the shopping and walked along the corridor and turned left into the dining and kitchen area; Simon placed the bags on a work surface and started putting things away.

'I tell you what, let's get the food going and then I'll give you the grand tour' Simon said, he took an apron and draped it over one of the dining chairs, took off his rugby shirt, so he had a polo neck sweater on, undid his sporran and belt then removed his kilt, she smiled.

'You can't cook in a kilt' he said blowing her a kiss and then putting the apron on and then went behind the breakfast bar to start to cook.

'Do you have an apron for me?' she asked.

Simon opened a draw and tossed her an apron, she sat down took off her boots, blouse, camisole, bra and jeans and bent down and picked up his rugby shirt, put it on and replaced her boots. Wow, she thought, that was a good idea, it smelt of him, his aftershave, it still had some of his warmth too; she put the apron and said 'you can't cook in designer clothes'.

Simon handed her a bowl with water, some carrots and a knife, she stood in the dining area side of the kitchen bar and started to peel. She helped Simon prepare the vegetables and loaded them into the steamer, he started to parboil the potatoes, and he prepared the meat and put in the oven and set the timer. He then tidied everything away and washed the surfaces down and made them a mug of coffee each.

Karen's phone rang, it was Emma.

'BK we got to North Berwick but the weather is so bad we decided to return but the police say the roads to Edinburgh are blocked, we don't know what to do'.

Karen relayed the information; Simon picked up his phone and wallet from his sporran and accessed his contacts and rang a number.

'Emma, Simon's up to something here, hang on a second' said Karen.

Simon took the phone from Karen. 'Emma, I have booked you a suite at the Macdonald Hotel in North Berwick, you should be able to find it it's by the sea, it's in my name, Macintosh'.

'Thank you, never thought of that' said Emma.

'Emma, the suite has a spa bath, did you take the Marmite?'

'Yes' replied Emma wickedly.

'Enjoy' Simon said, they sniggered naughtily together.

Simon tuned to Karen and said 'Would Madam like the grand tour, now?'

'Madam would like that very much' she replied, Simon undid his apron and put his kilt back on.

This is the kitchen, with all mod cons, and through here is the utility room, it's got the boiler, washing machine, freezer, etc. He opened the freezer rummaged around and put a dish on the work surface, 'pudding' he said.

They walked through into the dining area and then into the living room; Karen looked at the room, the artwork was good quality, mainly landscapes; the drapes really made the room come alive, it was male but warm; the big L shaped white leather settee looked just perfect in the room.

As she watched, Simon knelt and lit the fire; she wandered over to the dresser which was covered in photos, she could see the two girls, they were pretty and did look like him, there was one of Simon on a beach with a woman, she looked closer it must be his mother, there were several photos of Jane, for some totally strange irrational reason Karen suddenly felt guilty, like a mistress stealing Jane's man from her.

They walked back along the corridor and entered his bedroom, Karen stood and took in the scene, she actually quite liked it, the triple glazed windows and nets cast a bright light into the room which softened when he switched the lights on. The mirror wall worked very well and made the place very light, again the colour in the drapes was well thought through, good design.

'This is my bedroom, wardrobes and drawers behind the mirrors, dressing table here' he went over and switched on his laptop and then went next door to get his phone which he plugged into a lead on the laptop, it would charge and synchronise.

Whilst he was gone she inspected the bottle of aftershave, his razor, a daily pill box with several different types of pills in it and other stuff on his table; when he returned she sprayed some aftershave on him and stood very close to him to take in the aroma, they kissed.

They went into the bathroom, two sinks she noted, there was a toilet and an area with a monsoon shower, there were no screens.

'Not a lot of privacy here' she said 'depends whose watching,' he smiled.

'I thought you said you had a hot tub' Simon pointed above him and took her hand.

They left the bedroom and climbed the spiral staircase, at the top, Simon opened a door and there was a short corridor 'on this side are the water tanks and computer system for the whole building, on the other side are the tanks, air conditioning for the kitchen and bathroom and water heater for the hot tub. If you are into green, there are solar panels on the roof that power the lights in the stairwell; saves us a fortune' he explained.

They entered his office, there were two work places with desktop computers, a scanner and printer on a unit on the opposite wall, the entire office was in a glasshouse built against the wall. Snow covered the roof and cast an eerie light.

'The flat roof between these gables is laid out as a garden, with tubs and a small piece of grass,' he switched the lights on to reveal - snow; he unlocked and opened the large French windows and stepped out into the snow.

The hot tub was located in front of the chimney breast, it had a very restricted view across the valley, because of the roof of a turret but great views towards Carlton Hill and the Firth of Forth; neither of them stayed outside in the garden very long, it was too cold and still snowing.

They closed the French doors and went down the stairs to the living room; the fire was blazing in the grate. Karen went off to the toilet and Simon sat on the settee and started to read the newspaper, by the time Karen came back he was fast asleep; ah bless him, thought Karen, the old boy needs his afternoon nap. She lay down on the other part of the L shaped settee, put her head on his thigh using it as a pillow and within minutes was asleep herself.

Simon was woken by the alarm he had set to remind him to put in the oil for roast potatoes; he sat up and carefully lowered a sleeping Karen to the settee; he thought she looked so peaceful and beautiful when asleep. He used to watch Jane asleep sometimes, she was so lovely, so wonderful, he changed his thoughts.

He went into the kitchen, swapping his kilt for the apron and put the baking tray in the oven to heat the oil, once the oil was hot, he drained the parboiled potatoes and placed them in the hot oil and returned it to the oven, turning the heat up to crisp them. He then put the Yorkshire pudding tray into the oven to heat and set a reminder for 20 minutes to remind him to fill the pudding tray. He went into the utility room and came out carrying a bottle of wine; he carefully decanted one of his finest bottles of Barolo into his Edinburgh Crystal decanter.

As he was doing this, he had his back to the dining and living room; as he turned to use the sink, he was startled to find Karen was leaning over the breakfast bar, just watching him and smiling sweetly at him.

'What?' he said smiling at her.

'I was just thinking as I was watching you, that most guys I have known would have just stood up and woken me!' she said.

'But, gorgeous, you are with quality now, can you cook?' he asked.

'Nope' she replied.

'Iron?' he responded.

'Nope' she replied.

'Sew?' he tried.

'Nope'.

'What are you good at?' he said.

'I'm quite musical, I could make a living at that' she said.

'I'm not sure, I've heard some of your songs' he said with his impish smile.

'Naughty boy' she retorted throwing her apron at him.

Karen's phone rang.

'BK it's Hal, look, I'm still in Perth and there's no way I'm going to make it back tonight and I think the flight tomorrow morning is definitely off as I don't think they will have dug themselves out by then. Where is Emma, I've been ringing her and she doesn't reply?'

BK replied 'Emma is in North Berwick with Carrie and they are staying the night at a hotel, they hope to be back tomorrow some time.'

Hal replied 'It looks as though we will have to stay Monday night and charter something to get to Paris early Tuesday, who the hell is Carrie?'

'I've no idea' said BK 'some girl she met and slept with, Emma likes that type of thing, she sounded rather pleased they were snowed in'.

'BK I'm really sorry, but it looks like you will be in the hotel on your own tonight' said Hal.

'Hal, I'm not in the hotel and I'm in Simon's flat' Karen said.

'Jesus, you didn't sleep with him, did you?' Hal replied.

'Well, yes I suppose I did' she answered, the line went quiet, 'Hal are you still there?'

'Yes, I leave you two on your own for 24 hours; you both get laid and you leave a $3500 dollar a night hotel suite empty, damn bisexuals! BK, I've rung LA, they're going to try to arrange things I'll ring back in an hour or two when I have some news, can I remind you that you are on stage in Paris Tuesday evening and with what happened in Berlin you do need to rehearse.' Hal shouted.

'Hal, I'm about to sit down to roast beef and Yorkshire puddings cooked and prepared by a lovely. sexy man in and out of a kilt, I'm in heaven.' Karen said.

'BK you sound very relaxed, have you taken anything?' Hal enquired.

'Yes, Marmite - orally and I'm hoping for a second fix really soon' she looked at Simon and blew him a kiss.

'What?' asked Hal.

'Ask the people you're with, bye Hal' she replied and rang off.

Karen turned to Simon and said 'That was Hal, he's snowed in too'.

Karen watched as Simon deftly poured the Yorkshire pudding mix into the individual cups of the tin and then replaced the tin in the oven. He leant over the breakfast bar and kissed her very gently and said 'you look absolutely gorgeous standing there in my rugby shirt'.

Karen went and sat on the settee and started to read the New Musical Express she had brought from the hotel; twenty minutes later Karen sat down with Simon to a sumptuous feast, they sat side by side at the table facing the window onto Cockburn Street, the snow had all but stopped and some people were venturing out, sliding down the hill outside on sledges and kitchen trays.

There was easily enough food for four, a gorgeous juicy beef joint, just pink in the middle, roast potatoes, roast parsnips, carrots, cabbage and a plate of huge fluffy Yorkshire puddings.

'This is so good' said Karen 'how did you learn to cook like this, none of my previous boyfriends have ever cooked me anything other than in a microwave.' She suddenly thought, I said previous boyfriends, maybe he won't like that, maybe he doesn't see himself as my boyfriend yet, oh dear.

'Well, you clearly have been hunting the wrong age group' he said and smiled at her. Karen thought, by the present form he was correct, she had always gone for the mid 20 year old and in the music business, often to enhance her profile as Brad would say.

'My mother and sister taught me to cook, we had occasional lessons at school and I did a few courses, but I got better as the years went on. Jane was a reasonable cook but

I found it relaxing and got better and better with practice, I loved cooking for bigger numbers, 20 or so at family gatherings and I have cooked a few times in a professional restaurant serving the paying public.'

'Is that your mother in the photo on the beach?' Karen asked.

'Yes, she died over 20 years ago, that was about a year before her death' Simon replied vacantly.

'She couldn't have been very old when she died, what did she die from?' Karen asked and touched him on the arm, Simon noticed the touch, it was these tiny gestures that he really liked about Karen.

'She was only 67 and she died of cream' he said.

'What? Your mother died of cream!!!' she asked.

'And my father' Simon replied and explained 'They were from a different generation, they fought in the war, my dad was in Normandy, food was on heavy rationing, so when cream and other dairy products came off ration, they went a bit over the top. When Jane and I got married, my mother copied out all her recipes and gave it to Jane as a present, I still have it but I can feel my arteries hardening just taking it out the drawer. I could probably publish it as a guide as to how to have a cholesterol count in double digits; or maybe even a low fat cookery book in the US' he digged her in the ribs.

'That's so sad,' she said 'Not only was your mother a wonderful woman for having you, and a good cook, she was also a great teacher; these Yorkshire puddings are simply divine and the potatoes melt in your mouth, you are a first rate cook, and your ass looks dead cute in that apron' she said.

'Well, at least I'm good at something' he said sadly.

'Honey, believe me you are good in bed, breakfast this morning was rather special and you are so good for me' she said and kissed him on the cheek, leaving a gravy mark which she gently wiped off him with a napkin.

'I've never had any family other than my mom, how many brothers and sisters do you have?' Karen asked.

'My sisters were a lot older than me, eight and nine years, my younger sister died of cancer and my eldest sister and her husband live in England. I talk to my sister Caroline regularly by phone and we meet up once or twice a year, her husband's not too fit, cancer, but despite medical science he is still with her, they are so unbelievably happy together, I just hope it doesn't end for her, like it did ....' his voice trailed off and a tear ran down his cheek.

She caught the tear and sucked the moisture off her finger, she pulled him towards her chest and kissed him on his head, he was overcome with emotion and she held him tight and said, 'no-one has ever cried for me, I hate to see you hurt, you're some guy and I love being in your company; cry whenever you want but I might just join in' she said lovingly and softly.

Simon said 'have you never been in love?'

'Yes,' she replied 'many times but I don't think any of them loved me, I loved Jake but he beat me and abused me, I still love the nice him, not what he became'. Simon kissed and cuddled Karen.

Karen's phone rang; it was Hal, she was going to switch this damn thing off she thought.

'BK, the situation here is that we fly out at 9.00am Tuesday on an Air France plane and should make rehearsal on Tuesday afternoon, sound check about 6pm, it's tight but doable. We contacted the hotel and they have a hire for the suite for next week, can you pack your things tomorrow and move them into Emma's room, room service are on standby to help' said Hal.

'OK, bye gorgeous, speak to you soon' BK said and Hal rang off.

Simon poured Karen another glass of what had turned out to be a stunning bottle of wine.

Karen turned to Simon and said 'dearest, can I stay here tomorrow night? I'm getting thrown out of my suite'.

'That will be two nights in a row, I will have to charge you rent' Simon replied.

'I could always pay in kind' Karen said.

'Done' said Simon with a really impish grin on his face and pushed his hand up under the rugby shirt to fondled one of her breasts, Karen giggled.

'Naughty boy' said Karen, running her hand high up the inside of his thigh, to the top.

'That's nice and thank you' he kissed her.

'Tell me about Hal your manager' Simon said.

Hal's not my manager, he and Emma work for me, he's my executive manager and Emma is my executive assistant.'

'My manager is a guy called Brad Morgan' Karen said.

She told him all about Brad at work and at home about Lauren and the kids, she didn't tell him about Brad Junior and the other Karen.

Karen said 'Brad was brought up in the UK, in London his father was in the USAF, he talks often about the place he was staying at. I can't remember the name.'

'Ealing' said Simon.

'How in hell did you know that?' she turned and looked at him with her mouth full 'before you answer that can I say again, that this food is stunning, simply superb, you would pay top dollar for this in LA'.

'You are' said Simon running his hand to the top of her thigh; they laughed.

'I was brought up in Ealing on a housing estate with Americans, their fathers were all colonels in the USAF; there was the Morgans, the Roberts, the Sellers and a couple of others,' replied Simon, continuing 'Brad is the reason I am addicted to peanut butter and jelly sandwiches, his mother made them'. Simon looked wistfully into the past.

He looked out of the window and said 'the two of us used to play in the snow, we made this igloo one year by pushing large balls together and hollowing them out. Look Karen, it's stopped snowing let's go and play in the snow'; they cleared the table, putting the dirty plates in the dishwasher and set it going.

'I've got an old coat you can borrow, let's go and be kids again' he said.

He walked into the bedroom, stripped off his kilt and found some jeans and a warm top, in the meantime Karen had retrieved her clothes and redressed except for her blouse, she wanted to keep the rugby shirt on, it was nice and warm. She walked into the bedroom, walked up to him and they kissed, it was a slow meandering kiss, holding each other close. He looked into her eyes, stroked her left cheek with his fingers and said 'I am really enjoying your company, young lady'.

'I adore the way you touch me so tenderly and you are a very good kisser for an old man' she playfully slipped her hand over his bottom.

They put on their thick sweaters, scarves, socks as gloves and coats and went out into Princes Street gardens just opposite the end of Cockburn Street.

They had a snowball fight, made a snowman, made footprints in the snow, rolled in the snow, buried each other and stuffed snow into each other's clothing. An hour later, it started to get dark, they were exhausted, wet, starting to feel the cold and sore from laughter.

As they walked back through the front door Simon said 'Let's warm up in the hot tub'.

'Good idea' said Karen walking to his bedroom; as they

stripped they left little piles of snow to melt on the carpet.

Simon handed her a rugby shirt. 'No, I'm OK' Karen said, happy to be naked next to him.

'But it's a British and Irish Lions Shirt' he said, looking slightly hurt; she took the shirt, threw it on the bed and laid on it with her legs and arms open to welcome him. They made love, Karen knew it was making love, not sex, and there was not the urgency, the pornography of the night before; this was so sweet, caressing, and just a slow build to mutual pleasure.

Afterwards they lay on the bed, cuddling, not talking just enjoying their bodies being together, Karen laid there at a level of satisfaction she could not remember experiencing before, she thought of little Karen and Brad junior and the look of total satisfaction off her face. As Simon left to get the hot tub ready she watched him putting on his bathrobe, it occurred to her that she wanted to spend more time with him.

Simon looked into the bedroom to see Karen just putting on the rugby shirt, 'I've got the pudding and some coffee and I'll go up and start to fill the hot tub, come up in a couple of minutes'.

He disappeared; she heard the tank in the roof emptying its hot water; after a while she went up the staircase, taking their wine glasses, the decanter and her tub of Marmite, she saw Simon standing over what looked like a steaming cauldron.

He walked back to the office and picked up the tray and then returned for the wine and some towels, he turned the lights down, slipped off the bathrobe and walked across the roof and sat in the tub, Karen took off 'her' rugby shirt and went and joined him.

She found sitting there close to Simon sipping wine whilst it snowed a unique and much to be repeated experience. They sat there with the snow just starting again in those big flakes you remember from childhood; they played with Marmite, Karen found out that she didn't necessarily like the taste of Marmite but it was bearable for the effect.

When they got out of the tub, they took the towels and ran into the office, steam pouring from their bodies, they dried themselves and each other; Simon put on his bathrobe and Karen her rugby shirt.

'You really do look drop dead gorgeous in that shirt' he said to her.

She leant forward and kissed him, pulling the tie out of the bathrobe and throwing it across the room. 'That's better' she said.

They spent the rest of the evening with the drapes shut fast against the weather and fire blazing away, watching television, fondling and playing with each other.

When they went to bed, they didn't have sex; they didn't make love, they just slept together in the same bed, knowing that they could do that again the next day. Before, Karen went to sleep; she started to have thoughts about re-arranging 'Love Smiles' to a new beat and a new style flashed in her sleepy mind before sleep came.

Chapter Twelve

Goodbye is such a horrible word

Karen woke in Simon's bed, with his warm body next to her; she nestled into his back and gradually came to; she went to the bathroom and walked around to the kitchen and made two mugs of coffee.

When she returned, he was still asleep, lying over the area she had just vacated; she looked at his face and down across his body, he was in reasonable condition for a man of his age thought Karen. Mind you, he was the only man of his age she had seen asleep, she had seen a few older men at swim parties in their swimsuits and she remembered seeing naked older people the once or twice she had been to a nudist beach.

There was something very peaceful seeing another human being asleep somehow trusting, intimate yet common place, he rolled over onto his back, Karen smiled and straddled him 'Good morning Mr Macintosh' she said 'and what is sir up to today?'

'You by the feel of it' he said, he was very sleepy but there was such mischief in his eyes and smile. Their hands roamed over each other's bodies and gradually with Karen on top they enjoyed loving, gentle coupling, slow with a lingering level 12 kiss that brought them incredible intimacy and delight; all washed down with a tepid cup of coffee. They lay in each other's arms, Karen was beginning to like this too much, and Simon adored the intimacy the closeness, he had missed that; his phone rang and he reluctantly broke the cuddle and walked over to the dressing table.

'Simon Macintosh' he said 'Good morning, Peter and what have you got today; OK, I see when is the tender due?

that's a bit tight, no, I've got a friend staying at the moment. Look why don't we meet at the vaults at 3.30 and finalise it then; you've got my CV for inclusion.'

As Simon was standing talking on his phone, Karen lay on the bed enticing him with erotic views of her body; she noticed that he was beginning to respond. The person on the other end of the phone was clearly doing the talking as Simon was just saying 'aye' or 'yes' every now and again; she rose from the bed and knelt in front of him; he started to lose concentration; he rang off. He pulled her to her feet, he was actually slightly annoyed, 'if you did that every time I'm on the phone, I would never get any work done' he redialled the last caller.

'Peter, sorry, I was thinking of something else, we did just agree? Thanks see you then' throughout this phone call he had been slowly playing with her ring; he rang off.

'And another thing young lady, I am desperate for a pee' he said.

'Can I watch?' she said, he took her hand and led her into the bathroom.

They showered and gently towelled each other dry; 'Now listen, I need to work out, you don't get a temple like this without working out and swimming' he said smiling at her.

Karen said 'me too, I usually work out each day and run a few miles to keep fit and toned for the dance routines.'

Simon looked at her body, it was not overly muscular and she wasn't skinny, apparently size 10/12 European, although he had noticed that all her clothes were size 12; but at 5ft 9 she was almost as tall as Simon. Her arms were well muscled and her stomach was divine, flat but not heavily muscled, she had good definition through her chest and breasts; her thighs and buttocks was the area she clearly carried more weight and muscle, must be the dancing he thought.

'Do you have a spray tan?' he asked.

'Yes, virtually every time I go on stage, I get a tan, it's easier for the cameras, something to do with contrast also it shows off the costumes, what there is of them' she answered.

They dressed together, Karen put on her now dry clothes from the previous day, they weren't dirty she had hardly worn them.

'You know' she said looking at Simon 'I've known you for three days and I've spent most of it naked and or in bed with you, I've never done anything quite like this before and I have loved every minute of it'.

'Hey! not bad for an old man' Simon said with a wide grin 'I've not done this for a long time but I'm glad I have and I'm glad I met you, I do find it tiring though'.

'You're just a naughty boy and I have adored every second we have spent together and of course I will stay here tonight' she said kissing him on the cheek and fondling his buttocks.

They had breakfast in the kitchen, she had a slice of toast with Coopers marmalade and another with Marmite, its original use, as Simon had said; she still wasn't entirely convinced about the taste of it.

During breakfast Karen and Simon chatted about her life on the road, recording, groupies' adoration and being recognised.

'Do you get nervous before you go on stage?' he asked.

'Yes, of course, sometimes you need a little extra confidence, I could be performing in front of 20,000 as in Paris or 70,000 in Chicago and then there are TV studios. Actually, the smaller the audience the worse it is; playing in front of 100 people or a small studio audience can sometimes be even more stressful than a big venue, you can see them individually' she answered.

'Have you ever been on a chat show?' Simon asked.

Yes, I appeared on Jay Leno once and a couple of local ones

in the States, but only because people insisted; I'm actually a rather boring person, I'm not good at storytelling like you or jokes, I hate chat shows. I once saw George Hamilton on TV and he was a dead natural, I couldn't do that' she said.

Simon asked 'I don't think you're boring, so how would you answer the question how did you like Edinburgh?'

'Well' she said 'When I was in Edinburgh I met this guy, he was really nice, gentle and kind, we spent a lot of time together and had a lot of fun. He made me the happiest I have been in years and I do so much hope to see him again next week' she blushed.

'Funny' said Simon 'I had a very similar experience I met this incredible woman who shagged my brains out, was great fun and was the first person I had met since my wife died that I want to spend more time with, especially next week.'

He walked across the living room and took one of the false roses in the vase and handed it to her, kissing her lightly on the cheek.

'It's a false rose' she said.

'It's February and snowing, the gesture is genuine' he said, she kissed him on the cheek.

'Thank you Simon, you have made me very happy and I don't think I have ever spent quite so long with someone and never had an argument or disagreement and thanks for shagging my brains out too;' she said, they embraced for a loving, slow kiss.

Simon looked in her eyes and said 'Right, now I must go and work out and swim, it keeps depression away although I don't need help today because I am with you. Why don't we go to the Balmoral Hotel gym and pool, I've never been there and you might as well get some value out of all those empty rooms you've just paid for!!!'

'That is a great idea' said Karen.

'I'll get my gym stuff sorted' Simon said.

They left the flat and headed to the Balmoral Hotel; Simon went straight down to the fitness centre, signed in from the Royal Suite and changed. He had just finished his first 10 minutes stint on the cross trainer when Karen walked in looking stunning in a rather figure hugging leotard; 'sorry, I took so long, I had to organise the concierge to move my clothes and set up my keyboard'.

They were alone in the gym, just them, the machines, the weights and the CCTV camera blinking soullessly in the corner; they went about their separate routines with only the occasional glancing and fleeting touch betraying their relationship. After 45 minutes, Simon suggested a swim, they changed and met in the pool, they splashed, played and bobbed up and down in the corner and Karen liked the closeness.

As they sat in the Jacuzzi, Simon said 'I've got a lunch in George Street at 12.30, then I'm going down to Leith for my meeting with Peter, I shall be back about 5 -5.30pm. I've just got enough time now to dump my gym stuff back at the flat.'

'What is it like in Leith?' she said.

'Why don't you come and see' he said 'it's a bit cool for a long walk but we could meet in the Whisky Society vaults and walk over to Malmaison and then get a taxi back, if the snow is clearing OK. I'll ring you when I'm finishing with Peter and you can grab a cab and I'll meet you at the other end' Simon replied.

'That's a good idea' Karen said.

They went to get changed and met in the corridor outside the lift; Simon grabbed her and kissed her passionately, the lift arrived, he got out at the ground floor and she continued up to her suite. She had her day to organise and a song to re-arrange, within ten minutes she was on the phone to Clive Thompson in Paris; the re-arrangement of Love Smiles was done in her mind, now she had to share it with others and convince her band they could do the change.

Simon left the Balmoral Hotel and walked down across Waverley Bridge, the snow was still lying in the gutters but the gritting and salting had made the pavements and roads safe and passable. He went to the door of his stair and tapped in the pin number and opened the door, he tossed his gym bag in a box marked no8 and then walked back across Waverley Bridge. The path through Princes Street Gardens had been opened up by a single pass by a small tractor spreading salt, the trees dripped water and down across towards the railway was an almost virgin stretch of snow, Simon only just resisted the urge to go and walk in it; he could just see over the other side of the railway, to the small snowman they had built the day before, he smiled.

He walked up Hanover Street, along George Street passing the Opal lounge; a lot had happened since the last time he had been here, he had got his life back, he smiled and chuckled to himself, turned and walked into the Centro restaurant and switched into work mode.

Hal returned to the Balmoral Hotel around midday, he had left his cousins by walking to the main road and being picked up by a taxi that took him to Perth station, the train had arrived at Waverley Station right next to the Balmoral Hotel only 20 minutes late. The first thing he did was to run a hot bath and eased himself into the warm suds. He had taken his laptop with him to Perth and so had caught up with all his emails and paper work but it was still too early for direct contact with the Beach staff or Brad Morgan's office.

What Hal didn't know was that whilst he was lolling in the bath listening to his iPod, BK had come back and supervised the moving of her clothes into Emma's room so the hotel could re-let the suite. BK had taken her hand luggage bag, packed some clothes and equipment she thought she would need overnight. She was going to stay the extra night with Simon, despite the fact he had to get up early on the Tuesday morning so she could go to the airport to catch her early flight to Paris.

The concierge had helped her move her clothes and then unpack and set up the keyboard and her laptop, when everyone left she dialled a mobile number and talked to Clive Thompson in Paris. So between Skype and a music interface programme, cellphones and the built in cam of the laptops, they could talk to each other and both see the page of music on the laptop, sharing the re-arrangement. As she suggested changes and sang or played them, Clive was tweaking them on the SSL mixing board. BK had a mad idea, which was to re-arrange Love Smiles and get Clive to rehearse the band then sing it the next night as the last song. Clive was, as always, brutally honest, he was aware that BK had not composed or rearranged anything for a long time 'BK, it's bonkers, a nuts idea but let's see if it works' Clive said eventually.

BK had woken up early and spooned with Simon, he was asleep, she had dosed in and out of sleep and as she did a completely different version of Love Smiles started to form in her mind, by the time they made love it was fully formed in her mind and she ached to compose.

Emma walked into the corridor outside the suite to find the door to her room open, Hal was sat in the sitting area which doubled as an anti room or waiting area for the suite and the larger rooms off this corridor.

'Hi Hal babes' Emma kissed him on the cheek; she was in a good mood thought Hal 'I had to come back by train.'

She was cut short by Hal saying 'shush' and whispering 'you have some explaining to do and gossip to share young lady' he pointed at BK.

Through the open door she could see BK with her back to them, her long hair brushed straight and hanging down her back. She was sat at her keyboard, with ear phones on, on a table next to her was a laptop and Emma could clearly see Clive Thompson. They had lugged that damn keyboard half way around the world and Europe, just in case BK became interested in music again; she hadn't; until now.

'OK, I'll go from the top; I'll switch the speakers on here so I can sing along with it.' Emma heard BK say.

Emma recognised opening bars of 'Love Smiles', BK was playing it on her keyboard, she started with the raucous heavy beat, the song had originally been called Love Sucks but they had to change it because of the conservative nature of their America audience. As she started to sing the words the tune moderated into a slow, sickly, love ballad, Emma watched, she had never seen BK compose anything, as the song went on she realised she was thinking of Carrie and the wonderful sensitive way they had made love in the hotel that morning.

Emma started to cry, not weeping but tears welled up in her eyes, it was the most adorable love song and BK was singing it and swaying with the music. By the end, both Hal and Emma were in tears, not because of the song but that their employer and friend was composing and playing her music with glee. At this point, Emma knew that BK had connected with Simon at an emotional level; she was going to have problems when they parted, she also felt just a little jealous.

When BK finished singing, the laptop erupted into shouting, 'BK, I've got an idea let's play in the normal way and then end the show with this version, it's Paris, it will stick them dead' said Clive

Hal said to Emma 'What has been going on here?' Emma replied 'Hal, Simon happened, she doesn't know it and as sure as hell, he doesn't but BK is happy; we will have to make sure that no one destroys what she and Simon have together'.

BK jumped as Emma handed her her phone; it had rung whilst BK had been video rehearsing, which seemed to be what she had invented; listening to the music over the internet, through earphones and then singing along whilst someone else listened 1,000 miles way.

Emma had answered BK's personal number, she had been shocked to see the photo that displayed for the caller, it was fairly impressive, phallic and very pornographic and with the name Simon Macintosh underneath she recognised the subject of the photo, BK did surprise her sometimes.

'Hallo Simon, this is Emma, do you remember me?' she said.

'Yes, always' he said, 'down boy'. Emma said, blushing at the double entendre, the photo and all 'I'll get BK for you.'

'BK, it's Simon for you'; she tapped her on the shoulder, BK couldn't hear because she had earphones on, she looked at the picture; she instantly stopped what she was doing and took the call. She remembered taking that photo and thought it so funny at the time to assign it to Simon's contact details; she wondered if Emma had seen it, again, she had looked a little flushed.

'Hallo sweetheart' said Simon.

'Sorry' said Karen 'change of plan, I'm going to be another hour or so here so then I'll come over to your flat, I know where it is, actually from this room I can see the building'.

'OK' Simon replied 'I'll get on with some work; cook you something nice, a curry and we can slob out watching TV rather than go out, I'm exhausted'.

'Curry, hot tub, TV, early bed, sounds ideal to me' Karen said adding 'but not necessarily in that order.' Simon laughed; it was his naughty laugh Karen thought, an idea popped into her head and then was gone.

'See you soon honey, I can't wait' Karen said.

An hour and a half later BK pushed the button on the video entry system marked S Macintosh and stood looking at the video camera.

'Has anyone told you recently, you look gorgeous' was the reply.

Two oriental girls passing by giggled and BK turned to and smiled at them. One of the girls put her hand over her mouth and squealed; she had recognised BK Shore, her pop idol, but never expected to see her whilst on holiday in Edinburgh, she started talking to her friend. The door buzzed and BK walked in out of the cold and into the stairwell and made her way up to Simon's flat, she felt tired, a bit bloated and a little under the weather.

She was greeted by a smiling Simon and they walked into the flat together, he closed the door and they kissed and ran their hands over each other's bodies; every time they were apart the meeting was a little less tense, each time it was becoming easier. The phone rang, Simon said 'I am really sorry I'll have to take it, it's a potential client and an important one'. He pressed answer on the house phone in his hand and walked off up the spiral staircase to his office.

Karen wandered through to his bedroom, his wardrobe was open and she looked at the clothes hanging there, formal shirts, suits, jackets and an Edinburgh Rugby shirt, she took it off the hanger and decided to wear it as a dress, it was long enough.

Simon finished his call and scribbled a reminder on the board in his office, he went down stairs and was surprised to see that Karen wasn't in the living room, he looked in the bedroom and she wasn't there either. 'Karen?' he said.

'I'm in the bathroom, don't come, I have a problem' he stood by the door, 'I have a period' she said.

'God that takes me back' he said 'anything I can do?'

'Nothing unless you have a supply of tampons' she said 'I do actually, I'll be back in a minute' he said.

He returned with a box of tampons and knocked on the door, Karen said 'come in', he found her showering and placed the tampons on the surface by the basins. She stepped out of the shower and kissed him on the cheek, he left the room and went and sat in the living room and Karen emerged a few minutes later wearing his Edinburgh Rugby Shirt and knickers.

'I'm really sorry Simon, lousy timing, it's all closed down there for the duration' she said. He stood up and kissed her lightly on the lips and ran his hand under the shirt up her back and over her naked breasts. 'That's good, everything else seems to be in working order' he said and gave her his naughty boy smile; an idea popped in and out of her mind, flitting across her consciousness.

Simon had decanted a bottle of wine and poured two glasses, the fire was roaring in the grate and they sat in front of the fire, sipping wine and cuddling into each other and just idly chatting. Karen was lying using Simon's lap as a pillow and she just loved watching the firelight in his face, she was thinking of music.

'You were right about Love Smiles, I re-arranged it and it sounds much better, you have also given me several ideas for new songs, there has got to be a Bollywood themed one on the Calcutta Cup' she said.

'Bit difficult to get anything to rhyme with Calcutta Cup' Simon said and an alarm sounded in the kitchen.

Ironically, Simon served beef madras, naans, pickles and rice, it was very tasty and Karen was now convinced he was a very good chef. 'Is that one your mother taught you?' Karen asked 'no, it's off the BBC website, but I have changed it to make it easier using made-up pastes from the shops' he said.

They sat on the settees cuddling. Karen undid Simon's shirt so she could feel his chest hair, she really was developing quite a thing for his chest hair and lay across his body facing him and resting on one arm.

'Simon' she said 'You took the fact I have a period very calmly'.

'You can't help or avoid your biology and anyway I like apples' they laughed.

'I have to ask this question, but you are a bachelor, sorry widower, living on your own and you have a box of tampons in the house?' she asked.

'Ah, but I have two daughters, one of whom is far more organised than I would want to be and she equipped the flat for all eventualities, although I know she never thought the tampons would be used by my girlfriend, it's the third time it has been used; I mean the box not the tampons' he smiled a warm impish smile.

'That is so thoughtful; Jake used to make me sleep in a different room during my period, he used to call me unclean and not allow me in the pool' she said falteringly.

'What a bastard, why did he treat you so badly, you're wonderful' he said.

Karen started to cry, Simon remembered those deep sobs from his own experiences and he cradled her in his arms. She started to tell him about Jake, not the front story but more of the truth than before; how he would get stoned, hit her regularly, make her do things she didn't want to, broke her teeth and nose, whipped her, tied her up and left her and generally humiliated her. She sobbed throughout and hung onto Simon so tightly that on more than one occasion, he had to loosen the grip.

She simply could not stop crying, she had never told anyone these details before, she sobbed and cuddled into

Simon nestling against his chest. Simon said 'Karen, he raped you didn't he?' The change in the intensity of the sobbing and the firmer cuddle gave him his answer but she nodded and said 'Yes'.

After some time she had cried herself out 'I've never told anyone that, never' she started to cry again and said between the sobs 'and now you're going to dump me because I'm dirty, soiled and unclean'. He held her; he could feel tears streaming down his chest; he started to cry too, she could feel that, life had been hard on both of them.

'I hate the fact that you are so upset, you have cried your heart out and shared something very private with me, I appreciate your trust. Listen, your past is your past and my past is my past, we will share as we need to but it makes us the people we are now, it makes us better people not worse; I am sorry but I don't know how to react or support you.'

'You already have,' she nestled into him and to his surprise started to suckle on his nipple like a child.

She stood up, took his hand and said 'can we go to bed together please?' and handed him his rugby shirt back.

'It would be rude to refuse a lady,' he said.

Just before they settled for the night, they set some alarms; they fell asleep in each other's arms; Karen had kissed Simon all over his body and ensured he was comfortable before cuddling down next to him. Simon fell asleep thinking of Karen, her sobbing and how she must feel; Karen sleepily said 'Simon, thank you for being so kind and lovely, I'm growing very fond of you' but Simon was already asleep.

Simon woke to find Karen already dressed; he sat up in bed and said 'You should have woken me, is there anything I can do?'

'Yes' she said 'get out of that bed and stand over there I want some nude photos of you and yours.'

'Hey' he said 'I haven't got any of you naked.' 'Yes you have: I put them on your phone last night,' she smiled with mischief in her eyes.

They went and made some coffee and tidied the debris from the night before, Karen's phone rang; it was Hal to say the car was waiting downstairs.

They kissed by the front door, she in her fur coat, him naked; 'that tickles' he said, 'what about this?' she said kneeling in front of him 'yes that tickles too' laughed Simon gulping.

She stood and held his neck and said 'Simon, no-one has ever treated me like you have this weekend, you've been a true friend and a wonderful lover' she started to cry 'I don't want to leave, I don't want to say goodbye, I can't let you go, I can't,' tears flowed down her cheeks.

'Karen, I never thought from our meeting, we would end up friends, let alone lovers or that I would end up in a naked cuddle with a grizzly bear. We haven't started to have fun together, you will be back on Friday and we will be together then.' Simon said.

'Simon', 'Karen', they kissed, he opened the door and she was gone.

Simon leant against the wall, he felt emotional and he looked at the photograph that hung there; he said 'Jane, I wish she was you'.

Chapter Thirteen

Getting the act together

As the wheels touched the runway at Edinburgh Airport, BK realised she was wet between her legs; she was actually very aroused; she had drifted off to sleep and dreamt of the previous weekend, now she was all excited about meeting Simon again, it was ridiculous. She had only met him a week ago but the meeting had transformed her, for god's sake she thought, he's 20 years older than you and you're thinking about him like a teenager.

This weekend would be different, Hal and Emma were staying at the hotel and she would be staying at Simon's flat. He had texted her to say that the spare room was ready, they had texted a lot but he had been busy with his business and she had been rehearsing or performing but she wanted his bed, his arms and his smell.

She had found a bottle of that weird aftershave in the duty free at Edinburgh Airport on her way out, she bought it and had taken it with her; it was a lovely smell but on him it was very different, much better and incredibly arousing, for her anyway, he must add something; she smiled.

Emma leaned over and said 'I know what you're thinking'.

'Well enjoy it Emma, darling' she said and kissed her on the cheek, 'are you meeting up with Carrie?'

'Like I said I know what you're thinking' they smiled at each other, it was a really dirty smile.

Emma and BK locked eyes 'you were brilliant this week, I'm so proud of you' Emma said.

It had been a very different week; they had to cancel rehearsal on the Monday as they had to stay in Edinburgh, flying to Paris early morning on the Tuesday. So they had quickly rehearsed on the Tuesday and practiced the new arrangement for Love Smiles as part of sound check for the first concert

On the Wednesday after the first concert, she had woken up between wonderful crisp white sheets, she felt the softness against her ass and breasts, and she cuddled a pillow. She had slept like the dead, a deep satisfying sleep; Emma arrived and sat on the bed next to her.

'Hey girl since when have you been sleeping naked?' Emma said, as BK tossed the covers back and made off to the bathroom; returning she lay on the bed next to Emma and BK put the back of her head resting on Emma's stomach. They talked a girlie talk about life, men and clothes, BK told Emma all about the rugby, the people she met, the look-alike scam Simon made up and how they had sex and then made love. Emma told BK about Carrie, what they did and what a lovely time they had had together; they both laughed about Marmite, kissed and BK stood up and moved over to the bathroom for a shower Emma followed.

They had had precious little time to shop or sightsee in Paris, they had been driven around the sights, BK thought how wonderful it would be to be in Paris for a weekend with Simon. They got out of the limousine at the Moulin Rouge and walked around; as she and Emma were walking passed one of the sex shops a display caught BK's eye. 'Look at that' she signalled to the interpreter and they walked into the shop, placed an order and paid for the item and its delivery to their hotel by taxi the next day. She would have fun with that, she left the shop laughing, followed by a rather sullen interpreter who clearly did not appreciate being dragged into a sex shop to interpret such intimate questions. BK had also bought some bottles of fine French wine and shipped them to Simon's apartment; he knew it was coming because she rang him from the shop for an access code to the front door for the delivery in time for her to help drink it.

BK had three concerts in Paris on Tuesday, Wednesday and Thursday, not one of them had sold out although the 85% sales rate more than broke even. The concerts in Berlin had lacked any real sparkle or atmosphere; Clive Thompson had thought it was like listening to a record collection, he had his work cut out at the production deck keeping BK in tune, but she had also been a little off on timing and the computerised solid state logic mixers were good but not that good. On one song, 'Love Smiles', she had only been on key 30% of the time and the computers and producers had sweated blood to ensure she sounded OK.

He had then had this strange link up with BK who had re-arranged Love Smiles completely differently, it grabbed him, but he thought it needed more polish. She had phoned, from Edinburgh and even over a phone line he knew her singing was so much better.

BK had stepped into the rehearsal room in Paris on Tuesday afternoon, from the start she was different, she sang her signature song 'Get Down Now' with a passion Clive hadn't seen for years, and in tune. Half way through she stopped and coached the guitar section. Hal, and everyone else, was aware she wasn't swearing or shouting at them as usual but gently encouraging them to play better.

Four songs later, she called a break; Clive Thompson turned to Hal and said 'What happened in Edinburgh? Did you get her laid or something?' He was sitting at a huge Solid State Logic mixing deck, preening the settings for the concert. Over the last year Clive had bullied, pushed and dragged performances out of BK; Brad had insisted on this tour but she was too fragile, but now she was back to how she had been.

The rehearsal area was a large room which held all 37 performers in the band with three vocal recording rooms and two control rooms. All the performers were in the one room, playing and singing together but they were all wired up and so listening to their bit in their ears. The music was so much better, the timing, the tone and for a change BK's pitch all gelled perfectly and when he played it back there were nods around the room. The rehearsals went so well they simply moved to a longer sound check at the venue.

They had practiced their music and vocals for the re-arrangement of 'Love Smiles' but the sound check was the first time that BK and the band had performed and sung it live; this was an entirely new genre for them and when they saw her perform it they realised it was very special, the band had applauded her, unique.

The venue was part of the same complex; the Bercy-Paris Sports Palace was an incredible venue on the banks of the River Seine in Bercy Park. It is pyramid-shaped and has its walls covered with a sloping lawn. The structural steel roof, designed by Jean Prouvé, is supported by four huge concrete columns. This massive 55,000 square metre architectural wonder plays host to any event you can imagine. It can hold up to 18,000 people in its main hall, allowing singers and musicians of all types to perform in the centre of Paris.

This rehearsal had been something different, she had sung the same song 90% in tune, her timing was spot on, she had pulled the saxophonist up for missing his cue by a fraction of a second and she had sung the song with such a passion and feeling, the band had applauded her. Indeed Emma had sat there with tears coming down her cheek. Like Hal the bitch was utterly tight lipped about Edinburgh. BK burst into the control room and hugged Emma. Maybe those rumours about BK and Emma are true thought Clive; who cares, this was so much better.

The first concert had been a triumph; BK had worked the crowd like no-one had seen for ages. The songs were well delivered and the band had risen to the occasion, the atmosphere in the venue was electric.

Brad Morgan had sat in his office in LA munching another salad; he was determined to lose weight this time. He was watching the private internet feed from the cameras in Paris and several other venues on split screen.

Clive Thompson had emailed him to tell him that BK Shore was performing well and he should look in on the concert.

About time that bitch started getting her head together, every time he talked to her she cried so he had given up and talked to that faggot Hal. He didn't rate that Emma woman, her assistant, she was too close to BK; God sake they slept in the same bed and took showers together.

BK was on fire; she talked to the audience, even trying a few sentences in French and was running around the stage like a new born lamb, what the fuck had Hal done to her. She had insisted in not staying in Paris, Brad knew that Hal had only agreed to the Edinburgh trip because it was cheaper than Paris. Hal had now cancelled the hotel bookings in Madrid, because she wanted to go back to Edinburgh for the week, why?

Brad had wondered why Clive Thompson had changed the running order and put that song in, for a second time, just at the end of the concert during the 'spontaneous' encore. Brad has always rated the untidy Brit, his ear for a tune and his miraculous abilities at the mixing desk made him one of Blue's best properties.

Brad heard BK say to the audience 'Our very last song is 'Love Smiles'. Last week in Berlin I wasn't able to sing this song very well. But I went to Edinburgh last weekend; it's the most wonderful place in the world; I don't know what happened to me but I felt like singing the song differently'. She was choking back the tears but she turned to the camera sporting the biggest smile Emma had ever seen on her; the crowd roared and the music started.

She hit the first note, she had her eyes shut, she was swaying with the music and she started singing the lyrics of the most sensual love ballad.

'Oh my god' yelled Brad, dropping his coffee cup on the floor.

Terry, his assistant, rushed in to clear up, 'hey isn't that BK Shore? She's giving that some, it's so so...'

'Fucking fantastic, get me that fag Hal Riddick on the line and if not him that lezzy Emma Button' shouted Brad.

'Brad,' said Terry, 'she is doing that really well'. They stood in silence watching the TV screen with its hazy picture streaming live from Paris; at the end of the number the audience erupted.

Hal was standing in the sound-proof technical production booth, he had never seen BK perform like that, as the last bars rang out she stood in centre stage with darkness around her arm outstretched behind her, a gesture of total submission and love, the cameras picked up the tears rolling down her cheeks, it was a picture that appeared in newspapers and magazines around the world; she wiped the tears away and sniffed and waved at the crowd that went wild.

Hal dialled a number on his phone, it was to someone he hadn't met; Emma had stored the number on his phone.

It was answered, 'Simon Macintosh'.

Hal said 'we have never met but I'm Hall Riddick, I thought you might like to hear something.'

Hal moved out of the sound-proof box and held his phone

up to the tumultuous applause, he felt his phone vibrate with another call, and he ignored it.

'I'm sure BK will explain and I look forward to meeting you' said Hal.

'Thank you that was most kind and thoughtful of you' replied Simon.

Hal rang off and looked at his phone, Brad Morgan and Larry Packman had both rung; Hal was a man under pressure, Beach had been struggling, mainly because their principal asset was under performing, he had done his best but ever since the Jake incident it had been pretty much downhill. He had seen BK transform in one week from a nervous under confident wreck to a confident young woman; he really looked forward to meeting this guy, he knew everything about him, the agency had filed a full report, including his security clearance details. It was what Brad would call bank account to dick width; there was nothing to suggest he was anything other than an ordinary guy who life had crapped on.

Hal also knew that Simon was not a wealthy man but a very proud one and one regarded by those around him with true integrity, something he would have to manage carefully. He had already assigned a discrete bodyguard in Scotland to keep an eye on him, for Simon's own protection. He had briefed Judy the publicist, in the very strictest of confidence, who was already preparing scenarios and the legal team had reviewed the legal position; Hal also knew that if BK was back on form all those people who were so difficult to speak to or who yelled at him down the phone would suddenly became nice and available and with that thought his phone rang and it was Penny from Paramount records.

Emma was standing bolt upright her eyes wide open, the noise of the crowd hit her like a wall; BK had given that song a very new twist. She had noticed her working with the orchestral arranger and a couple of the other musicians; it had been changed into a wonderfully powerful love song, sang slowly and with vibrant lust and sensitive love; her phone vibrated, she looked at it and saw the name Brad Morgan.

That bastard hadn't talked to her for a year and treated her like shit; she stepped into the dressing room next to her and took the call.

'Emma, it's Brad, sitrep now young lady, what the fuck just happened?'

'Brad, I have no idea, she re-arranged the song and sang it from a heart I never knew she had' said Emma.

'She re-arranged the song, she's written diddly squat for years and then this!!!' Brad yelled.

'She's writing a new song, I saw her on the plane over and she's arranged for Peter Cairns, the keyboard player, to come over to the hotel tomorrow morning, to compose' Emma said.

'What brought all this on, you two become lovers or something?' Brad sneered.

'Brad that's cheap, what happened was Edinburgh' Emma said.

'What the fuck happened in Edinburgh, I know it's supposed to be beautiful but?' Brad asked.

'Brad, she met someone good for her,' said Emma.

'I want to know who he is, fuck sake, tell me it's a he, from bank account to dick width' Brad screeched down the phone.

'NO Brad, NO neither Hal nor I will tell you, leave it arsehole; just leave it to run and take your money; promise me that or nothing else; remember you owe me. You might think I'm a useless piece of shit, a feeling that is entirely mutual, but Brad just leave it,' Emma said calmly down the phone and then rang off.

Brad looked up to Terry who was listening to the phone call on speak phone and said 'Tell me T, am I going mad or did that spineless pussy licker just tell me to fuck off and mind my own business?'

'Glad, you didn't miss it Brad, she must have grown balls' he smiled 'but she's right, leave it Brad, it's Hal's business' Terry said.

'Everyone's ganging up on me now' Brad said, throwing his arms out in frustration.

Terry said 'Brad that song will have burst the hearts of every woman who hears it; puncture BK's bubble and you'll get nothing, keep it and you'll make another fortune'.

'Shit,' he stared at Terry, he knew he was right.

He asked Terry to get a call booked with BK Shore.

BK sat texting on her phone; Simon had sent her a text to say that Hal had rung him and said it had gone very well and he had heard the applause. BK had tried to ring him but the speeches at the dinner he was attending had started so texting was all they could do. They were excited like teenagers even though he was in a dinner in Edinburgh and she had just come off stage and was bathed in sweat. She was in mid text when the phone rang and Terry Moreland was on the line saying that Brad Morgan wanted to talk to her.

Brad Morgan came on the line 'BK, sweetie that was the performance of a lifetime, well done. I just adore that re arrangement of Love Smiles; we will have to get you into the studio to record that asap the record company are battering Hal's door down.

'BK, what brought this on, Emma said composing too, have you been sick? What happened in Edinburgh, you were totally crap in Berlin and now just fabulous. I remember looking in your eyes in hospital, sadness and to look at your eyes on the downlink and I saw joy; so babes, what is his name, only a heterosexual could make that difference?' Brad said.

BK replied 'Brad, you're a homophobic old fart. Edinburgh is a marvellous place and I did meet someone and yes *he* was very good for me, I have never had so much fun and love.'

'So are you going to tell me anything about him?' Brad demanded.

'No' said BK laughing, she was about to take control over the conversation.

'BK you have to protect him, the press will kill him' Brad advised.

'Brad, Judy is on to that but I want to keep him for myself, he's a very nice guy, he's 20 years older than me,' she said.

'My god, he's my age, dirty old man' Brad said.

'No, he's really just a naughty boy' BK said 'Yes, Brad, he is your age; Brad, that's it, I've got it, the title of my new song 'Naughty Boy'.

'Brad, you have to understand; he was hurt like me, his wife died in a plane crash and we just clicked, he was a good friend to you and is now a good friend and lover to me,' BK said, now she had control.

'Careful BK, please don't get trapped with another arsehole, he will dump you once he's made money out of you; what did you just say, repeat that BK' Brad said.

'Thought you missed it, you know him, he was a good friend to you and is now a wonderful friend and lover to me' she said.

'I know this guy?' Brad said.

'Yes; when you lived in Ealing who was your best Brit friend?' BK asked.

There was a long pause and Brad said quietly 'Simon'.

Brad went silent, 'that was a long time ago, when you had trouble with the snow, I remember we made an igloo once.'

'You pushed big balls of snow together and then hollowed them out' BK said.

'My god, so few people know that, you're being diddled by Simon!!! I'll get the contact details from Hal' Brad replied.

'As far as I know, Hal doesn't have them, I've got them on my phone, but I will talk it through with Simon first Brad, I will let you know when you can make contact, you will not do so without my permission' said BK and for the first time Brad submitted to her wishes, she was in control.

By the end of the next day, Hal Riddick, Brad Morgan and Larry Packman were happy men; they had been emailed and told that the Wednesday concert had sold out and that sales in Madrid were as good as full and London was already picking up; the wonders of social network sites and 24/7 internet booking systems. All three were overjoyed and were now looking forward to the American leg.

Chapter Fourteen

Worlds collide

BK walked through the terminal at Edinburgh Airport, she had a tune running in her mind, she was frustrated it wouldn't come out and she didn't know what it was about but some music and lyrics kept rolling around her mind. She walked straight into the person coming towards her, she apologised and looked at him and he was familiar.

'Hey, I'm Manus; you were with Simon last weekend weren't you?' he said.

She remembered they had met on George Street and Manus had been in the bar tent after the rugby, he was one of Simon's closest friends.

'Well, can I say you have made an old man very happy and I don't just mean me? I saw Simon during the week and he was laughing and joking, his laugh is legendary and has been silent; you're good for him and I'm glad you're back in Edinburgh'.

'That's very kind of you, is he alright?' she said smiling.

Manus paused and looked pensive. 'Can I say, after the match all his friends were watching him, we appreciated the way you supported him, it is very kind of you, he's an older man he still grieves for Jane; please be careful, don't hurt him'.

'I understand' she said kissing him on the cheek; Manus ran off to get his flight.

BK took one step forward and stopped, no it can't be she thought, she felt sick and rushed to the toilet and Emma rushed after her. BK had always had this talent for writing songs and music; she had inherited it from her mother; it was a talent that had made her and Brad Morgan rich but the talent had a sting in its tale; ideas for songs hung around her brain and then as an idea matured, there was a nervous reaction and without warning, she emptied the contents of her stomach and then was able to write out what she was thinking; Hal called it 'creative vomiting.'

BK came out of the stall and went to the basin, she looked pale and she reached into her bag and brought out a toothbrush and toothpaste and started to scrub; Emma was standing with her hand on BK's back, 'you OK?' she said.

'I've just finished an outline for a new song called Naughty Boy, Emma, I need to see him again to finish it, he has such an impish smile especially when he is being naughty' BK said smiling.

'I know, I've seen him with that grin and nothing else, remember' Emma said and smiled.

BK spat out, stood up and started to sing a song, very flatteringly.

'You were the most wonderful thing in my life
A kind and dutiful wife
A mother, a lover, a friend, a whore
But now you are no more
Jane, Jane why did you board that plane
Because now I will never see you again'

Emma said 'you will have to be careful with that material, I suggest you change the name and it needs a bit of polishing; not sure if it's wise to call your lover's dead wife a whore'.

'I suppose you have a point, but someone taught him to be that good in the sack! Hey, Emma, I'm being sick, creative vomiting has returned' BK smiled with the colour returning to her cheeks.

'Are you sure its creative vomiting?' said Emma.

'Oh no it's definitely not that, I've just had my period, and I know it's too soon for morning sickness from what my friend

Marsha, has told me, however hold that thought; Emma can you get me a doctor's appointment today, I'd better check these pills I'm taking for period pains are strong enough, I don't want that other type of vomiting'

They walked out of the ladies to see an anxious Hal stood waiting; 'Hal sweetie, get me a keyboard and some paper, creative vomiting is back'. He handed her some mints he had bought whilst waiting; all three laughed, mainly from relief.

'Yeehaa' yelled Hal.

'Hal' said BK 'I have ideas for a whole album in my head right now, give me space this weekend'. She rummaged in her bag and brought out hand written notes and said 'see naughty boy, crying by the fire, I can't let go, crazy, innocence and daddy'. Hal put his arm around BK's shoulder and they walked off towards the exit and their waiting car.

Emma was on the phone to the American Express Black concierge service finding a private doctor in Edinburgh. They had booked the same suite at the Balmoral Hotel with three bedrooms, but BK was going to stay at Simon's apartment. He was working today and would arrive at the hotel in about three hour's time; she texted him 'arrived safe Karen xx'.

They were in Edinburgh for almost four days, this was Friday and she had to be at rehearsals in Madrid on Tuesday, the concert was on the Wednesday and then straight to London for rehearsals three gigs at London Excel, Friday and Saturday and Monday, that was the end of the European tour and she would return to LA; all the concerts were fully booked and she had become newsworthy.

They arrived at the hotel to find photographers outside, the paparazzi were in full force, she said 'drop me around the corner and I'll walk in through Hadrian's; Simon showed me that trick.'

The van drew up to the front door and only Hal and

Emma got out, Emma left the door open deliberately so the photographers could see that it was empty. 'Where's BK?' one of them asked.

'Not here' said Hal; she wouldn't be able to wander around George Street this weekend thought Hal.

They met up in the Royal Suite; 'Emma, let's get some drinks, I'll have a bloody Mary and let me have the wine list I want a good bottle breathing for Simon for when he arrives' said BK.

Hal was in the corridor briefing the security guards, last weekend he had refused to pay for them, this week he had arranged 24-hour cover; securing his assets as Brad caringly phrased it, he thought.

The doctor arrived about ten minutes later, Emma and Hal sat outside in a little sitting area where the guards patrolled.

Doctor Paula Donaldson was a woman in her mid forties and after qualifying she had married a fellow doctor Gordon Donaldson, who had gone on to be a very able bowel consult-ant. She had stayed in general practice but once the children came she went into private practice with a friend of Gordon's. They had three children, Scott was now 14, Caroline was 11 and Duncan was 7, she was very happy with their life but in private practice she saw a lot of people not so happy.

The receptionist had put the phone call from American Express through to her and she found herself talking to an Emma Button who was BK Shore's assistant; how Caroline and probably even Scott would like to meet BK Shore. She had been featuring all week in the news and was the darling of the Scottish press for calling Edinburgh 'simply the most wonderful place in the world'.

Paula had been somewhat surprised to be asked to attend a consultation as soon as possible as Miss Shore required an examination and contraception advice and maybe a repeat of an existing prescription. She explained that the call out and half hour consultation would be £400 payable upfront. She had made an appointment an hour later and handed the caller back to the receptionist so they could pay; Donna came through and said the payment had been authorised.

'They must have some money; you are to go to the Royal Suite in the Balmoral' said the receptionist.

She had been taken to the suite by one of the concierges and met by two security guards, one six foot six inches and the other about five foot eight inches, they looked slightly comical but also rather sinister.

'Thank you for coming doctor, ah here is BK' said Emma Button.

'BK, this is Doctor Donaldson, I will leave you two alone' Emma left the room.

'Well, Miss Shore, how can I help you?' Doctor Donaldson asked.

'Please call me BK' BK said.

'I've started having sex again after some time, I'm taking a low level pill to easy period pains but I want to make sure it is OK as contraception.'

'Let me see the pills,' asked the doctor 'are you taking any other medication?'

The doctor fired up her laptop and recorded some basic information, age, height and weight; she accessed the details of the contraceptive pills and the anti depressants BK was taking. The doctor took her blood pressure, tested a urine sample and examined her. The doctor asked 'would you like me to examine you down there, to make sure everything is OK?'

They moved into the bedroom and BK removed her jeans and panties, she hated this it was so degrading, she lay on the Queen Size bed and spread her legs; the doctor had put on gloves and a mask and proceeded to examine her.

'When did you last have sex?' she asked.

'Monday morning, god it feels a long time ago' BK said.

'I see, you have had some piercings on the labia, you don't use them now?' the doctor said.

'They were pulled out, so I let them heal' BK said.

'Do you shave your pubic area?' the doctor asked.

'No, I or rather Emma waxes it, it grows in very uneven and different colours so I do without' she smiled.

'There is quite extensive scaring here in the inside of your thighs, across your hips and buttocks, these are the signs of, excuse me asking but have you ever been raped?' said Doctor Donaldson.

'My boyfriend was rather rough and yes, he did rape me, that's when the rings were ripped out of my labia, luckily I didn't have the clitty one in at the time' BK replied.

'You should try to keep your stud in your hood piercing; it will close up very fast' the doctor said.

'My boyfriend insisted I had it done, I really didn't want to, I felt like some cheap white trailer trash, I never really liked it but recently, I have found that it is very stimulating, it has become quite an asset; I was about to put in a new ring before my boyfriend arrived but waited until you had been' BK explained.

'Is that the same boyfriend?' the doctor asked.

'NO, Simon lives here in Edinburgh, he would never ask me to do anything I didn't want, having said that he likes the ring, he says he will never think of Trinity House the same, but I don't understand the joke' BK said.

The doctor laughed 'Trinity House is the organisation that runs lighthouses and navigation beacons around England and Wales'; BK laughed too, so that was the joke, he was a naughty boy!

'So I guess that he is why Edinburgh is simply the most wonderful place in the world?' the doctor asked.

'Yes, he's due here in a couple of hours, I can't wait to see him again' BK said.

'So I can see, everything seems OK down here, your cervix is normal and I can feel no internal damage, you have also healed well, your vulva is a bit swollen but that could be your cycle or errr anticipation, when was your last period?' the doctor asked.

'In the last few days, with these pills I only bleed for a few days, I didn't have any pains this time though' BK said, 'that's very unusual for me'.

'You might not if you are having regular sex' the doctor said.

'Would you like to get dressed please, BK' the doctor said walking into the bathroom to wash up; the doctor walked out to the sitting room and typed into her computer as BK got dressed.

'Your current prescription is probably OK as contraception but I will just increase the dosage a little to be sure' she said, filling out her prescription. What is the name on your passport?' The doctor had once got caught because her private client had a different name and a passport was needed to obtain the prescription.

'Sarah King' BK said.

'I have included some contraceptive pessaries as a precaution, use them after sex, they might help but are not 100% necessary but better be safe than sorry'.

'BK, why have you been prescribed anti-depressants?'

BK explained 'I loved my previous boyfriend and he hurt me so much, I felt dirty, worthless; I've always wanted to have children but he hurt me so badly, I was scared I might not be able to, or find anyone else I could love'. BK asked 'have you got children doctor?'

'Yes' Paula said 'three, and a loving husband, guess I'm lucky'.

'Is your new relationship a loving one?'

'I only met him last weekend, he's the most romantic, gentle and wonderful man in Edinburgh' BK said, thinking of Simon and smiling.

The doctor packed up her computer and equipment, handing the prescription to BK and as she turned to leave she said 'By the way, your boyfriend can't possibly be the most romantic and wonderful man in Edinburgh, you see that will be my husband' she smiled and suddenly looked a lot younger 'Miss Shore enjoy your weekend'.

'Thank you doctor I will' BK said; they were both smiling.

Hal and Emma came back in, Hal sat at his laptop and started replying to emails, he had arranged for Carolyn, their secretary to come over this time so he had some support, she was due in on the evening flight from Paris.

'BK' said Emma 'let's go and have a shower'. Hal looked surprised.

'Relax Hal, girls can't wax their own beavers you know' she said.

Simon's train from Perth pulled into Waverley Station; he had been to Perth and Kinross Council assessing their single equality scheme for the Human Rights Commission, he and two other consultants were carrying out a detailed analysis; it was hard work, not particularly well paid but it was work.

On Tuesday, after a workout, he had chaired a conference, running a workshop and a questions and answers session with the keynote speakers; it had gone well and he had had an enquiry about a similar event next month. His consultancy business was doing well, he had struggled in the beginning but now he was making a passable living but above all it was keeping him busy.

He had gone to the conference dinner on Tuesday night and had just gone out for the pre speech 'comfort break' when

Hal rang. He had stepped into a cubicle, it was nice of Hal to ring, he had wondered how she got on, and she was so worried that the tour was going from bad to worse.

He had spent Wednesday in the office, doing his accounts, writing reports; he had lunch with a friend and worked out in the evening. He had added some extra sequences into his work-out and then gone through it with the fitness advisor at his gym; the whole routine was now over an hour in the gym, and swimming, with changing and walking to and from the gym it took two hours, he was doing this daily. He had also looked out the abs frame and was doing exercises at home to strengthen his stomach muscles; he really was a vane old bugger, he thought.

Thursday had been an advisory day, he had spent the day with one of the small companies he advised and helped with management advice, in this case, he had helped finalise a tender document. By Thursday, he was exhausted from all the working out and thought he needed to build his strength for the weekend, keeping up with her sexually sapped his strength.

He had thought of her often, during the week in her different world, they had texted a bit, she had even suggested that she stayed at the flat whilst in Edinburgh, that would be nice. He was also an old man, twenty years was a long time to span and he was also a little scared of getting too involved, he was unsure of his emotions but did so like being with her.

Every time she rang him or sent him a message, a picture of her ring and private parts flashed on his phone, he had tried to change it but she had password protected it and in the end he just enjoyed the view, he had also looked at the pictures on his laptop, naughty girl.

Simon walked out of the lift in the Balmoral Hotel; a security guard walked up to him and said 'ID'. Simon looked for his security guarding license; the guard moved his arm to display the armband. 'No problem' he handed over his driving license; the guard checked his name against the list and spoke into his microphone 'Bob, this one's OK'.

The second guard knocked on the door and when he heard 'come in' opened the door and Simon walked in, to be enveloped by BK, when they moved out of the way the guard closed the door. He talked to his colleague over the radio, guess that's 'the dick' arrived. They had code names for their charges, BK was Brenda and now Tom, Dick and Fanny; Hal, Simon and Emma, they smiled at each other.

BK kissed and cuddled Simon, 'I've never seen your hair all fluffed up like that, it's very big' he said 'do you like it like this or flat,' Karen said, 'I think flat, it's less tarty, more you' she smiled, kissed him again. 'It will be changed when I wash it after our hot tub' she said.

Simon walked over to Emma and put his arms around her and gently kissed her on the cheek 'good to meet you again' she giggled, he's cute, she thought I can see what BK sees in him. He turned to Hal and shook his hand, placing his other hand on Hal's elbow, he continued to hold Hal's hand and said 'I really appreciated that phone call; it was very kind of you, and it's good to meet you'.

'Hey guys, it's 5pm on a Friday and I don't have a drink, do you want to go out somewhere, I noticed the scrum at the front door and came in via Hadrian's, but we could give them the slip and then Karen and I could go home to my flat' Simon said.

Hal said 'I'm not sure; we would have to take one of the security guards'.

'Ah, that reminds me, Hal' Simon said; he put an arm around Hal and steered him into a corner.

'Hal, I became aware of being followed and bumped into Jack Tobin a few times looking a bit sheepish, I eventually doubled back in an alleyway and caught him, Scotland is a small place and I presented him with his security license about six months ago and by the way don't blame him.' He wagged his finger at Hal; BK saw the gesture and looked at Emma who shrugged her shoulders.

'Why are you checking up on me mister?' Simon accused.

Hal answered 'Simon, the guard was commissioned to protect you, some of the press can be very dangerous if they find out who you are, I wasn't checking, honestly Simon'.

'What are you two up to?' said BK starting to walk towards them, Simon raised his hand and without looking at her made the stop sign, she stopped dead in her tracks and went back to Emma; Simon's phone warbled in his pocket.

'Hal, was it you who accessed my security details, they tell you if someone does that and I bet you have looked at my bank account details too' said Simon angrily.

'Sorry' said Hal looking sheepish.

'If you are worried about me or want anything, just ask, no more cloak and dagger, talk to me, that is the best way for you to protect your asset and my friend.' Simon pointed at Hal again 'Do I make myself clear, Hal?' Hal bowed his head and nodded; he was surprised that Simon then put his arm around him and gave him a man hug.

BK came over and screamed at Hal 'Scare him off and I'll kill you, bastard!!!' Simon pulled her hand down sharply and said 'Karen, listen, he was only protecting us, doing the job you pay him to do, I just didn't like the way he went about it, we have come to an understanding now, so apologise for shouting at Hal'. He put his arm around her and gently shook her 'Say sorry, that was unfair of you', she looked at him, he looked good when he was angry.

She looked at Hal and said 'Hal, I'm sorry, I apologise'. Hal's eyes bulged. *That* had definitely never happened before!

Emma could not believe what she had just seen, there was a stunned silence.

Hal raised his voice slightly and said 'Simon, what is it with you, you breeze into our lives, you have made BK really happy, her music is great, she's composing and she has just apologised to me for the very first time ever; I need that drink'.

'OK' said Simon 'line drawn, time for fun, Hal and I will raid the bar here, you girls have got fifteen minutes to make yourselves even more beautiful, is that enough time or do you need longer?' Emma and Karen disappeared into their rooms making rude gestures at Simon who stood laughing at them.

Hal and Simon poured themselves some drinks from the bar in the sitting room and drank a toast to good health and their common understanding. Simon looked at his phone and laughed, he nudged Hal and showed him the text, 'let's have some fun'.

Hal opened the door and invited the guard in and said 'we are going out briefly and one of you will come with us'.

Simon said 'so if you could tell Jack that Brenda, Tom, Dick and Harry (he winked) are going to the pub and we will need to leave by the staff entrance on the Waverley Steps' the guard looked shocked and nodded and silently left the room. Simon said to him 'hey pal, you're doing a great job and we appreciate it, love the nicknames, very accurate' they laughed.

Simon turned and walked into Karen's bedroom, she walked towards him in only her lingerie and kissed him 'I have wanted to be in your arms, in your bed, and have you in me all week. You are also extraordinarily beautiful when you are annoyed' they kissed again and Simon's hand roamed her body unchecked.

They assembled at the door and Jack Tobin stepped in to escort them, he introduced himself to Hal, who said 'don't worry, he got the better of me too' they smiled.

They left the hotel by the staff entrance; they were wearing hats, scarves and coats and were not recognisable as they stepped out into the cold. They walked down the steps and along the walkway in the station, with Karen and Simon walking with their arms around each other and Emma and Hal following with their arms linked. They exited the station onto Market Street and walked up the Fleshmarket Close to the Halfway House tavern, this is a tiny 30 seat pub, is about 400 years old, it has been there for centuries and originally served the workers in the meat market next door. They walked in and found a small table in the corner and sat down, Emma went and got the drinks, gin and tonics all around, she asked for doubles.

Emma and Hal sat opposite Simon and Karen as he called her, the two of them watched as their boss became more and more like a besotted teenager and increasingly flirty and Emma swore that Simon got younger too; it was clear that they were finding it difficult to keep their hands off each other. They all started to chat and joke, Simon related the link between him and Brad Morgan, Hal made a mental note of that one. Simon talked about rugby and how this weekend Ireland played Scotland at new Lansdowne Road and how he hoped to take Karen to watch it somewhere with atmosphere, Emma and Hal smiled, nodded politely and avoided eye contact. They had another round of drinks and everyone was beginning to feel the effects of the alcohol, Karen suggested they leave and go their separate ways; she and Simon wanted to spend some 'quality time' together.

They left the pub and walked down the steps, as they got to the bottom, they heard music coming from the sports bar. 'Hey' said Karen 'that's my song they are murdering in there, let's go'.

She took Simon's hand and with Hal and Emma in tow, walked into the bar and up the karaoke DJ. 'Can you play that one again; I can do better'. He was about to tell her to wait in line when she took off her hat and scarf and he recognised her. 'Bloody hell' he said 'this is going to be good'.

Karen pulled Simon into the middle of the space and kissed him on the lips, the crowd cheered. 'I wrote this song but don't actually perform it, it was a big hit for In Style' she said into the microphone.

Hal and Emma knew the song, she didn't perform it because it was about people who met, became friends, became more than just good friends and how the woman doesn't want to let go of her man, it had a strong instrumental, wonderful backing and several 'moaning' episodes.

She performed the song as if she was making love, she even licked Simon's chest; Emma thought it was incredibly erotic and an enormous turn on for a woman let alone a man, the crowd watched in silence.

Emma watched BK and saw that she never once took her eyes off Simon, Emma knew that look, she knew BK was very sexually aroused; something had really got her going. There were several parts where they danced together and she was surprised at the togetherness of the 'grinding' sequences, they must have done that type of dancing before, she found it a bit of a turn on.

BK's singing was immense, strong and confident; her timing, pitch and tone were perfect, she also changed some of the words to fit the circumstances. She finished the song standing in front of Simon passionately kissing him with her arms stretched behind her, it was sensitive and incredibly sensual and several women in the crowd gasped when the music stopped, they did not break their kiss and they got another cheer when they did. BK hadn't even noticed the crowd, she only saw Simon, standing in his shirt which was undone, he looked fit, she wanted him and she knew he wanted her, they had missed each other.

The crowd applauded and shouted for more, she asked the DJ for 'Get Down Now' and sang and danced; Emma watched BK, she had seen her sing this song countless times, this time she was singing looking directly at Simon, Emma knew that BK was highly aroused at this point; in fact from Emma's experience she thought BK was close to an orgasm.

Jack Tobin stepped forward and spoke to Hal.

When the song finished there was intense applause, whistling and cheering; Emma kissed BK and Simon, Hal then said 'we have to go, press'. They gathered up their coats and BK's suitcase and bustled out of the bar, despite the offer by the manager of free drinks for the evening. Hal and Emma crossed the road and walked back across the bridge in Waverley Station, as they got about half way across, Hal pushed Emma into the wall and kissed her, out of the corner of her eye she saw, Archie Fleming, a paparazzi photographer sprinting past. Hal said 'Sorry, I didn't mean to go hetero on you but that bastard would recognise both of us'. Emma roared with laughter as they walked on arm in arm. 'Hey, Hal, poor old Archie, he missed the picture of the year, Hal Riddick and Emma Button in heterosexual conversion shock.' They giggled all the way back to the suite.

Simon and Karen walked quickly up the slight hill to the bottom of Cockburn Street; Jack Tobin was walking next to them, looking furtively behind. They got to the door; Simon punched in his pin number and opened the door. 'Good night,' said Jack 'Miss Shore, those songs were lovely'. They stepped inside, Karen rounded on Simon and threw him against the door, ardently kissed him and said 'I need relief now this new ring is driving me nuts, please Simon please now' and pushed his hand down the front of her unfastened jeans.

Karen cuddled into Simon, muffling a scream as she

climaxed, once she had relaxed and was still getting her breath back. Simon said 'Guess it's open down there?'

'Certainly is, I'm sorry; the ring was supposed to be a surprise, I haven't worn it before and it's a bit too good' she said.

They climbed the stairs, whilst he was opening his front door, she pulled her jeans and panties off and once inside showed Simon her new ring, the normal semi circle was completed by a clasp and a bar which was made up of tiny letters SIMON, it was very stimulating and she had found out that if she wore jeans, way too simulating. They lay on the bed and made love, incredibly intensely, this was new to Karen but Simon had enjoyed it for decades, it was he said the most intimate thing two people can do. Karen sat cross legged on the bed next to Simon caressing his chest and stomach and brushing her hair out, after that session they had washed her hair and Simon had dried it.

Simon said 'Those songs in Sportsters were lovely and you sang the first one with great passion and rather erotically, you are a stunning singer'.

'Thank you, you should see me perform' she replied.

'I think I just did' he said.

'No, I mean on stage' she said, pinching one of his nipples ' OUCH, like I said I just did, it was very arousing dancing like that, next to you, we should practice' he smiled; she leant forward and kissed him.

'I have another surprise for you' she said, she left the room; his eyes followed her naked body as it moved around the room. She came back with her handbag, sat straddling him, he was propped up by the pillows, she retrieved some paper out of her bag and handed it to him. It was confirmation of two corporate hospitality tickets for the Ireland v Scotland match in Dublin the next day. 'Surprise!' she said 'we fly out of Edinburgh tomorrow morning and fly back at midnight, would you like to go?'

Simon calmly and carefully folded the letter, kissed it and replaced it in her bag and pulled her down, they kissed. 'We had better get an early bath and bed then' he said with his naughty boy smile, she just loved that smile.

'You know I can't say thank you enough or reciprocate, I adore the gesture but I will also relish the day because it is a chance to be with you again, thank you' Simon said.

They ate in the hot tub, talked about their respective weeks and what was to come in the next few days. Simon and Karen discussed the confrontation with Hal over security; Karen thought Hal had done wrong, Simon thought he had done the right thing but wrongly; they agreed to differ and go to bed.

They woke the next morning, played in the shower and were picked up about 9:20am when a car arrived to take them to their chartered business jet from Edinburgh to Dublin. They enjoyed the hospitality before and after the match and the rugby game itself. In the lounge afterwards, they met some of the Scotland team whom they had seen the weekend before in the Jamhouse; they tried to convince BK she should go for young flesh not a wrinkled old man.

They went to Temple Bar for some drinks, atmosphere and a cuddle then the car took them for dinner and a dance at Velvet, a nightclub by the airport, no-one bothered them, because BK Shore was in Edinburgh, it was just one of many kilted Scots but this one had a young bint.

From Simon's point of view there were two highlights to the day; Scotland won again by 14 points and on the flight back, both he and Karen joined the mile high club; they clambered into bed and almost instantly fell asleep in each other's arms.

Karen woke and felt the warm body next to her, she ran her hand over his sleeping body, she could not believe her luck, in two weeks she had met and got to know a thoroughly decent guy, probably the first decent guy she had met, who didn't care about her fame and status. She had discussed her feelings for Simon with her therapist in LA over the phone, Karen was now aware that she had become very fond of Simon and was scared, very scared about the next week and her return to LA. She was also aware that, for Simon to engage with her emotionally he had to let go a bit of Jane, something he clearly was not prepared to do, at present, Karen knew he had issues.

The sleeping body moved, they made love in spoons, he was very sleepy, Karen took the lead and was aware that it was one of the few times they had made love together and were not facing each other. Karen realised why Simon was different to everyone she had ever slept with, he made love to her like a man makes love to his wife, with care and gentleness, not a raunchy lover although he had done that too, it wasn't position, angle, thrust that did it for her it was the togetherness, it was also highly erotic. She had never been to bed with a married man; several friends had gone down that route but she had had experience of boyfriends leaving her for someone else or being unfaithful and simply couldn't steal another woman's man, Simon was as near to that she had come and she felt irrationally guilty about Jane.

They showered together; this definitely was not an Emma shower, but together under the water, soaping, playing and cuddling and then cleaned their teeth together, just like a couple living together; she liked that.

Karen knew that today was going to be either wonderful or a trial; Simon and Hal had discussed the impact that his relationship with Karen would have now the press were on the case, on him and his family. Simon's reaction was to invite them to Sunday lunch; she was going to meet Alex, his youngest daughter, Jane's daughter; she was going to see him in father mode.

Simon said he felt it too early to expose Karen to his girls but he was aware that the last place he wanted them to read of their Dad's new girlfriend was in the papers or chat mags. Karen, suddenly, thought that the father, Dad role, was as remote from her as her life in LA was from Simon; they would both have to work on that.

Simon told her about how difficult the phone calls had been for him, the girls knew this moment might come, when their dad would have a girlfriend. They accepted that as inevitable but it was the fact that she was less than 10 years older than them that had grated, especially with Fiona, his eldest daughter.

He was full of surprises because he invited Hal, Emma and Carolyn even though he had never met Carolyn, to his home. He said 'just because it will be difficult doesn't mean you shouldn't give duty hospitality'. She didn't understand the duty hospitality thing but Simon felt that they were in Scotland and he had a duty to admit them into his home. 'My parents and grandparents instilled it into me,' he said.

They had a quick breakfast, toast and marmite, Karen smiled at the marmite, they had used it for its alternative use in the hot tub the evening before, she was acquiring a taste for it in its original use.

Simon said 'right my love, you said you wanted a normal life, this is it, you go and tidy the bedroom and check the bathrooms for toilet rolls etc and can you also please make sure that your things are packed away, in case Alex goes in there; it's bad enough for her to admit that her parents had sex let alone us! I'll tidy up down here and sling the Hoover around'. Karen thought he called me 'my love' and happily went to tidy the bedroom and bathrooms, she was singing as she went about her chores.

Just before noon, they left the flat, wrapped up in their sweaters and coats and climbed the steps through the oldest part of the city to the High Street; Karen saw one doorway with a stone plaque that said ad 1423. She was about to do something she had never done with any of her boyfriends, it had never occurred to her or indeed them, she felt it was the correct thing to do, when Simon had suggested it, she had thought that no man or woman had asked her that question, she thought also how proud her mother would be and knew she would be startled by what she was about to do with Simon, but her mom would approve. Simon kissed her on the cheek; 'are you alright doing this, you are sure?' he asked 'yes my love, I would like it very much especially with you' she answered; Simon took her hand and they entered St Giles Cathedral for Sunday Eucharist.

After the church service, they dropped down the steps and took a car to the supermarket and Simon bought the provisions he needed for a meal for nine people 'I love cooking for large numbers; I get a real kick out of the planning, preparation and serving to people.' Simon said. They bought a couple of Sunday newspapers, they were stunned to find that there was a photo of BK on the front page of the Scotland on Sunday and inside an article about her singing karaoke in the bar; the man she had met and the change in her since so doing. Simon was mentioned in everything but name, they weren't sure and were being cautious, however by the end of the day one of the US papers named him and printed the photo of him from his website.

Karen adored the mundane shopping for food, it took two trips up the stairs each to get the provisions to the flat; Karen made an extra trip to bring up Simon's shirts which had been dropped off by the laundry he used. She had enjoyed being that domestic, perhaps even servile, she had never done that for any of her previous boyfriends and she got a curious kick out of it, it seemed silly that with staff and everyone waiting on her hand and foot, all she wanted was to do the shopping and be normal, she thought, as she hung Simon's shirts in his wardrobe.

They prepared the vegetables together, well almost; Simon explained he had a 'thing' about other people in the kitchen when he was cooking so Karen stood the other side of the kitchen bar just like they had the previous weekend. They actually worked well together and soon had the vegetables loaded in the steamer, the potatoes simmering and the meats cooking in the oven; Karen had watched spellbound as Simon made a Bakewell tart using a WWII recipe given to him by his mother.

Karen's phone rang and it was Emma, Karen talked to her for a few minutes and then rang off.

'God, she is a heartless bitch' said Karen, 'who?' Simon asked.

'Emma, she used my bedroom last night, licked the tits off poor Carrie and dumped her this morning, still she did well she usually throws them after two nights; she has a long line of well hung dorks and gorgeous women behind her'.

'She's young, she's got plenty of time to decide which way to swing' said Simon adding 'Can I say that having just said that I now feel positively ancient'. Karen walked up to him, felt his buttocks and kissed him on the lips 'Yup, you're right, you're quite old'. Simon gently tickled her in the embrace.

They chatted about the week to come. Karen invited him to the last concert in London. 'Carolyn will arrange everything; there is a party in the hotel after the concert on the Monday; I would love you to be my very special VIP guest'.

'I'd adore seeing you on stage and I'm always up for a party' he said.

Alex, Simon's youngest daughter arrived first; she was utterly charming and polite and she and Karen stood with a glass of wine and chatted in the dining area which was all set for the meal later in the afternoon; they chatted about music and the being on tour and Karen asked Alex about her research project and what her doctorate was about.

Alex looked at Karen and said 'So Karen, you like the smelly old man then?' Karen smiled and replied 'He doesn't seem old to me and his aftershave, on him, drives me wild, so I guess he's not smelly to me either'; this was more nerve racking than she had thought. She did find it really strange that Alex called Simon, Dad, of course, his daughter would but, she saw him as her friend and lover not someone's Dad. She wondered if Simon had the same problem when people called her BK and not Karen or indeed Sarah, if he ever met her mother. The video phone rang, it was Hal, Emma and Carolyn, and Simon said 'the door will buzz then come straight to the top of the stairs'.

As they moved into the living room Simon and Carolyn went and served drinks to everyone, there was a tension until Simon said 'Family and American friends, Karen and I wanted you all to meet because, although Karen and I have only known each other for a few weeks and we have become close friends, because of Karen's job the press and fans are wanting to know who I am and there are articles in today's papers; Alex, I didn't want you finding out in the press that your dad or grandad was dating BK Shore.'

There was silence.

'Hey Carolyn, grandad here is coming to the Monday gig in London and the party afterwards, can you organise everything for him?' said Karen.

'Of course BK, consider it done' Carolyn said.

'Dad' said Alex 'if Karen is BK Shore how come you call her Karen and they', she was pointing at Hal, Emma and Carolyn 'call her BK?'

Karen answered 'Alex, it is more complicated than that, my real name is Sarah King, my stage name is BK Shore, Karen is the name I made up so your Dad wouldn't know who I was when I first met him, he didn't recognise me. Karen is or was a friend's son's girlfriend, he treated her so gently and nicely; I wanted your dad, god it feels strange saying that, I wanted him to treat me that sweetly and he has, your dad's a lovely guy'.

Karen continued 'Listen Alex, my mother was single, she had a procession of guys, I never had a Dad but I know how difficult this is for you, especially as normally, Simon and I would know each other better before the family baptism of fire. Your father and I have no right to be together, our meeting was by chance, our friendship is accidental, everything else was a surprise, it's almost as if it was meant to be' she squeezed Simon's arm.

'Mum always said he would find someone else if anything happened to her; Dad, shame on you, you didn't recognise BK Shore?' Alex said.

Simon said 'No, I did not recognise her and actually when she told me who she was it didn't register with me, she had to explain' Hall and Emma looked at each other and then looked in different directions.

The alarm in the kitchen rang; Simon got up and asked Emma to refill the glasses; Carolyn followed him out to the kitchen 'Hi Simon anything I can do to help?'

'You could open those bottles of wine if you want; they are some of the stash Karen sent from Paris' Simon said.

Carolyn leant forward and kissed Simon on the cheek 'That was nice, what that was for?' he said.

Simon looked her over, she was tall about 6 ft, with quite broad shoulders, small breasts probably A, about 30 and well dressed, she was pleasant enough but did absolutely nothing for him, maybe he was getting old.

'That is from the band, when BK er Karen was snowed in the band were relieved because they didn't have to rehearse with her, then she started this video rehearsal, they began to ask what was happening, her spark was back. Emma told them to brace themselves; Karen rehearsed the band into the ground, non-stop right through to the sound check. I saw fully grown guitarists crying with joy and happiness at the music and at the end of the first performance of the re-arrangement of 'Love Smiles', she got a standing ovation from her own musicians, that is very rare and especially as several had been ready to walk,' she explained.

Simon said 'Well, I've only seen her perform in the kara-oke bar, last night and that was...' he was interrupted.

'Hal told me it was one of the most touching things he had ever seen, you have had a great impact on BK, she has never performed that song in public, she wrote it during the Jake era, you know about Jake?' Simon nodded.

'Listen' said Carolyn; 'before we leave can we have a quick chat about London'.

'Sure' said Simon.

When Carolyn and Simon returned, he saw that Alex and Karen were in deep conversation, Hal and Emma were talking at the other end of the settee.

'Chums, food is about 30 minutes, would you guys like the guided tour?' Simon said.

Simon showed Emma, Carolyn and Hal around; when they were in the office Simon looked at his diary and discussed it with Carolyn. 'No, I can't do earlier because I must do that engagement but I can cancel these they are personal' he indicated.

'Look here's my contact details' Simon said.

'I've already got those' said Carolyn, Simon looked at Hal 'She organises security' Hal said shrugging.

'Tomorrow morning, I'm doing a key note speech on corporate governance as a marketing tool, at the Edinburgh International Conference Centre, I'm going to go do my bit and leave' Simon said.

Hal surprised Simon by saying 'I would like to come and see you do that'.

'No problem, I'll send you the details' Simon replied.

'Simon' said Carolyn 'can I get on line here? I'll transfer contact details for Hal, Emma and I and Judy the publicist and book a flight for you on Monday'. Carolyn sat at the PC and tapped away at the keyboard.

Hall and Emma walked out into the garden area; being February the troughs were empty and the small piece of grass not at its best, they walked to the end, by the hot tub; Emma started to snigger, it was a crude snigger and she touched Simon's arm and pointed at the tub of marmite sitting on the side of the hot tub.

Simon smiled 'Karen is getting quite a taste for it'. Emma roared with laughter and Hall looked blank and Emma said to Hal 'One day, I'm get drunk enough to tell you'.

They went down stairs, Carolyn stayed in the office, she was on the phone and organising a ticket and backstage passes, she said to Simon 'I need an electronic photo of you'.

'If you look under documents and bios there is a selection of bios and photos, Judy might like those' he said; they left Carolyn to her organising and went downstairs.

Simon walked through to the kitchen, Hal and Emma went and sat talking with Karen and Alex; everyone was getting on rather well and were laughing and joking, but there was an underlying tension. He started to serve up the food. 'Lunch in five people' he yelled.

They sat around the table, the kitchen bar acted as a servery with the pork, beef and vegetables in serving dishes like a buffet; once everyone had food, Simon said Grace.

Karen remembered their conversation about religion, it had led to the two of them going to church together, she put her hand on his and said 'that was nice'; they smiled at each other. If they had not been so engrossed in each other, they would have not only seen Alex watching her father's eyes but Carolyn watching the two of them intently too.

The table erupted into conversation, Carolyn was sat next to Simon and he asked her about herself and how she ended up doing her job. In ten minutes or so, she had booked his flights to London, had organised a pick up at the airport, tickets and passes for the concert; she said that after lunch she would pull it all together in a briefing note. Carolyn explained that she had studied business and psychology at UCLA and was working as a logistics manager in a haulage firm in Santa Monica when her brother met a new guy, who turned out to be Hal and she ended up working for Beach.

Simon asked 'so are you er?' Carolyn put her hand on Simon's thigh and said 'Oh no, I'm a full-on hetero bitch, give me a dick any day'. They laughed.

Alex started to talk to her father and said 'Dad, I didn't expect you to find someone who could be my sister' comments flew around the table followed by laughter. Karen protested 'I'm from California not Alabama'.

The meal progressed in the way family meals do, slightly fraught, with breaks as the table was cleared and reset, people laughing and joking, moving around the table. Stories being told to individuals, the whole table or groups and then everyone helped to wash up and tidy the meal away, talking whilst doing chores.

Hal watched as BK took the bins down stairs, he had never seen her doing domestic things; in LA, she had staff to do that; she wasn't asked, she just did it, she also brought some logs up for the fire and organised Carolyn and Emma to fill the log basket and hauled it up the stairs.

The time passed very quickly, Carolyn disappeared and arrived back and briefed Simon on the trip to London on Monday week; both Hal and Karen decided to attend Simon's speech the next day. Hal explained that they flew to Madrid late afternoon on Monday so they had time to drop into the conference in the morning.

It was gone seven o'clock when Alex, Hal, Emma and Carolyn decided to leave; Simon had disappeared for a while into the bedroom with Alex.

Alex said 'Dad, you know I can never accept anyone other than Mum, Karen is nice but she will never replace Mum, Karen is a nice person I'll give you that and you are clearly good for each other.'

Simon replied 'Alex, no one can replace your mother in our lives, she is always with me, I would not have told you or Fiona about Karen if it wasn't because of the press; I would have kept her away like I have the others'.

'What others?' Alex said. 'There have been some' Simon said.

They continued to talk for a few more minutes and then joined the others but not before Alex said 'Dad, since when have you been using eye make-up remover?' picking up a pot from the dressing table.

As everyone left, Karen made a coffee and she and Simon curled up together on the settee; Karen said 'Alex is a credit to her parents, what an intelligent, charming young lady'.

'Thank you, I just wish I had an idea what the hell she does,

I know she is Dr Alex Macintosh and tells me she is going to fix the mess I have made of the planet, she has explained her doctorate and project to me many times but it swoops right over my head' Simon replied.

Karen smiled and said 'Thank god you said that, I thought it was just me, she and Hal got on well but he did ecology as a major in College, at one stage she was drawing something on paper and they looked totally engrossed' they laughed.

Simon said 'I did enjoy the karaoke last night, you are a good singer'.

'Should be honey, I do it for a living, dancing with you was wonderful, with a little practice we could be very sexy together' Karen replied.

'OK let's practice, you're a dancer, teach me' he said.

'What here?' Karen said.

'Yes, we can move the furniture back and learn our special dance' he said.

He dropped to his knees next to her, she wondered what he was doing but he undid the retaining bolt for the settees and they moved them back against the walls, they carried the coffee tables into the corridor and moved lamps out of the way; Simon put the guard on the fire. There was a passable area for a dance floor, not big enough to really do anything, but big enough to have some fun.

Simon hooked up his laptop to the sound system and Karen accessed her website to download some songs but especially 'Don't Let Go' by In Style.

'I will record this song for my next album, just for you' Karen said.

She sang along with the lyrics and they practiced dancing together, it was sexy but Karen wasn't sure if they had captured the lustiness correctly and Simon needed a lot of practice to be fluid.

'OK strip' she said, undoing his trousers.

'What?' said Simon.

'You may have sanitary towels but I bet you don't have leotards, if we are going to make this sexy we need to dance it nude, strip get those clothes off' she stood pointing at him, she was already naked and walked off into the bedroom.

She returned, lay on the floor and inserted her special ring in front of him, something she thought ironically Jake had always wanted her to do but she had refused. Jake had also wanted to fit it but he had been disappointed there too, the only person to have done that was Emma and that was only because Karen had a dislocated arm and broken wrist and needed to get the stud in to stop the piercing healing up, as she had it she might as well keep it; she had always regretted having it done, she felt cheap and it had hurt like hell; but now it was an asset.

They danced together to the music, laughing and enjoying the closeness, it was very sensual and very good fun, Simon was such a good sport but not a natural dancer, but he gradually improved.

'Listen Karen, my love,' he said 'we will have to stop; I'm bathed in sweat, the twenty years are telling'. She laughed 'you're doing well; when you're in London I'll get Jill, my choreographer, to give us some ideas, this will be our tune and our dance' she said; in her mind she noted that he had called her 'my love' again.

They rearranged the furniture and sat on the settees and watched TV with just the light from the fire illuminating the room; Simon got his things ready for the next day; at one point he came down, he was annoyed about something and took Karen upstairs to show her something on his office computer. They spent an hour or so curled up on the sofa making plans; eventually they went to bed and lay next to each other, chatting until they fell asleep.

The alarm clock went off and they turned and cuddled each other, Karen rolled over on top of Simon and they both enjoyed sweet, gentle, intimate moments, beyond the lust of first love, moments when two bodies join in mutual satisfaction, comfort and love. Simon adored the closeness but hated himself for loving it. He did like Karen but wished it was Jane - that had been their favourite position, he pushed those thoughts away.

They arrived at the Edinburgh International Conference Centre by taxi just after 9am, the conference started at 9.30 with a keynote address by a Scottish Government Minister, a speech by an economist from the Royal Bank of Scotland and then Simon on 'Governance for Good', followed by a question and answers session with the three speakers and then a break. Hal had explained to Simon that he had a friend in LA who ran business conferences and governance was always a hot subject that he had difficulties finding good speakers for in the US. Karen just wanted to see Simon in business mode, she was curious about this part of his life.

They listened to the other speakers and then Simon came on, his delivery was good. He had clear slides and Hal found himself agreeing with Simon's opinion on how good governance in business could yield business advantage. Hal thought of the businesses he had links with and how one or two of them would benefit from that type of thinking especially the bail bond company he ran with his brother. Karen thought Simon looked gorgeous; she did try to listen to what he was saying but just loved the sound of his voice, seeing him stood there on the stage, she realised she was rather proud of him.

Hal was interested that a Minister was willing to take open unscripted questions from the audience and the way that no definitive answer was ever given by the politician; some things never change he thought. Simon's answers were clear, precise and generally rather witty. Hal thought Simon was good at this and he had an idea, if he needed it. They stayed around for the coffee break and then all three left to go back to the Balmoral Hotel by taxi. Simon would return later for the evening reception and conference dinner after they had left for Madrid.

The taxi dropped them off on the North Bridge and they walked into the Hotel though the side door, and along the corridor and took the lift and up to the suite; they had avoided the press again. Hal noticed that as they walked along the corridors, Karen was holding Simon's hand and kept grabbing it when they separated, he made a mental note.

Simon was sat reading the Scotsman newspaper and making the occasional phone call, Hal was sat at the table on his laptop, with Carolyn and Emma sat next to him on laptops and phones, they were running their business and organising, BK was working with Carolyn and was doing her blog on the fan website.

This was the 'spontaneous' communication which was sent to Judy and her team in the publicity unit to edit prior to going on the website. Judy had decided that this would be the first time that BK would mention that she had met a 'friend' in Edinburgh. The press knew that she had a new boyfriend, few knew exactly who he was although several were aware but without complete proof and were waiting for confirmation. Judy had found Simon's bio very useful, Carolyn had been on his computer and also sent a resume and his contacts list, some documents and a load of pictures of Simon and his family to Judy who had assigned a researcher to look into his background, his family, the plane crash and other details that the press might try to drag up, he was what the researcher had called 'an ordinary guy'.

Karen walked over to Simon and said 'would you like some lunch honey?' He stopped what he was doing and grabbed her so she was sat on his lap, he kissed her, he was sat on a settee facing the window, and the others were all sat at the table with their backs to the window; they could never see them kissing.

The others heard a silence and looked up into the mirror on the wall in front of them, in the reflection in the window they could easily see BK and Simon kissing and every time they broke she re-established contact and they saw her clearly move his hand onto her breast.

The three people sat at the table were sending each other messages.

Carolyn typed 'I think she is more besotted with him, than he is of her, he has issues!!'

Hal replied 'I noticed this morning that she was very excitable while watching him speaking'.

Emma chipped in 'Guys, he is not an unwilling participant, I think they are very fond of each other, it will never last, never does'.

Hal typed 'What do we do when they get to London and she goes back to LA and he goes to Edinburgh will it finish then?'

Emma thought 'Yes, he'll dump her; she's really scared of that'.

Carolyn said 'No way, I'm not usually the romantic but I think they are in love but don't know it; if he can he will come to LA.'

Hal wrote 'I have an idea, I will have to wait until we get to Madrid, when it's working time in LA, we had better provide him with a business reason to come to LA'.

To the question 'would you like some lunch honey?' Simon answered 'did you mean something to eat?' Karen sniggered 'I did mean food, first!'

The people at the table all looked at each other and sneered silently.

Karen stood up and said 'Simon, take me somewhere for lunch'.

He stood up, readjusted himself and Karen watched him smiling and air kissed at him.

BK said 'Simon and I are going out for lunch see you soon guys'.

Hal said 'Take one of the security guys with you, just in case'.

Carolyn asked the concierge to get a taxi waiting so they could get a quick getaway, the press had given up since they had been told when BK Shore would leave the hotel and that she would make herself available for photographs but the paparazzi were probably around.

Carolyn had also organised a table at Chez Jules on Hanover Street, a small French restaurant Simon had recommended; she was very good, he thought. The taxi was waiting and the two of them and their security guard jumped into the cab and they were away; at the restaurant the guard sat at the bar whilst Karen and Simon were placed in a quiet corner out of the view of most of the other diners.

After a quiet lunch generally chatting and discussing some of their more distant family, they returned to the hotel and walked into an empty suite, the others having gone out. Karen grabbed Simon's hand and pulled him into the bedroom 'please, I need you' she said to him; they kissed and cuddled, slowly taking each other's clothes off and made love, lying together for a long time, warm and comfortable.

As they lay in each other's arms, Karen said 'that was lovely; I will miss you this week'. She propped herself up on one arm and looked into his eyes 'I've become very fond of you; I would hate to lose it, I'm scared we will'. He said 'I have adored every minute that I'm with you'. They showered together, just enjoying being with each other.

The others had arrived back and the concierge came to collect the luggage, Carolyn and Emma went downstairs to organise their departure. Two people carriers with black windows arrived at the main door, Carolyn supervised the loading of the luggage. There were four photographers waiting and about 30 diehard fans, Judy had tipped off the local fan club, always looked good to have fans around for the pictures.

Upstairs in the bedroom of the suite, BK was in floods of tears with Emma consoling her, she did not want to leave, she was petrified of losing Simon, she realised that she was being stupid but she so liked his touch, his smell, his presence and his wit. Simon was next door in the sitting room talking to Hal, although he didn't show it, he was going through similar turmoil but he also felt guilty for having feelings for another woman.

Karen walked out of the bedroom, Emma bundled a protesting Hal out into the corridor, Karen was in tears, she hung onto to Simon like a limpet, saying 'I don't want to leave you, please don't leave me'.

He sat her down and took her hands, 'Karen' he said. 'No, please don't dump me' she grabbed him close to her, she knelt on the floor in front of him 'I'll do anything you want, please don't dump me, I so like you please.' Tears rolled down her cheeks, she wailed.

He gently traced his finger down her cheek, 'I'm not going to dump you whatever gave you that idea?' he said 'I'm more scared of you dumping me, an old man, set in his ways with a family and you will probably fly back to LA without even a goodbye.'

'I wouldn't do that, I'm not sure I could' said Karen.

'So neither of us are going to get dumped, thank god for that' said Simon, 'we have existed in my world, we will struggle when your world collides with mine but hell, you only live once, let's do our best and see what comes'. He pulled Karen off her knees and she nestled into his chest, there was a knock on the door.

'Listen, my love, we have grown very close, very quick,' he said kissing the top of her head 'you could always pop up from London and spend the night with me' he said laughingly.

They kissed slowly - a level three kiss. They parted and looked into each other's eyes, she gave him a small velvet pouch, he opened it and he looked at the small gold ring with the letters spelling his name. She said 'the next time we meet you can fit it'.

She turned and left the room with Hal and the guards in tow.

Simon sat down and for a moment and lost his composure; Emma walked in and saw him, Emma sat next to him and said 'Simon, she really likes you, stay with it, please, I've never seen her so happy', he hugged Emma.

He sat a few minutes longer to compose himself, then went down stairs and left the hotel. He stood next to a group of autograph hunters, BK Shore walked down the steps and waved at the paparazzi that had not been allowed in the hotel. Simon watched as she stopped and signed autographs for the group opposite, she turned and started to sign autographs and have photos taken with her fans, just in front of him. This was Karen as BK Shore, in her world, he wasn't sure he liked it.

She looked up and saw Simon watching her, their eyes locked, she could not stop looking at him, a few of the people in front of him turned to see what she was looking at, all they saw was more young people and some old man staring at BK Shore. They looked back to see their idol, staring back at the old guy, tears welled in her eyes; she turned towards the vehicle and smiled at Hal; he had never seen that smile before, it was very impish, 'sorry' she said.

Simon turned away, he hated goodbyes, his shoulders dropped and he took one step towards home, with a heavy heart and torn in every way. He heard a commotion behind him and then someone grabbed him from behind, before he realised what was going on lips covered his and he felt a tongue dart in and out of his mouth. Karen kissed him with passion, she felt warm, calm, happy, it was that moment that she acknowledged in her mind that she was falling in love with him, she realised she hadn't loved Jake because it had never felt like this, she had never wanted to do anything like this with him.

Simon was petrified, he knew BK Shore the star would never do something like that, this was Sarah King he was kissing, he never wanted to have an emotional attachment with anyone again, he knew she was falling for him, but denied it, he was too old, she was too young; and he still yearned for Jane.

They looked deep into each other's eyes, the world around them was in chaos but they took no notice; he slowly drew his fingers down her cheek, picking up the tears as they rolled down her face 'that was lovely, thank you, Sarah' he said.

The fans around had gone wild but had deliberately formed a barrier between them and the cameras who were jostling for the money shot. People in the street had stopped and were clapping, the pavement was full of people, one of the security guards arrived and bundled the two of them into the front vehicle which drove off, turned left onto Waverley Bridge; no one, except Jack Tobin, sitting in a car at the bottom of Cockburn Street, noticed it stop and let off one passenger.

Chapter Fifteen

el venir hacia fuera luchando – coming out fighting

BK Shore had a large Latino and Spanish following because she had recorded a Spanish version of some of her songs, the legacy of being left as a young child with a Mexican family whilst her mother worked or toured. The concert in Madrid had been arranged by Larry Packman, the promoter but was bound to boost sales record sales.

BK had a two hour tour of the sights of Madrid accompanied by Emma, Carrie, her assistant publicist, a photographer and a couple of security guards; she also met invited members of the press in a café on Plaza Mayor. The press, which included a television crew, were delighted that her Spanish was good enough for interviews, although she needed a little prompting here and there. They asked general questions about the tour, how she was performing, where she was going next but also wanted to know about 'su novio' (your boyfriend), she smiled sweetly and said 'eso es privado' (that is private).

The interviews were going well when one female reporter asked 'usted lo ama' (do you love him), BK looked at her and said in English 'your interview with me is now finished, I said that was private and I meant it' and repeated it in Spanish, 'Su entrevista conmigo se termina, dije que que era privado y la signifiqué'.

The fact that BK had acquired a new determination and drive had not been lost on her staff on the evening before, when they arrived at their hotel in Madrid. BK had called a meeting of all those closest to her and linked in Judy and

Barry, the head of the Beach legal department via video conferencing from LA.

Judy, BK's publicist, was a tough, straight-talking New Yorker who ate prisoners for breakfast; she had worked for Beach for about a year. Judy had gone ballistic at BK's 'irresponsible behaviour' in Edinburgh, not only had she met a complete stranger, a nobody, some old guy off the street but had been photographed, uncontrolled, hugging him, crying and kissing him in public, free! Judy had wanted to manage the gradual build-up of the opportunity, a friendship developing; now the chat magazines were doing their own thing with BK Shore's new lover; the tabloids already had them in and out of bed like yoyos.

By the time they got to their hotel in Madrid on the Monday evening it was the beginning of the working day in LA. There was plenty to do, organise and talk about, to run the business that was BK Shore; Hal had been talking to Brad Morgan and Larry Packman because as well as organising the European tour they were finalising the American mini tour of six gigs which followed on.

The record company was also keen that BK spent time at the Paramount recording studios in Los Angeles, to record some new songs and especially the new version of 'Love Smiles' and she wanted to record 'Don't Let Go'. BK had created four new songs which were now in the hands of lyricists and composers to polish the product; she had recorded a very rough live demo tape of Love Smiles, Naughty Boy, Snow and Don't Let Go, which the company had liked. She owed them an album, she was a year late according to contract; she was already working on other songs and Emma had reported that creating vomiting was taking place; BK was losing weight.

The conference started with Judy, who was not pleased; Emma looked at BK, she remained uncharacteristically quiet and calm throughout the tirade from LA, a small tick on her cheek betrayed her thoughts; Judy finished with 'I just don't know what you were thinking, what have you got to say for yourself?'

BK muttered something to herself; Judy said 'I can't hear what you are saying BK, speak up please dear'; it was highly condescending.

There was silence, BK was looking at her lap 'I said, it was the right thing to do' she said.

'It wasn't BK, it could never have been and if you thought it was, why did you apologise to Hal beforehand, BK it was idiotic and so are you' Judy said.

BK sat in silence; everyone in the room looked at her.

BK slowly stood and looked at the camera, Hal saw the look in her eye, he knew that look; yes Oh yes, he felt himself welling up, he had waited a long time to see that look again, it was well over two years, he wiped a tear from his eye; BK Shore was coming out fighting, this was going to be good, he sat back smiling.

Emma had never seen that look in BK's eyes; they had a steely determination and fire, Carolyn looked at Hal, sitting back and clearly enjoying the moment. 'What is going to happen?' she asked. Hal said 'It's been a long time but you are about to see the reason I work for BK Shore, brace yourself'.

BK spoke in a slow deliberate voice, looking right into the camera.

'I knew you wouldn't like it and it would cause hassle for Hal, but I had to do it and I feel sorry for you because you have never experienced what I have felt that makes those actions not just right but essential' she was looking directly into the camera.

She turned and faced everyone in the room and slammed her hand on the table 'OK listen up, know your place, I will not tolerate YOUR 'unacceptable behaviour'. I'm the talent here, I'm the boss, without me you are all washed up, this is my business and I am back running it' she said calmly.

She continued 'Judy, get this in your head and get it right into your head. I was right, it was the right thing to do, I am now convinced of that, 110% because for probably the first time in my life I have fallen for a decent guy, not lust but love and yes, he is twenty years older than me. One false move by any of you and I could lose him, any of you make that move and you are fired. He is not ready to be in love with me or anyone else; he still loves his wife, he needs more time to get over her death; protect him not my reputation. Judy, I will have total editorial control over anything and I mean anything missy, that is about Simon and I; you are NOT to release one thing, understand Judy'.

Judy offered a muttered 'I'm not sure that's right'.

'Judy, I want that clear and precise, I have full editorial control, let me hear a loud 'Yes BK'' she demanded.

'Yes BK' shouted Judy between gritted teeth.

'Hal, you are to support and protect him as you see fit but you must tell me and more importantly him. Simon is way too clever for you; if he needs resources, management anything give it to him it is in your best interests, do I make myself clear?'

'Yes BK' Hal said loudly and smiling.

BK span around and locked eyes with Carolyn 'Carolyn, the next time you raid someone's computer, delete the history file, you betrayed his trust and his hospitality; I was going to fire you; you have Simon's good nature to thank that instead you owe him an apology and I want to hear he has received it face to face from you'.

BK pointed at Carolyn who was blushing to her boots; 'grovel bitch' she said with menacing venom.

'Yes BK' shouted Carolyn, who was crying and shaking.

'With that in mind, Barry, can you escort Judy to her desk and ensure that the images of Simon and this family are deleted, I want a sworn statement from her that no other copies exist and Judy, if I ever find out you actually did call Simon a decrepit dirty old man I will scratch your eyes out, personally and one by one. But before that, you encouraged Carolyn to steal information and kept it when you knew you shouldn't have it, you betrayed his trust, my trust and the trust of all of us at Beach. Judy, you're fired, whilst you are at your desk clear it' BK said with authority.

Judy said 'under the circumstances BK, I think I should quit.'

BK said 'You don't have that option Judy, you're fired; Barry, ensure that Judy leaves with three months' salary and I want a gagging agreement; then escort Judy to her desk and ensure she leaves the premises; by the way, Judy, the payoff is Simon's idea, not bad for a decrepit dirty old man.'

'Thank him for me' Judy spat back with more than a hint of sarcasm.

BK turned to Hal and said 'Hal can you please authorise all of that and get us a new publicist'.

'On to it BK' Hal said, he noted that by making that comment, she had acknowledged his authority, she was good, did she think of that?

BK looked down at Emma whose mouth was open in shock. She gently closed Emma's mouth with one of her fingers and said 'Emma, you keep that shut, no gossip, not a word, understand and I want to see all the managers in this room in two hours, organise it and let it be known, it's time this crew got its act together, we have America next.'

'Yes BK' said Emma loudly, with a quiver of excitement running down her back.

'Now, Colin' she said turning to Colin Thompson, who

until now was enjoying the spectacle; but started to shake, he was a bit of a gossip and he was worried about what BK was going to say next but he hated that bitch Judy and so did most of the crew and band.

'You and I have a rehearsal schedule for Madrid and London to map out, and a playing order to finalise, we will do Madrid tonight and London early tomorrow morning' said BK. Colin thought, she always used to take great pride and interest in the schedules and organising everyone's time and the running order of each gig but hadn't for a while, it was nice to have her back.

'Yes BK' he smiled broadly.

'Emma dear, can you get me a large Bloody Mary and an equally large gin and tonic for Colin' BK said; Colin thought that only the BK he had known would remember his penchant for G&T.

'Not a word outside this room OK, go, people, we have work to do' said BK clapping her hands and ushering them out of the room. By the time she got to the bar and met some of the band for dinner, something she used to do but hadn't done all tour, they cheered her. The word was out that BK had personally fired the wicked witch from the east as she found out Judy was called. However far more significant for them was that BK, the musician was back and they loved it; although no one would admit it they all knew about Simon and the effect he had had on their BK; information about him from the web and other sources was being texted around the entourage.

Hal walked up to BK and flung his arms around her. 'Welcome back, Simon has brought my BK back so I'll take the bullets for the guy; that was some display; you fired Judy, boy that took guts' he said.

'Hal, thank you for standing by me, I think you understand

from the security discussion you had with Simon that neither of us will take any bullshit. I talked everything through with him and he gave me good advice, Hal, he has a very high opinion of you and so do I' she said and kissed him on the cheek.

Carolyn was crying at the end of the table, BK sat next to her. 'I'm so sorry BK, I never thought' she said.

'We all make mistakes as the Dalek said climbing out of the dustbin' said BK.

'What's a Dalek?' Carolyn said.

'I have no idea, Simon is always using that phrase' BK said, Carolyn smiled.

'It was the betrayal of his hospitality that hurt him and therefore me the most, he had never met you but invited you into his home, Carolyn that was a shit of a thing to do, but remember both Simon and I are expecting you to apologise to him in person when you see him on Sunday and let me say again, I would have fired you, he wouldn't hear of it and it is his trust you betrayed, so let's be friends' BK said and hugged her.

Just before BK started work with Colin, she disappeared and rang Simon to tell him how things had gone and how she appreciated his business advice and support, she was glowing, buzzing; she also told him, she missed him and was looking forward to seeing him again.

The next morning rehearsals started at 08:30 sharp and for the first time in a year, BK rehearsed the band, the singers and the production crew, there was a snack lunch and then straight on to the sound check and the dance dress rehearsal, she worked them hard and drove them as hard as she drove herself. There was a quick move back to the hotel for a meal, a brief rest and then back to the venue for hair, make-up and finally costume.

The rehearsals and the concert in Madrid had gone well;

the venue was a complete sell out, 13,000 Spanish fans packed the Palacio De Deportes de la Comunidad; the reviews were superb. She had enjoyed the concert, before they had been rather mechanical, like going to the office. However she was getting pleasure in doing her best, Simon had used the phrase 'being the best because you want to be rather than you have to be'. The concert had ended with the 'loving' version of Love Smiles as the press called it, she explained the song in Spanish and said she was singing it for a special person in her life. As she sang the song, she was thinking of Simon, the crowd certainly sensed the emotion in her at the end, she found she could not stop crying, they were happy tears though.

The moment she walked off the stage the roadies started the breakdown of the band's equipment and instruments; the sound system and staging stayed in place as it would be modified and used over the next few days by another of Larry's groups.

A separate system was in construction at the Excel in London, BK Shore would play to three sold out houses on Friday, Saturday and Monday and a redressed staging and system would be used by the Soweto Gospel Choir on the Sunday for an evening 'service'.

BK laughed when Brad found out what Larry had organised. He said 'Jesus there must be some money in god'.

They had chartered a plane that could land at London City Airport, it would have to land and refuel in France but the process saved hours. The plane was loaded with BK's 57-strong entourage and their guitars and other instruments stowed on seats under cargo nets and luggage and equipment in the hold. The process of loading, transporting and then loading into the plane took place as the performers slept; they were scheduled to leave at 9am the next morning.

Chapter Sixteen
Excelling in London

The plane swooped down across the Thames and landed on the improbable airstrip in the heart of the London docklands. It taxied to the cargo unloading area where customs officers waited to clear the load and a different group of roadies sat with vehicles ready to move the equipment to the Excel centre. BK was the first to leave the plane and was escorted through passport control along with Hal, Emma and Carolyn; a car took them the short distance to their hotel.

BK spent most of the flight sat next to Jill the choreographer, talking through ideas for a dance. Several times they practiced something in the aisle. BK would be rehearsing the dance routines that afternoon on stage whilst the rest of the team assembled, equipped and tested the stage system. There was a sound rehearsal scheduled on the stage which included vocals but unknown to everyone, except for Carolyn and Emma, BK was booked on a flight to Edinburgh, returning the next morning; this was only made possible because the Excel London is next door to the airport.

The centre has no facilities that could be described as dressing rooms; indeed most places had appalling dressing rooms, tiny pokey rooms with no or inadequate facilities. The advantage of the Excel centre was they used trailers; BK's trailer was 28 ft long and had a sitting area, bedroom, shower room and kitchenette, it was comfortable and warm.

They arrived and looked around the centre; the building was vast and was configured to hold 18,000 people in a concert layout, it had hosted concerts three nights previously, they started to prepare for their concert.

Simon worked all day in the office and pottered around the flat and did some shopping. Hal rang to keep him updated on events and on security but Simon spotted Jack Tobin in his car when he went to the gym in the morning. After Hal rang, Simon made contact with Jack, they had lunch together in the wine bar immediately below Simon's flat and Simon shared his diary with Jack and agreed communications and an emergency text or call system.

Karen knew that Simon would be hosting a networking event at Le Monde, in George Street, it was open to all members and their guests so she guessed that included her.

'You are going to fly to Edinburgh with just the clothes you are wearing?' said Emma

'I'll have a clean pair of panties and some spare stockings in my handbag' said BK 'I don't need too many clothes for this trip' she winked at Emma. 'You horny bitch' Emma replied and they laughed.

BK was wearing a white top that revealed an interesting but not vulgar amount of breast, a black soft leather skirt and a matching leather jacket and her big faux fur coat. She had selected some really sexy and skimpy underwear which felt nice but made her feel very sexy. She felt really good, things were going better than she thought, the band were now on their toes and playing extremely well, she was now back into her music and feeling the rhythm again.

The taxi swung into the entrance of London City Airport and she left, went up the escalator and presented her boarding pass, she passed through security and headed for the executive lounge. Ten minutes later she was boarding the British Airways flight to Edinburgh, she sat in her seat and felt excited but a little apprehensive, she didn't know if Simon liked surprises, she would also surprise him in a business context, she was sure he would like her arriving unannounced.

Simon spent the entire day working in the Health Trust of which he was chairman, discussing the strategy; he had a two hour meeting with the chief executive and gave advice on management issues, and external relations. They were to have a meeting with the Scottish government cabinet secretary next Thursday and they discussed the issues to be raised. Since becoming chairman, Simon had driven the Trust hard and instigated considerable changes, it was beginning to produce first rate results but was still very patchy, there was much left to do. Simon and the Chief Executive went out for lunch at Browns, Simon texted Jack Tobin to tell him and Jack said that the paparazzi were camped outside his flat.

Simon planned to return to his flat before going out to the Institute of Directors event but, instead he dropped down the hill to the Royal Scots Club, he was able to freshen up, have a cup of coffee and have ten minutes to relax and check his emails. He also took the precaution of changing all the access codes for the door of the stairwell to his flat keeping just his, Alex's and the emergency one he had given Jack Tobin. Those changes were made on the same webpage that controlled the heating and the water heater for the hot tub; looking at that his mind drifted off and he thought of Karen and being in the hot tub with her.

When he snapped out of the daydream he was aware that he had an erection, he felt guilty, he remembered stopping halfway down the stairs this morning and realising that he hadn't talked to Jane before he left the flat, he always talked to the photo; he went back up the stairs and looked at her in the photo. 'I'm so sorry Jane, I forgot you today, I feel so bad, I was thinking of someone else, not you' he slowly moved his fingers over her cheek. 'I will always love you Jane but I've started to have feelings for someone else, will you ever forgive me?' He looked into her young eyes, a tear at the corner of one of his eyes.

Simon walked up the hill across Queen Street, whilst waiting for the lights to change, he looked along Queen Street and saw the flagpoles of the Jamhouse, he smiled to himself and those were nice memories. He walked into Le Monde and made his way to the lounge bar at the back, he always joked to his fellow IOD members that they had to walk fast through the ever so trendy bar so as not to raise the average age too high. There was considerable discussion about Simon and the fact that he had a new 'woman'; their children had informed them of all the latest BK Shore gossip and were keen to know more about BK Shore's new man.

Susan the chair of the committee watched as Simon moved effortlessly around the group with a joke here and a laugh there, he was so good at this and on very good form tonight, these events attracted over 100 members during their two hours and had been a great success, mainly because Simon made them so much fun. Susan was facing Simon who had his back to the main bar; he was in deep conversation with another woman. Susan saw a commotion in the bar beyond, the manager was running to the front door; Bob one of the event regulars emerged from the throng and made his way towards the group. 'What's happening there, don't know, there seems to be a problem with a woman in a fur coat.'

Susan entered into the discussion in front of her but her concentration wavered as her eye caught more movement at the far end of the bar by the entrance. A woman left the throng and walked through the bar towards their part of the bar; Susan recognised the woman, walked passed Simon and his group and went to meet her. 'Hallo,' she said 'I guess you have come to the IOD network event, I am Susan you are very welcome' Susan shook the hand of BK Shore.

BK put a finger up to her mouth to signify quiet and walked towards Simon, the others facing the bar knew what was going on and smiled, but kept quiet, they watched as the young woman circled Simon's waist with her arms and said 'Good evening, I've come to network'. The whole group laughed, Simon's face was a picture, he span around and embraced her, she went to kiss him but he stopped her, he looked around and quickly pushed Karen into the Gents toilet; they kissed and fondled each other. 'Karen what a lovely surprise, you look fantastic, I can hardly keep my hands off you' Simon said, 'I have longed to be with you again; it's not easy for me to keep my hands off you either honey' Karen replied.

They emerged a minute later, Karen held Simon's hand, he tried to break the hold but she wouldn't let him, he introduced her to the group as 'Karen my girlfriend'. Karen was rather interested in some of the business issues they were talking about; after all she ran a multi-million dollar organisation, she was soon drawn into the event.

A couple of minutes later, Simon stood in the corner using his mobile phone, he was switching on the water heater for the hot tub; he would need it after all. He texted the intervention message to Jack Tobin, who rushed through the bar, caught Simon's eye and nodded at him, Jack thought 'good call, big man'; he dialled for back-up.

Susan watched BK and Simon, they could hardly stop looking at each other, she knew what that was like, she went up to BK and said 'Can I have a word?' they parted slightly from the group 'This is none of my business but I'm 39 and David my partner is 58'.

BK said 'wonderful, how do you deal with the age thing, got any tips?'

'Just go with the flow, older men take longer to express their emotions, and are much better in bed in my opinion, I really enjoy my life with David, we never notice the age difference, it's other people who do and have a problem with it, we just get on with it' said Susan. They talked about how they met their partners, both by complete accident, both had not expected what happened and both had gelled very quickly, feelings had developed very fast and very intensely.

Simon suggested to BK that they should go and get something to eat, they left the group and walked towards the front of the bar, to be met by Jack Tobin 'follow me' he said and he took them out through the kitchen to a back entrance, free of paparazzi. They walked down into Rose Street, with two guards in tow. 'I'm going to take you to the best restaurant in town' he said and walked into the food store on the corner, Simon bought a pizza, a can of anchovies and a large tub of Mackies honeycomb ice cream; Karen held the basket in one arm and Simon's hand with the other; at one time she had undone his tie and unbuttoned his shirt a little, that's better she had said 'I like to see your chest hair, what's this your wearing a chain, she fished the gold chain out of his shirt' he smiled his naughty boy smile, Karen looked at the locket on the chain, it was a small gold ring with small letters that read SIMON, it was her special ring. She kissed him briefly; it is difficult to get too passionate in a supermarket, especially before the check-out. 'Careful BK' said a young girl passing 'you'll melt the ice cream'; they looked up and laughed.

Jack had sent on the other guard to look at the flat, he reported two cameras at the door, as they got to the corner of Cockburn Street, Jack stopped them, talked to his colleague who used the emergency access code and opened the door to the stairwell to Simon's flat, Simon and Karen ran round the corner and in through the open door, the guard slammed the door shut behind them, safe and not one photo taken.

They walked up the stairs and Simon opened the door to the flat, he turned to her and said 'welcome home'; as the door closed she fell into his arms and they stood kissing for a long time.

Simon moved through to the kitchen, turned on the oven, he topped the pizza with the anchovies and popped it in the oven and set an alarm; Karen just loved these domestic scenes and always watched him in awe, she wanted him.

Karen emerged from the bedroom, wearing Simon's Scotland rugby top, nothing else just his rugby top. He washed his hands and walked towards her, gently laid her on the dining table, threw his clothes off and they let vent to their lust, this was not slow love making, it was lust and thrust and lasted the time it took for the pizza to cook!!!.

Simon put on a bathrobe and went upstairs and filled the hot tub. Karen, back in her rugby shirt, brought up the wine and glasses. Once filled, the hot tub steamed in the cold evening air, the warm bubbles simmering in the light from the office, they sat in the hot tub eating pizza, intimately close and entwined. They sat talking and discussing the events since they last met, they decided to lick the ice cream off each other using their bodies as plates, it was very impractical, rather cold and far from erotic and in the end they gave up and just pigged it, out of the tub with spoons.

They had spilt so much ice cream and pizza in the hot tub that they had to have a shower afterwards to clean up Simon said smiling 'I wouldn't want you to smell of anchovies'. Karen flicked her towel at him and he lifted her up and sat her next to the basin, he raised her legs and stood back, he removed his necklace and in silence, very gently and rather nervously did something Karen had never let any man do before, he fitted her clitoral ring. She said to him 'I have never let any man do that' he smiled at her, sat there in an erotically undignified pose and said 'another thing to put in my resume, I suppose' they laughed.

For Karen, it was far more than a symbolic sexual act, she had never thought she could trust a man in that way, she hadn't felt threatened, she hadn't thought about it, it felt natural; she dropped her legs to the ground and thought wow! it feels good too. The ring was the usual horseshoe shape but the letters of his name formed a clasp across the ends of the horseshoe, the effect was to add weight to the ring and the letters kept touching her and stimulating her and during sex it was out of this world, for both of them.

They never dressed , Simon turned the heating up a few degrees instead, and they practiced their dancing and incorporated a few steps Karen had picked up from Jill, her choreographer. They talked about Monday, the concert and the party afterwards, they had hatched a cunning plan; they would dance the first dance at the party together.

They went to bed early, lying in each other's arms, they gently made love, hardly moving just enjoying being one entity; two people joined in peace. They had started talking to each other during these sessions, usually to encourage or reassure each other and to aid mutual satisfaction.

Karen said 'I need to ask you why you never have sex with me from behind with me on all fours? Is it something to do with me?'

'Not at all, Jane was never too keen on that position and it is a bit lonely as a man stood there pumping away on your own, so we got into the habit of not doing it that way, you only have to ask and we will' Simon answered, she kissed him a slow level 12 kiss; they were lying facing each other with Simon on one side, they were just lying there joined.

Karen asked 'do you ever think of Jane while we are doing this, she clearly shapes how we have sex, I know you must have done this with her, it is absolutely gorgeous'.

'I do think of her a lot' he said, he stirred, moving himself.

'I try not to when I am making love to you, it could turn into a bit of a threesome, I have to admit to you that on several occasions I have imagined you were Jane, especially when you are on top' he said, in the dim light she could see him smile, but she felt his erection wane slightly.

'Did she ever share?' Karen said.

'No, have you ever shared with another woman?' he asked.

'Yes, I don't mind being with women but prefer men,' she flexed her pelvic floor muscles slightly; 'Emma and I have been lovers and I have shared with other women with men,' Karen said.

'Would you share me?' he asked. 'Only with Jane' she replied.

'That is a lovely thing to say, not sure what Jane might say, but the thought is just wonderful, thank you' they kissed and he rolled over on top of her, afterwards they lay in each other's arms and fell into a deep sleep.

Friday morning buzzed into life at the ungodly hour of 6.30am, they had an hour before the car would arrive to take her to the airport, it was a sad moment, saying good bye.

The performances and rehearsals passed without incident, the band was getting even better; the dance routines had been honed to something approaching perfection; BK had found a new confidence in her music and in the way she managed the audience; the mood in the camp was positive and smiles and laughter abounded on stage and off it.

But it was the reviews that highlighted the change, the New Musical Express, which had panned the Berlin concerts and had suggested that fans didn't waste their money, printed an excellent review and talked about her concerts being the hottest ticket in town.

Hal borrowed an experienced publicist from another company that wasn't on tour and Samantha flew to London to join the team; BK was now relaxed doing interviews with the press but the rules were no questions about her private life. If you did, the interview ended, as one reporter found out to his peril. The closest anyone got to Simon was MTV who questioned her on Edinburgh and how she liked the city; she was asked 'it must be a very special place for you?' to which she answered 'he is' and then blushed. When they looked at it in play back, Samantha was overjoyed, 'it looked so natural,' she said; BK held her hand, smiled at her and said 'I didn't know I said that, so you see it was natural'; Samantha said 'that's lovely, it's so romantic'.

On the Saturday evening, she rang her mother, who was in good health and lucid thanks to a new drugs regime. Karen, or Sarah as her mother called her, discussed Simon with her mother, she said she wanted her mother to meet Simon; she had never discussed her men with her mother other than when they had gone. She talked to her mother for over an hour, crying as she described how she felt.

Her mother said to her 'Sarah, my darling daughter, you are in love with him, careful I don't think you have fallen like this before; is he in love with you?'

She didn't know the answer to that question but explained about his age and Jane and his girls and that he was a widower and not still married; she explained it all twice to ensure that her mother understood.

After the phone call, an emotional BK and Emma discussed her relationship with Simon, how Emma felt about it, how BK had developed a strong emotional bond and thought she was falling in love. Emma confessed that she felt a little jealous and shut out, finding BK's closeness to Simon very emotional and arousing especially when she saw them together.

By the Sunday, BK was exhausted and slept in until just after midday, she would work out, practicing some of the dance routines as part of her exercise regime, have some rest and talk to Simon. He was going to the Scotland v France rugby match on the Sunday afternoon; she had considered going but it simply wasn't practical, she had so much to do, needed to rest and wanted a little time to practice and compose her new songs. Simon was due on the plane that was due to arrive at 6pm at London City Airport on the Monday; he had a client he had to see on the Monday morning and lunch time.

Simon was in the Hampton Hotel near Murrayfield Stadium after the match, when his phone rang, it was Iain from Media Inc the company he would see tomorrow morning. Simon answered the phone and walked out of the bar and stood outside, it was quiet but there was a slow drizzle of sleet and snow.

'Simon, its Iain, look I'm going to have to cancel tomorrow, I've got a tummy bug, something I ate and I'm not going to be in a fit state by tomorrow' he said.

'That's awful, did you eat out?' asked Simon.

'No, but there is a bug doing the rounds in the office, I thought I would let you know early so you could drown your sorrows without worrying about the hangover' they laughed.

'Really appreciate the call, hope you feel better' Simon rang off.

Simon left about an hour later, went straight to his office and changed his flight to one arriving early afternoon. He rang Emma and made arrangements to meet her at the airport and then go to the venue where BK would be preparing for the evening performance so he could surprise her. He found it difficult to sleep that night, imagining being with Karen at the party in the evening and in her arms when he arrived, eventually he gave up and took a sleeping pill.

He was greeted by Emma who hugged and kissed him like

a long lost brother 'I'm so glad to see you and BK will be so surprised, getting your own back for the other day?' she said. 'Simon, she has been talking a lot about you'; they walked out of the airport arm in arm and got into the waiting car.

The end of tour party was to be held in the Cafe Royal Hotel in Central London and Simon and Karen were booked into a suite with Emma and Hall in adjoining rooms; the rest of the entourage were in a hotel just around the corner; Emma was the organising link for the party and would be going straight there after ensuring Simon was through security and reunited with BK.

They arrived at the London Excel and Emma took Simon to the security office and he got his ticket for the concert and his access to all areas pass, she introduced him to the head of security, he radioed his staff to say that 'Jock' was on site. They had been briefed about Simon, shown his photo and told to which areas he could have unescorted access; the security manager briefed Simon especially that he wasn't allowed anywhere near the stage unescorted for health and safety reasons.

Emma took Simon to BK's trailer, looked at her schedule and said 'she should have just finished having a spray tan before her nails and hair, guess she will run late!!'

Simon nodded at the security guard outside, they could both hear the motor of the power shower, she smiled back at him and winked, he winked back. In the sitting area was a large tent like structure and some machinery, he walked through into the bedroom area; there were clothes thrown on the bed and BK was singing in the shower, he could just see her through the glass shower door; he had an idea, he stripped, waited until she had her back to the door and stepped into the shower with her. The guard outside heard a scream, then silence then laughter, she smiled to herself, her husband sometimes did that, one time he had returned early from a business trip, a week away, she was in the bath and he had just sat in the bath with her fully clothed; it had been a great romp.

Carolyn and Leigh-ann, the beauty therapist, arrived and entered the trailer, Carolyn was worried, BK was running late, Leigh-ann had found Carolyn to say that, she was ready but there was no sign of BK. As they entered the trailer, they realised BK was in the shower, hopefully exfoliating ready for the spray tan, they could hear her singing 'Singing in the rain', she kept missing words out as if she couldn't remember them. Carolyn looked at her watch, BK was now at least 10 minutes off schedule she decided to push her on and walked into the bedroom, turned the corner to find the door of the shower propped open, she walked up to the shower and said 'BK you are running 15 minutes late'.

She nearly dropped her tablet PC, in front of her was a copulating couple, the view she had definitely proved that neither Simon nor BK were virgins! The way they were wedged into the cubicle gave them no opportunity to cover themselves, or preserve any modesty.

Carolyn flushed, it was embarrassing and arousing. 'Oh god, I'm so sorry' she turned her back.

'Don't worry she's just coming' Simon said. All three of them sniggered and Carolyn ran out the room, flustered, she had seen things like that on the internet but never in real life.

Karen towelled herself dry, 'Leigh-ann, can Simon have a spray too?' she shouted.

'What!?' said Simon.

'Come on sweetie, you are all exfoliated, I'd like to see you all tanned, come and watch me have mine,' she said and grabbed him; he was now in no position to say no.

Karen gave him her towel which he put around his waist and they walked out into the sitting area; Leigh-ann started to use a hair dryer on Karen's naked body, once dry Karen stood in the tent and was sprayed. For Simon, it was strange and slightly arousing to see someone else around the body of his lover, even if it was a beauty therapist, Carolyn was stood, watching and leaning against the wall. Karen stepped out of the tent and stood around to dry; Carolyn was using the hair drier on her; Simon stepped into the tent, removed the gold chain around his neck and threw his towel out. Unlike Karen, he had a small pair of paper pants on. After a while, Leigh-ann said 'that's you done Simon except for your bits, I can't do them' Karen said, 'I will.'

Leigh-ann stood next to Carolyn behind the tent, she watched as the pants were thrown out and Karen crouched down, it was an unusual sight, as she worked on Simon's 'bits'. Carolyn nudged Leigh-ann who looked at her and Carolyn licked her lips and pointed at BK, they smiled, she was drooling at her task.

'OK close your eyes girls he's coming out' Simon left the tent naked and walked towards the bedroom, Karen noticed that Carolyn was watching him, Leigh-ann had her eyes shut; Simon continued into the bedroom to dry off.

BK stood with her hand on the wall just above Carolyn's head, her body close to Carolyn, who blushed; BK knew exactly how uncomfortable Carolyn would feel with a naked woman that close to her but she was annoyed that Carolyn had watched Simon, her Simon. 'I hope you enjoyed the view, he has a very nice penis, doesn't he? Carolyn when I said grovel I meant apologise not ogle his dick as you know it's all mine, eyes off'. Carolyn blushed, started to feel really threatened but BK smiled at her, kissed her full on the lips and felt a slight arousal, groaned, winced and turned away. 'Simon, you are so going to have to take this ring out' and walked into the bedroom.

Five minutes later Simon emerged with a towel around his waist and retrieved his bag from the sitting area, as he passed Carolyn, she was on the phone rearranging the schedule, BK was now running nearly half an hour late, she noticed that he had put his gold chain back on and hanging from it was a small gold ring.

Karen emerged from the bedroom wearing a red British Lions rugby shirt and three quarters leggings, Leigh-ann gave her a manicure and pedicure and painted her finger and toe nails dark brown. Simon was wearing a t-shirt and his kilt, he was going to have a dancing lesson with Jill and Carolyn had reluctantly rearranged the schedule so BK could dance with Simon for part of his lesson.

Leigh-ann then gave Simon a pedicure and a manicure, men's hands were so much different, bigger and needed more scraping and polishing; before she went on this tour she had only done a few men's hands and most of those were at college. But the band had valuable hands, as Bob, the pianist, a regular, said 'my hands are my greatest asset'; he wore gloves most of the time and had regular hand massages and manicures.

Simon and Karen practiced their dancing on the landing outside the circle of the venue; Jill had marked out with chairs the space they had to work in. The sequence followed the 'Don't Let Go' music; there were turns, grinds, seducers and waltzes and some jive type movements, for Karen this was easy, for Simon, it was unbelievably difficult and complex and he had to concentrate very hard. The song started with Karen holding Simon by the back of the neck and leading him around in the dance, at one specific moment, they swapped roles and he led her around the floor, the sequence finished with them kissing and Karen with her hands outstretched behind her and Simon holding her neck in the kiss; if he let go she would fall.

They practiced for the best part of an hour and then Karen went to her hair appointment in one of the other trailers which was kitted out as a salon; Simon practiced some more with Jill, he also asked Jill to show him some general dance steps he could use. As he was finishing, Carolyn arrived and asked to speak to Simon, she was very nervous and almost in tears, they sat in a corner, close together, it was an intense and tense conversation, someone looking in would have seen Carolyn's body language as submissive and Simon's as aggressive, both postures changed over the conversation and it ended with Carolyn kissing Simon on the cheek and hugging him. They walked together to BK's trailer and found the sitting area full of people with costumes, microphones and clipboards. Simon retreated to the bedroom, had a quick shower and then decided to have a sleep; he was woken up by a brown leather clad rock star with big bushy hair, who was gently running her hands up and down his chest hair; Karen was BK Shore and was ready for the stage 'How on earth did you sleep through the support band,' she said; Carolyn rushed in and said '25 minutes!!'

'Out' yelled Karen, Carolyn retreated; she was not having one of her best of days.

Simon dressed whilst Karen discussed her nerves, they shared a medicinal cigarette and she told him how much she was looking forward to the fact that he would be in the audience. Simon was escorted to the VIP green room ready for the concert to begin, he managed to grab a gin and tonic and talked to one of the guests who he vaguely recognised but couldn't place; it turned out to be an American chat show host called Jay Leno, who Simon only knew because Jay owned a DeLorean car and had reviewed it on Top Gear, Simon's favourite TV programme.

All the guests had their tickets collected, it was a fire regulation requirement the steward was extraordinarily keen to tell them and they were escorted down to the front three rows; Simon was put in a specific seat next to, of all people, Nathan Macleod, the Scotland Rugby captain. The music started and BK Shore strode onto the vast stage and the crowd went wild, the sound system was pretty awesome, Simon had made a point of listening to the play list several times during the last week, he had started to quite like her music, which was probably just as well. She had also explained some of the events or stories around each song and what her thoughts were in writing it or performing it in a particular way.

The performance lasted one and a half hours, Carolyn had told Simon that there were huge fines from the unions if they went over by more than 5 minutes and the police were insistent that the crowd should be dispersing before by 11pm. Simon could not believe that it was his friend and lover on the stage. She looked different, in control and was very good, he realised about half way through that he was proud of her, she had clearly mastered this strange world of hers, a world as alien to him as his was to her.

As the concert drew to its close, a steward approached Simon. 'Excuse me sir, are you Simon Macintosh?' he asked. 'Yes' said Simon. 'Can you come with me please sir' the steward replied and took Simon the other side of the security barrier to a spot in front of the stage. BK Shore was about to sing the now famous 'hot' version of Love Smiles, the music started and Simon could see her looking at him. She was singing the song to him, it was highly sensual and rather romantic; at the end she jumped down from the stage and kissed him, the fans around them screamed, they had sensed the emotion within the delivery of the song. Karen ripped her microphone off and threw it on the floor and nuzzled to his ear and said 'I've fallen in love with you', gave him a deep level two kiss and then she was gone, acknowledging the applause and cheers; Simon returned to his seat.

Simon knew too well what he had heard, he never thought and was totally unprepared that another woman would have feelings for him; let alone him for her, he shut out the thought, end NO! Men don't feel like this, no, never, he knew there were feelings, he knew there were, no, think of Jane, you can't no; he couldn't, he thought of the kids, Jane.

In his turmoil he looked at his hands, he thought deeply, he was going to have to end their relationship, he couldn't have her falling for him, but he couldn't finish their relationship it would hurt Karen and he didn't want to do that, he knew he had become rather fond of her. He clasped his hands to his chest and felt the chain and the ring under his shirt, he realised he was losing a bit of Jane, her face appeared in his thoughts 'Simon, darling, just go with the flow, do what feels right, I will always be there for you' he could almost hear her saying. To the backdrop of the chaos of thoughts and the slightly bizarre and very loud broadcasting of 'always look on the bright side of life' over the Tannoy as the venue emptied, he made his decision.

To avoid the traffic, they had chartered a boat to take them from near the Excel to Westminster Pier, where a car would meet them and take them to their hotel; Karen was still in her stage costume with her fur coat over the top. They stepped onto the speed boat and it sailed along the Thames, this journey meant they would have a chance to change and briefly rest before they had to be at the party downstairs in their hotel. Simon and Karen cuddled into each other and watched the docks, warehouses, apartments and hotels on the water's edge pass by as they sped to their destination.

They landed at Westminster Pier and switched to a car;

Karen and Simon lay in the back of the limousine, kissing and hugging each other.

'Simon' said Karen 'please don't leave me, just because I'm going back to LA' she started to cry 'I want to cancel the American tour and stay with you. Hal said I should talk to you, so did my mom'.

'No, you can't cancel the tour' said Simon 'that is not fair on everyone' she hugged him and said 'Jane please forgive me, but I adore your man; Simon, I have fallen in love with you.'

Simon thought for a long while and said 'I heard what you said at the concert and I have become very fond of you too. I'm not ready to reciprocate your love, I need more time, I, I still love Jane.' Karen started to sob.

'I don't want you ever to stop loving Jane but please don't leave me, I beg you, give me a chance,' she sobbed.

'There is a part of me, the sensible part, that says I should finish our relationship here and now,' Simon said.

'No please, I beg you I'll do anything,' said Karen, Simon put his finger over her mouth and silenced her.

'Jane loved me for my unpredictability and not always being sensible, so why don't you come and stay with me immediately after you finish the American tour, that is of course, if you haven't got bored with me'.

Karen screamed and shouted 'I'd love to do that, oh baby that would be just wonderful'.

'There is a but' Simon said 'I'm not the easiest person to live with, I can get moody, I get frustrated, tired, angry, I suffer from depression and I snore for Scotland, but you know that and I probably drink too much, I'm set in my ways and I'm not always the wonder guy.'

'Listen, my love, I have the same failings, I get PMT, I like my own way, I'm a bitch and I can be really mean to the guys I love, I snore too but you know that too' Karen said 'I know you will always love Jane, but I'm willing to share, can we try, please?'

The car stopped at the Cafe Royal and the door was opened by the footman, no one emerged, Simon said 'Driver, we are not ready, drive around the block' the door was shut and they drove off. Simon was about to do the most romantic thing that anyone had every done to Karen; not one of her boyfriends had made such a gesture; he had planned it as a joke but it now had acquired a potency he had not anticipated; he was about to give her a gift of no value that was priceless.

The car drew up, for a second time, and a beaming BK Shore emerged still in her stage outfit, she walked up the red carpet and into reception to be met by the duty manager, who introduced herself. BK Shore was holding the hand of an older gentleman and repeatedly looked back at him, making eye contact and giving him broad smiles. The manager's mind momentarily wandered, she knew that look, that behaviour, she was deeply in love with her boyfriend and yearned for the end of her shift so she could join him in bed, she smiled politely and escorted her VIP guests to the lift.

They met up with Emma at the elevator, Emma noticed how happy and radiant BK was, positively glowing and that around her neck was a simple gold chain and on it was a gold coloured key which had 1911 engraved on it. As the doors closed, BK kissed Emma on the lips, it was more than just friendly and they hugged each other; Emma picked up the key and said 'Why 1911?' Simon said 'it's the initials for Sarah King, SK in numbers'. Emma looked puzzled, 'it's my own entry code to his apartment block and the key to his front door, he has given me part of him, part of his home' BK said. Emma put her hand on Simon's chest and flicked out his chain with BK's ring hanging from it, she smiled, a tear ran down her cheek and as she held the key in one hand and the ring in the other she kissed Simon rather passionately and she, Karen and Simon stood hugging each other, next to a highly bemused and embarrassed duty manager.

Karen stripped out of her stage clothes and quickly showered with Simon who soaped her down and rubbed her back, Emma brought them some coffee whilst Karen was drying her hair and Simon was changing his clothes, he was getting used to Emma being around them. He left the bedroom and sat eating sandwiches with a gin and tonic, chatting to Hal; Karen had Jenny from costume, a hair dresser and a makeup artist with her in order to prepare her for her entrance to the party in just over an hour.

Karen emerged, with her hair brushed straight, with perfect make-up including bright red nails and lip-gloss; she wore a bright red strapless satin top that resembled a Basque and exposed her shoulders and showed a daring level of cleavage. Her dress had petticoats under it, like a ballroom dress but was made of Clan Macintosh tartan, white sheer stockings and matching red shoes finished the ensemble. A simple gold chain hung around her neck and nestling between her breasts was a key, held in place by tit tape. Simon walked forward and kissed her 'you look stunning', they turned; Hal and Emma were taking photos of the two of them, they looked at themselves in the mirror. 'Yes,' said Hal 'you two do make a great looking couple'.

They enjoyed the party, it was full of 'A' list celebrities that Simon had only ever seen on TV, they danced the first dance which was 'Don't Let Go', using the steps they had learnt together. At 2.30am, they left the party, which was still in full swing and returned upstairs to bed, they cuddled into each other in the massive bed, Simon watched as Karen fell asleep in his arms, she looked so at peace and relaxed, a few minutes later he too was asleep.

Emma had an eventful party, dancing and chatting and ended up in bed with Nathan MacLeod. He was, she said, a never to be missed experience, the rumours were accurate; she was exhausted, satisfied and sore; Emma had fallen asleep after he left but that was only a few hours ago, she had showered and dressed.

Emma woke BK and Simon, walking into their bedroom with coffees, 'I'm sorry guys but it is time for you to get up and you have things to do today' she said.

They had been awake some time and had made love; they had enjoyed some of the most intimate moments of their relationship and were basking in the afterglow of pleasure, desire and comfort, falling in and out of sleep together.

A naked Karen got out of bed and walked into the bathroom and started to run the water in the big bath, as she passed Emma she kissed her on the cheek, Emma could smell their sex, something she did not find unpleasant. Karen came back in and threw the bedclothes off Simon and pulled him out the bed and said 'time for your bath, old man'. Emma watched the two of them, as they walked naked into the bathroom, hand in hand oblivious to her presence; Karen turned and said 'Emma, I have something I want you to arrange so you had better come and talk to us whilst we are in the bath'.

As Emma walked towards the bathroom she noticed their gold chains, lying on the dressing table, the ring on Simon's was missing and Emma smiled, she had seen where that was! Karen and Simon sat in the bath drinking coffee, she began to realise that the two of them had a deeper confidence in their relationship than she had seen before; she was also overjoyed as clearly BK trusted her around Simon and Simon seemed to accept her presence, she appreciated the trust. She stripped, placed her clothes on the bathroom stool and joined Karen and Simon in their bath.

Afterwards, Karen and Simon laughed about Emma getting into the bath with them, Karen said 'I really didn't mean for her to get naked and join us, I expected her to sit on the bathroom stool which is why I put it there!! Emma told me that she felt locked out, a little jealous, I wanted her to be our trusted friend and include her a bit but probably not that much; anyway I know you enjoyed it, you naughty boy'.

Simon said 'Listen, I'm over fifty and I'm in a bath with two beautiful naked young women, twenty years younger than me, I thought I had downloaded myself onto a website. Once over the shock, it was very pleasant and rather exciting; we should do it again,' he smiled his naughty smile.

'Listen, buster, I'll decide that not you, OK!!' Karen said, holding him with a tight grip, Simon gulped and nodded.

Emma had sat in the bath opposite them and Karen had told her about what they had decided about their future together, Simon would return to Edinburgh the next day, she would do the American tour and go to the Paramount recording studios in Los Angeles to record some songs in between the gigs, a few of which were a week apart. The day after the end of tour party in LA, she would fly to Edinburgh to live with Simon but that was in nearly six weeks time.

Their day in London was punctuated by publicity shots, so when they visited the London Eye, Karen was photographed and went on the wheel with photographers; Simon sat in a cafe with Emma who told him all about her encounter with international rugby or Nathan as he was called.

Immediately before the photo shoot, Simon and Karen had taken one of the gondolas alone and he had pointed out the landmarks of the city in which he was brought up; they did so enjoy being together. They visited St Paul's Cathedral and walked across the bridge to the Globe theatre and took a private boat for the last photo shoot.

Simon had asked that it drop them at the Embankment Quay and that he and Karen would make their way on foot, back to the hotel in Piccadilly, followed by a security guard. They stopped at Gordon's Wine bar and for tea and cakes in the splendour of the Institute of Directors in Pall Mall. He explained that he had brought Jane there and told Karen about the struggle they had when he started his consultancy business.

They dined in their suite, they wanted to spend time on their own; once finished, everyone was banned from entering the suite; even Emma and Hal; they enjoyed the time together but there was a looming sadness for both of them, they would soon be parted. They stayed awake into the small hours, before going to bed because they kept falling asleep, having taken several hours to travel around the sexual world. When they eventually fell asleep, they knew each other's bodies in every detail, an intense and penetrating intimacy between two people falling in love with each other.

The next day they spent time together in their hotel room; they had lunch in the Ritz Hotel something that Karen had always wanted to do; they were allowed to use a small lounge to say goodbye, and they asked their security guards to ensure that no one was allowed to enter the room. Simon and Karen cuddled into a corner and they kissed, he pushed her skirt up, she wore no panties, not with that ring, it would be far to stimulating; he knelt in front of her and gently removed the ring; he ran the ring just inside her and threaded it onto his chain and tucked it away, still wet, under his shirt. They had sex in that corner, this was lustful, rather dirty and absolutely satisfying and afterwards they stood by the door kissing and said their goodbyes. Simon left, he walked out of the Ritz and down the stairs of Green Park Underground Station to catch the tube to London City Airport.

The woman sat opposite him on the tube train was reading a copy of Hallo magazine and was startled to see a man whose picture was in her magazine sat opposite her, pretending not to be in tears.

Emma, who had been waiting outside, came into the room and went to hug BK, but she saw BK's legs buckle, she had fainted; Emma caught her and although BK recovered, she was very pale and sat down and cried, sobbed, Emma hadn't seen her this upset before, she cuddled her friend.

BK rang Simon from mid-Atlantic to ensure that Simon got home alright; it was going to be a long five and a half weeks, for both of them.

Chapter Seventeen

A whole new world

Simon had been on line using the webcam to Karen who was in Denver preparing to go on stage, and she was at the end of week three of her American mini tour. She had spent the week at the Paramount recording studios, near her house, recording some new songs; she was now just two short of an album, assuming everything was accepted.

Emma had also rung him to say that she was worried because Karen was not as happy as she had been and she had noticed that she was eating spasmodically, had creative vomiting, had lost weight and she was finding composing difficult. Emma was surprised to hear that Simon was losing weight too; Emma had discussed her concerns with Hal, she knew BK had lost nearly 7lbs; alterations were being made to costumes, Hal had said he would see what he could do, but Emma had not seen any action.

It was just before midnight when the phone in Simon's flat in Edinburgh rang and an American voice explained that he had been sent Simon's speaking notes about management and Simon had been recommended by Hal as a speaker. Jed was running a business conference in Chicago in two weeks time and was short of a speaker, if he used Simon he could call it an International Conference and boost sales.

These late night phone calls from America were causing havoc with his sleep pattern, he was woken a week or so ago at 3am by a call from Erin, Karen's mom from Bakersfield; Hal had given her Simon's number. She told him that Sarah, as she called Karen, had been to see her, had told her all about him and she had never seen her daughter this enamoured, she had never discussed her men with her mom whilst she was going out with them; Erin was worried because Sarah had asked her mom if she could bring Simon to see her if he was ever in LA. However, for Erin it was when Sarah told her that they had gone to church together that she realised how committed her daughter was to her relationship with Simon.

A concerned Erin had rung Simon mainly to ensure that he was genuine, he had talked to Erin for an hour and been given something of a grilling to the extent that he wondered if Karen was right that in her opinion this lady was losing it as she seemed to be very with it as far as he was concerned. He was left with the clear picture that Karen had fallen in love with him heavily but that mom was worried she would end up hurt again. They had discussed Jane and his children, his feelings for Jane and Karen or Sarah and the age gap; they had shared the irony that the age gap between Karen and Simon was about the same as the age gap between Simon and Erin.

In the end, they had finished their call understanding each other's position rather well because they agreed they were both in different ways concerned parents, neither of them told Sarah or Karen of their discussion.

The night after Jed's call, Simon had a dreadful night's sleep, thinking through what he could do, but when he woke, he had the outline of his speech and seminar and emailed it to Jed who by now was asleep. Later that day, Jed accepted Simon's proposal and a deal was struck. Simon had business class expenses, in-country costs and would be paid $5,000 per day for two days, this was good money. What Simon didn't know was that Beach had underwritten his involvement, Hal wanted him in LA so BK would finish her album before going to Edinburgh.

Simon would arrive in Chicago two days before the end of tour party, he would work the two days and wondered if he could get from Chicago to LA and the party in time; he rang Hal's office. It was a four and a half hour flight from Chicago to LA, the logistics that Simon had looked at were not good.

When Hal returned to the office, he was presented with a detailed analysis that said it could not be done; assuming all the airlines had seats, the timings didn't work. He thought for a moment, recalling his planning and said 'have a driver standing, charter a jet for takeoff instantly and get him from LA airport to the Plaza Regency Hotel, that WILL work' he knew it would, he smiled to himself. An hour later, Hal rang Simon and told him the arrangements that had been made, he had pushed back BK's arrival by half an hour and Simon would arrive at the hotel with about an hour to spare before BK, who as the hostess would be the last to arrive; it was tight but possible.

Simon asked that no one say anything, it was going to be a surprise, Hal did not even tell Emma and swore his staff to secrecy, the only other people who knew were Maria, BK's maid who would prepare BK's house for occupation rather than packing it up and one person Simon had told, unbeknown to Hal.

Chicago was a good break for Simon and Jed was supportive. He made his speech to 2,000 delegates, something he was very nervous about, the smaller seminar for 150 the next day was oversubscribed but it was the questions and answers session that went the best, Simon's angle on the answers was fresh and far more forthright than the normal business replies, it was a great success. Simon had been approached by several people to see if he could speak at their conferences or events, he had three proposals to put forward; he also gave out lots of business cards.

On the Friday, he attended the conference and took part in that questions and answers session; when the conference ended, Simon met his driver who took him to the chartered plane which took off early and Simon arrived, fully changed at the hotel with just over an hour to spare. Simon was, understandably, keen to see Karen, but there was someone else at the party he was almost as excited about meeting.

When he arrived at the hotel, he said hallo to Hal and Emma kissed him on the lips, a surprising level two kiss, it had thrown him completely, he hadn't expected it. He put his arm around Emma and talked to her, she pointed out a man sat at the bar; when the man saw Simon looking over towards him, he came trotting nearly running over, with his wife in tow. Several guests and the band members were confused as the two men met in an emotional embrace, like brothers; all of BK's entourage knew the guy at the bar and most of them knew Simon if only as the guy in the kilt but none of them knew what the link between the two men could be other than BK Shore, none of them understood why the meeting was so emotional.

Simon Macintosh and Brad Morgan stood holding each other; they had over 40 years to fill in; Brad introduced Lauren and they sat in a corner until Emma came and got Simon. Brad and Simon had been emailing each other for weeks and had spoken on the phone, once. Simon had told Brad of his plan to surprise Karen by welcoming her to the party, he had swore Brad to secrecy; Lauren knew that this was the first time that Simon and Brad had met since they were both thirteen, by which time they had been friends for six years; she knew those emotions would run deep.

Lauren watched the two of them, they were both talking excitedly and very fast, laughing and joking and looking at each other, it was rather touching; she was convinced the bond of friendship was still present. When Simon left she looked at Brad, he was standing facing into the corner blowing his nose, she recognised his sensitive and loving side, he had talked about this moment ever since BK Shore had told him of the link and almost constantly since he knew he would meet Simon; Lauren placed her hand on the small of Brad's back, she did so love him.

Lauren had discussed Simon with BK who had told her of her feelings especially the trust and love she felt for him. Having met Simon briefly and seeing how he reacted to the meeting with Brad she could see exactly what BK had seen in Simon and how difficult it would be for her to keep him. Lauren knew that BK was beside herself with dread and worrying herself sick that when she and Simon met again the spark would not be there, that the moment might have passed and that he did not feel for her the way she felt for him. As Simon left Brad, Lauren knew what was about to happen, she was also positive that this man did have feelings for BK, he was the sort of guy that would; besides, he would not have flown half way around the world to surprise her just to say hallo or goodbye.

BK Shore waited as the liveried doorman opened the door to the limousine, the last gig of her US tour, the previous evening had been a success, it hadn't been as good as some of the others; she missed Simon and now she was arriving at the end of tour party, alone. She clenched her thighs together and stood up out of the car, smiling broadly as the cameras flashed.

She was wearing a gray silk figure-hugging dress which ended just above the knee; it was designed as a sash with one shoulder bare and finished with a wide belt of tartan – Macintosh tartan, with a large gold Celtic knot buckle and dark gray high-heeled shoes. She had asked Simon for a photograph of his daughter Alex, so she could show it to her mom but she had also used it to show her hair stylist who had dyed her hair the same colour, so she emerged from the limousine as a ginger redhead, it was a surprise for Simon; she would see him in just over 24 hours.

A simple gold chain with a gold plated key hung from her neck and nestled between her breasts; the only times she had taken it off since Simon had given it to her was when she was on stage and when it went to the jewellers to be gold plated. BK would play with the key and remember talking to, being with and making love to Simon, especially his gentle hands on her body, she would suck the key like a dummy; Emma had admitted to her that she also found the whole ring and key thing hugely romantic, very erotic and more than a little sexually exciting.

BK went over to the people she recognised from her fan club and signed autographs, there was Jean from Fresno and that geeky girl Sam from LA. She gave an interview to an incredibly young looking reporter from a local radio station, signed autographs and talked to members of the public; she then made her way across the red carpet to the other side.

It was a quiet presence she felt first, above the screams and the shouts and the noise of cameras and traffic, it said 'Karen' and she knew it was in her mind, that soft accent, she remembered his aftershave, her hand moved down and touched the key and she paused. She thought; it was five nearly six long weeks since she had seen Simon, she longed for him, for her ring, to smell his aftershave on him, to be lying next to him in bed and that special cuddle that made them sleep entwined, in her mind she saw his smile and remembered how happy she felt with him.

'Are you alright?' it was the woman in front of her who woke her from her day dream.

'Er yes, I was just thinking about something' she said.

She was startled by the reply 'No, BK, you weren't, you're crying, don't be sad'.

BK kissed the woman on the cheek and said to her 'no, I'm not sad, you see, I was just thinking of him' the woman in front of her held her hand, smiled and said 'Well honey if you were thinking of him, you're in love'.

Before BK could answer, Hal and Emma arrived and stood hand in hand next to BK, she looked at them, why were they there? Why were they holding hands and smiling like idiots? Why was Emma in tears?

Emma kissed BK on the cheek and said 'I am so happy for you'. BK looked puzzled; Hal said 'BK you deserve this, enjoy', he handed her an electronic card for one of the rooms in the hotel; she was about to ask what the hell was going on when there was a shout.

'KAREN!' The crowd hushed, BK looked at Hal and Emma, who was now in sheets of tears, and then at the woman in front of her, who was pointing and shouting 'GO honey go!'

BK turned; there at the top of the red carpet was a familiar figure, just in focus, damn contact lenses. He stood there in full Highland dress, looking immaculate, very Scottish; he had lost weight, he was even wearing his clan plaid draped casually over the shoulder; she recognised the tartan – Macintosh tartan.

Simon had seen her emerging from the limousine, her hair ginger red in the lights, brushed straight and shining, in her dress she looked stunning, gorgeous, he could not believe his luck in meeting her and being with her.

Karen, for she was no longer BK Shore, went numb, from her toes to her head, she felt instantly strange, light headed and slightly faint. She screamed. She kicked off her $2000, 4inch heeled shoes - who needs them when he is here? - and ran up the red carpet, barging camera crews, reporters and flunkies out of the way. It seemed to be in slow motion, it seemed to be a long way, the crowd and reporters were silent in her mind and very quiet in reality and she was oblivious to the flashes and cameras around her.

Karen screamed at the top of her voice 'SIMON' and launched herself into his arms; their lips met, tears rolling down her cheeks, she opened her eyes in the kiss and realised it was dark but there were also huge cheers around her.

As she launched herself at him, Simon had brought his plaid over and covered their embrace and kisses from all around them. They were kissing long and hard under a cover of Macintosh tartan; momentarily, it felt safe and private; Karen placed her hand on his chest and could feel her or was it his ring, a pang of excitement spurted through her body.

There was enough light for them to see each other and Simon pulled back and held her gently with his hand behind her neck. He looked into her eyes and said 'Sarah King, I love you'.

Karen blinked back tears and looked at him and said 'Simon, I love you and please, always call me Karen, it's our special name', they stood there under their cover just looking at each other. 'Karen, I love you' Simon said.

Simon lowered the plaid with his back to the crowd. BK Shore turned and waived at the crowd with tears of joy rolling down her face and a broad smile. Simon and Karen walked towards the hotel with their arms around each other and entered the party.

THE END

Lightning Source UK Ltd.
Milton Keynes UK
08 July 2010

156620UK00012B/1/P